Family Secrets

Alan Sakell

Family Secrets

Vanguard Press

VANGUARD PAPERBACK

© Copyright 2024
Alan Sakell

The right of Alan Sakell to be identified as the author of
this work has been asserted by him in accordance with the
Copyright, Designs, and Patents Act 1988.

A CIP catalog record for this title is
available from the British Library.

ISBN 978 1 80016 976 0

This is a work of fiction. Names, characters, businesses, places, events, and incidents are
either the product of the author's imagination or used in a fictitious manner. Any
resemblance to actual persons, living or dead, or actual events is purely coincidental.

*Vanguard Press is an imprint of
Pegasus Elliot Mackenzie Publishers Ltd.*
www.pegasuspublishers.com

First Published in 2024

**Vanguard Press
Sheraton House Castle Park
Cambridge England**

Printed & Bound in Great Britain

For Peter and John

The oldest and the youngest of the Sakell boys

Part One

The Women

Robin
2017

CHAPTER 1

I first met Zach during my junior year of high school. He was on the football team, and I was a cheerleader. Everyone always said what a perfect couple we made. He was my first steady boyfriend. Yes, he stole my virginity when I was only sixteen years old. We were joined at the hip pretty much every day for the rest of our high school days. We had a close group of friends that we hung out with and did stupid teenage things with. My parents were already planning our wedding and future together. My mother could not wait for me to give her two grandchildren.

Zach had spent quite a bit of time at my house during those days. My parents adored him, and he adored them. My parents even invited him to go along with us on our family vacations. The same could not be said about Zach's parents. I take that back. The same could not be said about Zach's father. His mother was great. It was obvious how much she loved Zach. He was definitely a mama's boy. She was always super sweet and kind to me.

The problem was Zach's father. Anytime I thought of him, the first word that came to mind was 'controlling'. Zach's mother had been a stay-at-home mom. It wasn't that she didn't want to work, it was that her husband didn't want her to work. Any time she even dared to bring up the idea of getting a job it would turn into a full-blown argument. Zach's father would insult and belittle his mother until she broke down crying. If he had allowed her to get a job, he would have been giving up control of her and that was never going to happen.

Zach's father was the same way with him. He had to tell his father everywhere he was going, who he was going with, and when he would be home. He had a ten p.m. curfew even after we graduated from high school. As soon as Zach got his first job, he had to start paying his father fifty dollars a week to continue living in his house. It wasn't like his father needed the money. Zach was hardly ever home except after his curfew. It was all about keeping whatever amount of control he could over Zach.

Any time we did happen to end up at Zach's house, the change that would happen with his mother as soon as his father walked through the door after work would amaze me. Amaze is probably not the correct word to use. Anytime I hear the word 'amaze' it makes me think of something good, great, or even spectacular. There was nothing good, great, or spectacular about the way Zach's mother would change as soon as her husband walked through their front door. It was as if all the happiness, joy, and life were sucked right out of her. Gone was the bounce in her step. Gone was the smile on her face. Gone was the voice he stole from her repeatedly.

I tried talking to Zach about the way his father treated his mother, but he never wanted to talk about it. It was none of our business. Best to leave it alone. Never once did I leave that house without my heart breaking for Zach's mother. She was a smart, beautiful, loving woman, trapped in a loveless marriage, with a man who did not deserve her. I could only imagine what living with a man who puts you down and disrespects you all the time for years does to your self-esteem.

The couple of times that Zach was allowed to go on our family vacations with us he spent most of it worrying about his mother being home alone with his father. It weighed on him.

My parents were nothing like Zach's parents. My mother noticed something was bothering Zach during one of our vacations. When she asked him what was wrong all he would say was, "I am worried about my mom." My mother knew just by the way he had said it that it was best to leave it alone. The next time I was alone with my mother she asked me why Zach would be worried about his mom. I filled her in on the little I knew. That was probably a mistake. Like Zach said, 'It is none of our business.'

CHAPTER 2

One day Zach just showed up at my house. We had not made plans to see each other until later in the evening. I knew something was wrong before I even opened the door. Zach had a special knock he always did so I would know it was him at the door. Knock-knock stop, knock-knock stop, knock-knock. That day he just kept pounding on the door nonstop until I opened it. What I saw standing before me was a broken man.

While we sat there on my couch, Zach told me how he had found his mother dead at the bottom of their basement stairs. The paramedics and police officers had just left his house. He had rushed right over to my house. He didn't want to be inside his house. He kept seeing his mother's lifeless body just lying there in a pool of blood. It was hard to make sense of most of what he was saying. If I had to guess I would say he was in a state of shock. He kept staring into space and zoning out.

As the days passed, I learned more about what had happened that day or at least what the police believe happened that day. I had no idea if any of it was the truth. I will tell you the important parts and you can judge for yourself.

Zach was the first one in the house to get up that morning. He had left the house before his father or mother were out of bed. He went to the gym for an early morning workout which he did five days a week. After his workout, he went back home to shower and get dressed for work. When he got out of the shower, he saw his father coming out of his parents' bedroom, which was right across from the bathroom. He then saw his father close the bedroom door behind him. When Zach was finished getting dressed, he went down to the kitchen expecting to find his mother making breakfast like she did every morning for him and his father. Instead, he found his father eating a bowl of cereal all by himself. When Zach asked his father about his mother, he was told that she was not feeling well. She was still in bed sleeping. That was why he had closed the bedroom door. To keep as much light and noise out of the bedroom as possible.

Zach and his father left the house at the same time that morning. When Zach returned home after work he was surprised to not see or hear his mother. He thought for sure she would be up and about, or at least sitting in her rocking chair watching television. He headed up the stairs to make sure she was okay. The bedroom door was still closed. He knocked lightly on the door a few times. Getting no response, he slowly opened the bedroom door. What he saw alarmed him. The first thing he noticed was that his mother was not in bed sleeping. In fact, she was not in the bedroom at all. The second thing he noticed alarmed him just as much, if not more. The bed wasn't made.

Zach knew something was terribly wrong. His mother would never dare leave the bed unmade for his father to find. That would be an automatic argument that she would never win. He didn't live in a pigsty after all. Zach did his best to make his parents' bed the way his father liked it to be made. As he was fluffing the last pillow it hit him: why had his father closed the bedroom door if the room was empty? Better yet, where was his mother?

With the bed made to the best of his ability, Zach set out to find his mother. The house wasn't that big so there weren't too many places she could be. He looked behind the shower curtain in case she had slipped and fallen and couldn't get up. He looked in the backyard in case she was out there in her garden, which needed immediate attention. Then he stood in the hallway and yelled out for her. That was when he noticed it.

Back when Zach was about twelve years old, his father had gone into one of his fits of rage over something ridiculous. He was so worked up that he punched a hole in the door that led down to the basement. He tried to patch the hole the next day, but it ended up being easier to buy a new door. The new door was about a quarter of an inch too short. Any time the basement light was on, and the door was closed, the light would pour out onto the kitchen floor.

That was what had caught Zach's attention. He tried to remember if the basement light was on before he had left for work, but with the morning sun shining through the windows on that side of the house, it would have been impossible to notice the light making itself known as it was then. Zach went over to the door, turned the knob, and slowly pushed the door open. He didn't want to go down to the basement. He knew whatever he was about to find wasn't going to be good. It took all the strength he had to make himself walk up to the door opening. When he looked down the staircase, he saw his mother lying there in a pool of her own blood.

Zach didn't even go down the stairs. He knew his mother was dead just by the way her head was turned. He dialed 911 and waited outside the house for the police to show up. Zach's father got home right before the first police cruiser showed up. The police officers wouldn't let Zach or his father into the house until they had finished processing the scene. When the police officers were finished in the house, they asked Zach and his father some preliminary questions before leaving. Then Zach showed up at my door.

CHAPTER 3

In the following days, Zach and his father made a few trips to the police station for more questioning. Although there was no way to prove foul play, there were a couple of things that didn't make sense to the detectives on the case. One of those things had bothered me right from the start. Why was the basement door closed? Zach had told the police officers that his mother hated going down to the basement. She would have never closed the door behind her while she was down there. She was always worried she would get locked in the dark, dungy basement with no way out. The only times she ever went down to the basement were to do laundry. She had just done all the laundry the day before.

Another thing that bothered the detectives was the time of death which was determined by the medical examiner. According to the medical examiner, Zach's mother had been dead anywhere from twelve to fifteen hours. How was that possible if Zach's father had closed her in their bedroom when he got up in the morning? All the blood tests came back clean for drugs or alcohol, so what made her fall down the stairs?

I had my own theory of what really happened in that house, but I didn't dare say it aloud. Zach was already in a bad way. The last thing he needed was for me to be telling him what I thought really happened. That his father had closed the bedroom door so that Zach couldn't see his mother wasn't in their bed before heading to work. That his father had thrown his mother down the basement stairs the night before. That his father had closed the basement door so Zach wouldn't see his mother until after he had left for work. Therefore, giving himself an alibi.

After a few months, the case was closed. It was classified as an accidental death. Zach's father collected a nice chunk of change from the life insurance policy he had taken out on his wife. Zach spent as little time at his father's house as possible, spending most nights at my house. I waited and waited for him to say something about the possibility that his father had killed his mother, but it never happened. I don't know whether he ever thought about it, or he didn't want me to think about it. I can tell you, I thought about it every single time I had the misfortune of having to be anywhere near his father.

Eventually, Zach started acting like the Zach I had fallen in love with. He had seen up close and personal how to be a horrible husband. He had no intention of following in his father's footsteps. He made me the center of his universe. We both loved going to the movies, so we made that our regular Friday night date. We didn't always agree on which movie to see so we took turns from week to week. We saw so many movies.

Somehow Zach had managed to continue living with his father in the house his mother had died in. To be honest, they hardly saw each other, which was the main reason Zach had stayed. He wanted to be able to save up enough money for a down payment on a house. His father had managed to find a woman desperate enough to move in with them. She became his new live-in maid. I only met her twice, which was twice too often. I try to not speak ill of anyone, so I will let you draw your own conclusions about the kind of woman who would voluntarily move in with a man like Zach's father.

I started questioning whether Zach and I had a future together. We had been together for over five years. We had gone through some rough patches but for the most part, we were happy together. With that said, we had never actually lived together. Things change, people change, and relationships change once you live together. Would those changes make us a stronger couple, or would they break us? I had heard the saying, 'Together we are one' a few times. Sometimes it made me feel warm and fuzzy inside. Sometimes it scared the crap out of me.

CHAPTER 4

When Zach dropped down on his knee in the movie theater during my favorite part of *Titanic*, I thought he was looking for something he had dropped. I had seen the movie twice before, but this was a special Twentieth Anniversary Limited Release screening. The first time Zach said my name, I shushed him. Leo was helping Kate step up onto the rail: "Do you trust me?" he asked. "I trust you," Kate responded. My eyes were glued to the screen as Kate stepped up onto the rail with her eyes closed.

It was only when Zach tapped me on my knee that I actually looked down at him. He was looking up at me with puppy dog eyes and an uncertain smile on his face. Then I saw the twinkle coming from the diamond ring he had between his fingers. Instead of asking me to marry him, he said, "You're here in my heart, and if you say yes, my heart will go on and on."

Our engagement only lasted six months. Why put off until tomorrow what you can accomplish today? We had a small wedding in the same church I was baptized in. I hadn't been to church except on Christmas Eve, for as long as I could remember. I was raised a Catholic, but in those days I considered myself a non-practicing Catholic. The Catholic church has too many restrictions on what made me a good or bad person. Heaven or Hell. Those were my only two options. I never bought into God forgiving my sins if I confessed them and then said a few Hail Marys.

Zach's father gave us $10,000 for a down payment on a house as our wedding gift. Part of his dead wife's life insurance. When Zach showed me the check, I could swear I saw the words 'hush money' written in the memo section. We bought a quaint cottage in Somerset, MA. If you looked out of one of the windows on the second floor, you could say we had a water view. We had a big backyard with a large, beautiful maple tree that dropped its leaves into the koi fish pond we had installed shortly after we moved in. I spent many mornings out on our deck, drinking my coffee, and watching the fish as they continued to pop up for air.

The honeymoon phase lasted a lot longer for Zach than it did for me. Being married was a lot like being a Catholic. As soon as that ring is placed on your finger, you lose your independence, your sense of self. The marriage vows you promised to keep until death do you part, came with their own list of restrictions. You can no longer do whatever you want, when you want, how you want. You have to always be thinking and planning for two instead of just one. Granted, there were some advantages to being married, but I was quickly learning there were not enough of them to justify my loss of freedom.

I did my best to acclimate to married life. We closed our separate bank accounts and opened a new joint one. Zach had better health insurance at his job, so I canceled mine and he added me to his. I became known as his spouse. We both took out life insurance policies. We adopted a two-year-old Yorkie named Spaz, which suited him to a T. I even changed my last name. We still did our scheduled date night every Friday night, just the two of us. Most of them were still spent in the movie theater. Our sex life was more than adequate.

I often found myself wondering if all married people felt the same way I did, or if there was something wrong with my wiring. I once saw a poll in a magazine about what women want most in their lives. Marriage was at the top of the list, followed by a career, children, and money. Career and money I could understand, but marriage and children were much farther down on my poll answers. Having that wedding ring on my finger was making me feel like I had an ankle bracelet on, that was attached to an anchor. I was like one of our koi fish, always fighting my way to the surface for air. The restrictions involved with being married were suffocating me.

CHAPTER 5

When I was hired for my new job as the editor for our local newspaper and was told it would be long days for at least the first few months while I went through their training program, I felt relieved. More time out of the house was exactly what I needed. It wasn't that I wanted to be working night and day, I just wanted to be away from the house, from Zach, from the restrictions of my marriage. I needed time to be just Robin again, not Zach's wife, Robin. I know this is going to sound absurd, but when I was at work, I felt free again.

I had always been an outgoing, friendly person and people usually gravitated toward me. I had been known to be the life of the party on many occasions. I missed that! Zach was much more reserved than I was. We had fun together, couples' fun, but it wasn't the same. I missed the excitement of deciding in a moment's notice that I was going to get dressed up and paint the town red. Zach wasn't a club-hopping kind of guy. The only time we had ever danced together was at our wedding. To say he had two left feet was putting it mildly.

I wasn't a failure. I had succeeded at everything I had ever tried. Married life might just be the toughest challenge I had ever faced. We celebrated our six-month anniversary last weekend. If you call sharing a bottle of wine and having sex a celebration. Zach had no idea how unhappy I was. He only got to see what I let him see. I know I wasn't being fair to him. I should have been open and honest with him about how I was feeling, but the last thing I wanted to do was talk about it. The problem was me; it wasn't Zach. He was a great guy. He doted on me every chance he got. Maybe that was part of the problem. Maybe that was part of what was holding me under the water fighting for another breath. I didn't want to drown.

The first full weekend I had off from my new job we decided to go visit my parents. I was secretly hoping to have some time alone with my mother. She was the only person I felt I could talk to about my dilemma. I knew no matter what, my mother would always be on my side. She has always been my rock. I needed to know how she had managed to be married to my father for so long. If my mother could make her marriage last thirty-six years, why was I having such a tough time making my marriage last nine months?

By the second day of our visit, I was convinced I had made a big mistake. Watching how my mother and my father acted around Zach was making me feel like someone was holding a pillow over my face. They were treating him like he was the best thing since sliced bread. He was the center of their attention, and he was eating it up. I am quite sure I could have spent the entire visit locked away in my old bedroom and not one of them would have noticed. Why was I feeling that way? I should have been happy my parents were getting along with my... Zach.

On our ride back home from my parents' house, Zach had replayed most of the weekend's events for me. Had he forgotten I was there for it? I found myself starting to wonder if I would have been happier in my marriage if Zach was less loving and less caring. Would I have been happier if he didn't pay so much attention to me? Maybe if he had started drinking more and calling me horrible names like his father used to do with his mother, I would want to fight for my marriage. When Zach pulled into our driveway and shut the car off, I realized I had not heard a word he had said for a good half hour. If we were going to make it to our one-year anniversary, something, or someone, needed to change.

CHAPTER 6

I didn't get the chance to talk to my mother alone during our weekend visit. The mystery of how she had managed to stay married to my father for so long, had remained just that, a mystery. Zach was still in the dark about how unhappy I was. Either I was a darn good actress, or he was just not paying close enough attention. My long days at work had turned into normal days since I had finished the training program. More time in the house, less time out.

I had started contemplating having an affair. I know that sounds crazy but hear me out. Cheating on your spouse is like breaking a wedding vow and a commandment at the same time. Maybe that was just what I needed to do to stop feeling like I couldn't breathe. In my crazy mind, I thought if I rebelled against the restrictions of my marriage, I would feel free again. The craziest part of it all was that I really did love Zach. He was a nice guy, a great husband. He hadn't done anything wrong, yet I wanted to punish him in hopes of feeling happier. How messed up was that?

I knew I would never go through with an affair. The guilt would have eaten me alive. Maybe a little innocent flirting with one of the married men at work would have done the trick. I had even thought about going to see a shrink. The problem with that was, if I did go see a shrink, I would be admitting there was something wrong with me. What would I have told the shrink anyway? 'Can you please tell me why I have felt like I am suffocating ever since my husband slid my wedding ring on my finger?' A few times I had started hyperventilating just from looking at the rings on my finger.

One night while Zach and I were lying in bed after a quick roll in the hay, he asked me what I thought about getting off the pill. I had never been so grateful that Zach only liked having sex with the lights off. If he had seen the expression on my face, we would still be talking about it now. Instead, I snuggled up close to him, kissed him on his cheek, and said, 'I am really tired, let's save that for another day.'

I started making circles in his chest hair after that. He was fast asleep and snoring within five minutes. Trust me, it worked every time.

I was having very mixed feelings about being married as it was. The thought of having a baby had not even entered my mind. I needed time to come up with an excuse for staying on the pill. I know, I know, I was handling it all wrong. I should have just been honest with Zach about everything I was feeling and thinking. Lying and making excuses would never make things better. If anything, they could make things a lot worse. Getting caught in a lie typically leads to telling more lies or broken trust if you are brave enough to admit to the lie.

When my phone rang while I was driving home from work, I looked at the Caller ID. It was Zach's name that showed up on the screen. My finger kept going back and forth between the red 'decline' button and the green 'accept' button. Before I could choose one it had sent him to my voicemail. If it was important enough, he would leave me a voicemail. If not, he could tell me when I got home. After about three minutes I heard the notification go off letting me know I had a new voicemail. I guess it was important.

I pulled into our driveway and was surprised to not see Zach's car there. He was always home before me. Maybe he had to work late and that was why he was calling me. I got out of the car and headed to our front door. As I got closer I could see there was mail in our mailbox. I knew right away that Zach had not come home from work yet. He had a strange obsession with getting the mail. I grabbed the mail and let myself into the house. Spaz met me at the door. He hadn't gone to the bathroom in almost nine hours. I opened the back door and let him out into the backyard. Our backyard was completely fenced in, so I just let him go do his own thing.

I put the mail, my purse, and my phone down on the kitchen counter. Then I kicked off my shoes and let my hair down. Spaz started barking at the back door, so I let him back in the house. I gave him some new water and a couple of his favorite treats. I was about to pick up the mail to see if any of it was for me with my new last name when I noticed the little red light flashing on my phone. I had never listened to Zach's voicemail.

I dialed my own voicemail. The nice robotic voice let me know I had one new voicemail. I pressed one for play. It was Zach, but it didn't sound like Zach. There was something different about his voice. It sounded like he was trying to talk while he was crying. I was having a tough time making out what he was saying. I pressed rewind and let it play again. The second time I had the volume all the way up in hopes of hearing more of what he was saying. The only words I could make out were, 'Dad-hospital-hurry.'

CHAPTER 7

I don't know about you, but I hate hospitals. Hospitals are where sick people go. Some of which never get the chance to leave. The second the doors to a hospital open I start getting lightheaded and dizzy. There is a specific smell in the air as you walk down the halls of a hospital that makes me start feeling nauseous.

When I made it to the hospital I sat in my car and stalled for as long as I could. I knew I needed to go in and be there for Zach the same way he would have been there for me if one of my parents had just been rushed to the hospital. It was the right thing to do. No one wants to be sitting alone in the waiting room of a hospital. The sound of my text message alert startled me. I took my cell phone out of my jacket pocket and saw the new text message was from Zach: *Are you almost here?* It was time to man up.

I got out of my car and walked as slowly as I could across the parking lot. As I was approaching the entrance the doors slid open. A nurse pushing a wheelchair with a woman holding a newborn baby sitting in it was coming right at me. A man, presumably the proud father, was walking right behind them. I stepped to the side so they could pass. Most women get excited when they see newborn babies. I was not one of them. Newborn babies frightened me. I was too afraid I would break one. Give me a six-month-old baby and I was good to go.

By the time I made it to the waiting room, I could feel myself starting to sweat and flush. I spotted Zach sitting by himself in the far corner. He looked up as I approached him. He tried unsuccessfully to smile. I sat down in the chair on the side of his. I put my left hand on his knee and my right hand on his back. I tried to soothe him the best I could. His eyes were bloodshot from crying. He looked broken and defeated. I asked him what had happened to his father.

"He had a stroke," Zach replied.

A few minutes later, Bonnie, Zach's father's replacement for his dead wife, came walking into the waiting room. I had not seen her for some time, which wasn't a terrible thing. She had just been in to see Zach's father. She filled us in on what the doctor had told her. He had suffered a mini-stroke. The doctor wanted to keep him in the hospital for a couple of days to keep an eye on him. Turns out mini-strokes are usually a warning before a major stroke. It could've been much worse.

I stayed in the waiting room while Zach went to sit with his father for a while. Between you and me, I had no desire to see the man. Call me cold-hearted if you must, but every time I was in the presence of Zach's father, all I could think of was him throwing his wife down the basement stairs and leaving her lifeless body there for Zach to find. What kind of man does that to his wife, and his son? Not one I want to be anywhere near even if he did just have a mini-stroke.

By the time we left the hospital and made it home, I was exhausted. All I wanted to do was crawl into our nice comfortable bed, but Zach wanted to stay up and talk about his father. My least favorite topic of conversation. I poured us both a glass of wine and joined him on the couch. I suddenly had a bad feeling in the pit of my stomach. Before my glass had a chance to reach my lips, Zach asked, "Why don't you like my father?" I knew this day would come eventually. I had promised myself that when it did come, I was going to be completely honest. Zach was my husband. He deserved my honesty. I just didn't think it would come on the same day his father had suffered a mini-stroke.

CHAPTER 8

I drank half my glass of wine in one big gulp hoping it would go straight to my head. Zach just sat there looking at me. Waiting for me to answer his question. What good would lying do either of us? I put my wine glass down on the table and turned to face him. I contemplated lying to him, but the look on his face made it impossible.

I was struggling to find the right words. I didn't want to just blurt it out. I was afraid of what his reaction might be.

Instead of answering his question, I asked him a question.

"What do you think really happened the day your mother died?"

The expression on his face changed completely. He scrunched up his eyebrows and put on his confused face. He definitely hadn't been expecting me to bring up his mother's death. This wasn't going to go the way I had hoped it would.

"Why are you asking me about how my mother died? You know how she died. She fell down the basement stairs."

We had never talked about his mother's death since the day it happened. It was too painful for Zach to talk about. I honestly had no idea whether he believed it was an accident or not. For all I knew he could believe it was a suicide. Being trapped in that house with a husband that treated her the way Zach's father did, could have certainly made her entertain the thought of suicide.

I needed to tread lightly. The last thing I wanted to do was to upset Zach after the day he had had already. I picked up my wine glass and took another big gulp, almost finishing what was left in the glass before placing it back on the table.

"We have never talked about that day since it happened. I have always been curious about what you believe happened. I know it says accidental death on her death certificate. Is that what you believe really happened?"

I had always been able to read Zach's facial expressions, but the one I was seeing then was one I had never seen before. I had no idea what he was thinking. I may have pushed a button that should've been left alone.

In an almost accusatory tone, he asked, "Are you saying you don't believe it was an accident?"

There was my answer. He really did believe it was an accidental death. How could that be?

I was really doubting whether I should continue the conversation. It was becoming clear that Zach and I had different beliefs about his mother's death. His body language and the tone of his voice were already making me feel uncomfortable. Maybe it was being exaggerated in my mind by my quick consumption of the wine. I could tell he wasn't going to let me get away without answering him.

I needed to get him to say the words aloud, rather than me saying them. That way if he got angry, I could simply say, 'You said that, not me.' Here goes nothing.

"I just never understood how the basement door got closed after she fell, and before you found her. We both know she would never have closed the door while she was down in the basement. It doesn't add up." I said it perfectly if I say so myself. I didn't accuse his father of throwing his mother down the stairs. I simply pointed out the facts.

Zach's face turned a light shade of red. Almost as if he were blushing, but this was not a man blushing. I had seen that shade of red before on his father's face pretty much every time I saw him.

"What are you saying, Robin? Do you think my mother closed the basement door right before she purposely fell down the stairs?"

Was he really that deep in denial? Instead of his mind going to the possibility of his abusive father throwing his mother down the basement stairs, it went to his mother possibly committing suicide. I hadn't even thought about the possibility of suicide until that day.

Before I had a chance to say anything, the pieces fell into place.

"Wait a minute. This all started because I asked you why you don't like my father. Are you saying you think my father is responsible for my mother falling down the basement stairs?"

Finally, the cards were on the table. For some reason, I felt like I had the losing hand.

CHAPTER 9

Zach's father was released from the hospital two days later. Considering Bonnie didn't have a driver's license, Zach and I had the privilege of picking him up from the hospital and driving him home. After the conversation Zach and I had had two nights earlier, it was a rather uncomfortable outing. I waited in the car while Zach helped his father into the house. Luckily, Zach had to work that afternoon, or we probably would have ended up staying with his father for most of the day.

In case you are wondering how our conversation had ended two nights earlier, the words 'not good' would be an understatement. Zach kept pushing me to explain myself. I didn't want to lie to him, but I knew if I told him the truth all hell would've broken loose. Which was the lesser of the two evils? In the end, I compromised. I didn't actually lie, but I also didn't tell Zach that I believed his father was responsible for his mother's death. I simply said that I had no idea what had happened. I just couldn't accept that it was an accident. Not with the basement door being closed. Eventually, Zach gave up and went to sleep on the couch. It was the first time since we got married that we didn't sleep in the same bed.

I wish I could say things were better the next morning but that wasn't the case. By the time I got out of bed, Zach had already left to visit his father in the hospital. From the hospital, he went straight to work. I didn't see or speak to him until he got home at dinner time. I tried my best to have a conversation with him that night but all I was getting out of him were one-word answers. I even asked him how his father was doing, not that I really cared. His one-word answer to that question was 'better'. After dinner, we watched some television shows that we normally laugh during, but that night there was no laughter. In fact, the only sounds came from the television. Zach spent that night on the couch too.

I had to find a way to get us back on track. The issue I was having with that was that I wasn't sure what I had done wrong. Zach had initially asked me why I didn't like his father. I managed to dodge that bullet. Though in all honesty, Zach had known I wasn't a fan of his father since before we got married. Which meant I was in the doghouse because I told him I couldn't accept that his mother's death was an accident. Did that mean he did believe it was an accident? Was there something I was missing?

When we got back home after dropping Zach's father off at his house, Zach didn't even get out of the car. I had tried to lean across the front seat to give him a kiss goodbye, but he turned his head. I never knew how good he was at holding a grudge. I was seeing a side of him that I didn't even know existed. I got out of the car and watched as he drove away. My husband was choosing his feelings for his father over his feelings for me.

I tried to put myself in Zach's shoes. How would I feel if the roles were reversed? If one of my parents had died and it was ruled an accidental death, but Zach didn't believe it was an accident. How would that make me feel? Would I treat him the way he was treating me, or would I just accept that we had different beliefs? The more I thought about it, the more guilty I started feeling. Zach obviously believed it was an accidental death. Yet there I was trying to get him to believe that it was anything but an accidental death. There were only two other options. Either his mother committed suicide, or his father murdered his mother. What son would want to believe either of those two options?

That was what I had done wrong. I am sure Zach must have had his doubts at first. Even the police officers had their doubts when Zach told them the basement door had been closed when he got home. How long had it taken Zach to ignore the closed door? Had he thought even for a second that his father was responsible for his mother's death, or had he thought his mother had committed suicide? The last thing he needed was for his own wife to be putting doubts in his head.

CHAPTER 10

When Zach got home that night, I had his favorite dinner, spaghetti and meatballs waiting for him. I was by no means a good cook. Luckily, Zach was easy to please when it came to what he ate. He didn't even care that my spaghetti sauce came out of a jar. I had left the garlic bread in the oven a little too long, so I had to scrape some of the burnt edges off. I filled our glasses with what was left of the bottle of wine we had opened the other night.

Our conversation was light, but at least he was giving me more than one-word answers this time. I knew things were looking brighter when Zach offered to dry the dishes after I washed them. After we finished cleaning up the kitchen Zach went to take a shower. While he was in the shower, I prepared my second surprise. I logged into our Netflix app and searched for his favorite movie. Nothing says 'I'm sorry' like watching your husband's favorite movie for at least the tenth time, when you didn't like it the first time.

I put a bag of popcorn in the microwave and carried our wine glasses into the living room. By the time Zach joined me on the couch we had a nice big bowl of hot popcorn with extra melted butter to enjoy with the movie. When Zach turned the television on and saw that I had queued up Twins for us to watch his face lit up. Don't get me wrong, I love Danny DeVito, but Arnold Schwarzenegger's acting left a lot to be desired. I faked a laugh when Zach laughed, just like I had done every time we had watched the movie before.

I started falling asleep on the couch toward the end of the movie. It had been another emotionally draining day and it was taking its toll on me. I was relieved when the movie ended, and Zach shut the television off. There was no way I could've made it through a half-hour sitcom, never mind another movie. I just sat there on the couch waiting to see what Zach was going to do. Had he planned to spend another night on the couch or was he going to sleep in our bed? I was having a challenging time keeping my eyes open. My eyelids felt like they weighed ten pounds each.

Zach stood up and looked down at me.

"Do you need me to carry you?" he asked in a kind voice. As I went to stand up, he reached for my hand and helped me up. I leaned my head on his shoulder and we walked to the bedroom hand in hand. We didn't have sex that night, which was totally fine with me. I had no energy for anything of the sort. Within minutes Zach was snoring away. I, on the other hand, couldn't fall asleep. I was dead tired, but my mind started racing as soon as my head hit the pillow.

I couldn't stop thinking that something had changed in the last few days. What it was that had changed, was what was keeping me awake. If you remember a short while back, I was sure my marriage was on the outs. I didn't think I could make it work. I was quite sure I didn't want to make it work. I had even briefly contemplated having an affair. Yet now, there was nothing I wanted more than to make it work. What changed? Was it something to do with me, or was it something to do with Zach? I finally dozed off after what seemed like hours.

When I woke up the next morning, I felt like I hadn't slept at all. The scent of coffee brewing was the only thing that made me get out of bed. I made my way to the kitchen and was surprised to see Zach with my apron on at the stove.

"I hope you are in the mood for scrambled eggs," he said. Just then the toaster popped. I asked him if he needed help, but he instructed me to sit down at the table. A glass of orange juice was at both of our seats. It seemed all was forgiven.

Zach finished the eggs and put an even serving on both of our plates before buttering the toast. Then he joined me at the table. The eggs were a little overcooked and dry, but I wasn't about to complain. It had been quite some time since Zach made us breakfast.

About halfway through breakfast, Zach said, "I remembered something this morning."

To which I replied, "What's that?" I should have seen this coming.

"You never answered my question the other night."

I nearly choked on my dry eggs. Maybe all wasn't forgiven after all. I played the innocent.

"Which question is that?" I could tell by the look on his face he wasn't buying what I was trying so hard to sell.

In a bit more of a serious tone, he said, "Why don't you like my father?" I had really hoped he had forgotten that I hadn't answered him. The last thing I wanted was to make things worse again. I knew I had to answer him this time. I also knew it wasn't going to be the whole truth.

"It's not that I don't like your father. I just didn't like the way he treated your mother. He disrespected her and talked down to her every chance he got. She didn't deserve to be treated that way." I wasn't prepared for Zach's response at all.

"How was what happened between my mother and father any of your business? What gives you the right to judge my father that way?" With that, he got up from the dining room table without finishing his breakfast and walked out the door.

CHAPTER 11

Another thing had changed recently. I had started working from home. At first, I thought it was a bad idea. But not having to get dressed or having to leave the house to go to work was growing on me. After hearing Zach pull out of the driveway, I made my way out onto the back deck. I needed to relax and clear my mind. I looked over the railing and watched the fish as they swam around the pond looking for food. With all the craziness that had happened the last couple of days, I had forgotten to feed them. I grabbed a handful of fish food from the container we had hanging from the railing and dropped it into the pond. Lots of fish lips popped up instantly and devoured every pellet I had dropped in. Poor things must have been starving.

After dropping a second handful of fish food into the pond, I made my way back into the house. I couldn't stop thinking about how much the dynamics of my marriage had changed in the past few days. Zach went from being the loving, caring, sometimes overly romantic husband, to the husband who slept on the couch and walked out of the house without even saying goodbye. I, on the other hand, went from being the wife that felt like she was suffocating in her marriage, to the wife that would do anything to save her marriage.

After a quick shower, I got dressed and took Spaz for a walk. It was a bright sunny day. The birds were chirping in unison. I could feel my spirits starting to lift. I had to come up with a way to fix whatever it was that was now broken between me and Zach. As I walked, I replayed the conversation we had had during breakfast before he got up and left. Everything came back to Zach's father. My least favorite person in the world was the cause of the problems in my marriage. Zach was upset with me because I had told him I didn't like his father because of the way he had treated his mother. After all, it was none of my business as he so nicely told me.

How in the world was I supposed to fix that? Was I supposed to erase all the memories I had of his father mistreating his mother? The more I thought about it, the more it started to irritate me. If Zach's father treated his mother the way he did with me there in their house, how had he treated her when I wasn't there? How much worse had Zach witnessed than I had, and why was he so forgiving of his father? I think that was the part that confused me more than anything else. I can tell you with complete certainty that if my father had ever treated my mother the way Zach's father had treated his mother just once, I would never have forgiven him for it.

Spaz's poor little legs had had it by the time we walked around one block. When we got home, he lapped up most of the water in his bowl before heading straight to his bed and passing out. I went straight to the kitchen and cleaned up the mess Zach had made while preparing our breakfast. I found myself wondering if he knew the whole time he was over-cooking the eggs, that he was going to bring up the unanswered question, or if he had just thought about it after he sat down at the table. Why had he gone through the trouble of making us breakfast, just to ruin it and storm off?

After I finished in the kitchen, I grabbed my phone and went back out on the deck. With Zach out of the house, it seemed like the perfect time to call my mother and fill her in on what was going on. There really was no one else I would've trusted to talk to about such a personal thing. She answered on the second ring. It was so good to hear her voice after the day I had been having. She knew just from the way I said 'Hello' that something was wrong. Mothers always know.

Over the next thirty minutes, I filled her in on everything that had happened over the last few days. She was a little upset that I hadn't called to tell her about Zach's father having his mini-stroke. She was more concerned about him than I was. I asked for her advice on how I could mend my marriage. When I heard her answer, I dropped the phone.

CHAPTER 12

Two days later I found myself walking the aisles of Stop & Shop buying the ingredients for lasagna. It was going to be my first time making it. I had no idea there are three different kinds of cheese in lasagna. I would have much rather been making spaghetti and meatballs, but when I asked Zach what his father's favorite meal was, he said lasagna. So, there I was buying the ingredients to make lasagna for my least favorite person in the world.

You should have seen the look on Zach's face when I told him we should invite his father and Bonnie over for dinner. He thought he misunderstood what I had said. He asked me three times if I was serious. To be completely honest, having Zach's father in our house, never mind cooking for him, was the last thing I wanted, but my mother assured me it would help save my marriage. A small sacrifice for the greater good. I had even gone the extra mile and bought a nice bouquet of flowers to put in the center of the dining room table. I needed to have something that would make me smile.

By the time Zach arrived home from work, the lasagna was in the oven, and I was making homemade garlic bread. I must admit, it smelled amazing in our kitchen that night. Zach had picked up two bottles of red wine. I was quite sure his father was not supposed to be drinking wine with all the medications he was on after his mini-stroke, but that was none of my business. If he didn't care, why should I? I shouldn't tell you this, but just the thought of Zach's father having a bad reaction from mixing wine with his medications put a spring in my step.

For the first time in almost a week, Zach came up behind me, wrapped his arms around me, and told me he loved me. I couldn't believe it. My mother had been right. Little did Zach know that everything I was doing was for him not for his father. I looked over at the clock and realized our company would be arriving in twenty minutes. Twenty more minutes before my skin would start to crawl.

Zach went to take a shower and change while I put the garlic bread in the oven and set the table. I considered lighting candles but decided against it. There was definitely nothing romantic about that evening's dinner. I heard the sound of Zach's father's car pulling into the driveway at the same time I heard Zach coming out of the bathroom. Thank God for small miracles. If Zach's father had shown up before Zach had finished in the bathroom, I would have been left alone with his father and Bonnie. What a horrible thought.

I took my time taking the lasagna and the garlic bread out of the oven. I didn't want to be the one to open the door when they rang the doorbell. Every second counted. Ding-dong. Zach went to open the door while I put the garlic bread into a breadbasket I had just bought earlier at Stop & Shop. Ever the hostess. Reality hit the second I heard Zach's father's voice. I couldn't even remember the last time he had been in our house. It was show time. Fake it until you make it as they say.

Zach came into the kitchen with his father right behind him and then Bonnie pulling up the rear. I wasn't sure if they wanted to shake my hand or God forbid hug me, so I took my time cutting the lasagna into serving-size pieces while we all exchanged pleasantries. Just the thought of Zach's father hugging me brought the taste of throw up into my mouth.

Zach and I sat in our usual seats at the ends of the table, while Zach's father and Bonnie sat at opposite sides facing each other. I silently cursed myself for not planning this out better. I should have placed the vase of flowers off-center so it would have blocked my direct line of sight I now had of Zach's father. It was the first time I had seen him since he had his mini-stroke. From the looks of him, it had taken a toll on him. I almost felt a little sorry for him. As they say, 'Almost doesn't count except in horseshoes.'

After we finished eating, Zach and his father went into the living room to watch the local news, while Bonnie and I cleaned up in the kitchen. I had assumed we would be doing so in silence, but Bonnie had other plans. As soon as she heard them both sit down on the couch and the television turn on, she started bombarding me with questions about Zach's mother. She caught me completely off guard. I don't think we had ever spoken more than ten words to each other. I didn't know what was going on. Was she testing me to see what I would tell her? Had Zach or his father put her up to this?

I had tried really hard to read her. Though her questions seemed like they could be a trap being laid for me, her tone, and her body language seemed sincere and almost desperate. Maybe we were becoming allies without either of us knowing it. From what Bonnie was asking and telling me, it became rather obvious that Zach's father was losing his shine to her rather quickly. Their relationship had taken a turn for the worse when Bonnie started asking questions about Zach's mother. Seemed I was not the only one that was told it was none of my business. The subject of Zach's mother and her death was never to be brought up again. After being told that, Bonnie became more curious and more suspicious. I still wasn't one hundred percent convinced I wasn't being tricked into saying something I would later regret, so I stuck to the facts and kept my suspicions to myself.

"I am not sure how much I can tell you. I really didn't spend much time with Zach's parents. Mostly because I always felt uncomfortable. From the time I did spend with Zach's mother without his father around I can tell you she was a warm, loving, caring woman. I really enjoyed our conversations. She loved to tell me stories about when Zach was a baby and a young boy. She did everything for Zach and his father. Sadly, it was never appreciated."

I stopped there. I didn't want to get into the way Zach's father treated his own wife or the day she died. I could see by the reaction Bonnie had when I told her about how Zach's mother had done everything for them, and that it was never appreciated, that she was living the same hell. She too was being treated as a servant instead of as a partner. Although I didn't really know her, my heart ached for her. She had put herself into a dire situation with a bad man. At least she hadn't married him.

CHAPTER 13

Shortly after Bonnie and I had finished in the kitchen, our dinner guests left. Zach's father had started feeling sick. My guess was it was from mixing wine with his medications. Trust me, I am not complaining. The less time I had to spend with that man the better. Besides, Zach was so pleased with me for suggesting we invite them over for dinner that he showed his appreciation when we went to bed later. He was very appreciative.

While Zach was snoring away, I was too deep in thought to fall asleep. I kept replaying all the things Bonnie had told me in the kitchen earlier. Zach's father's attitude toward her had changed dramatically ever since she started asking him about his dead wife. I understand that talking about a loved one that you have lost can be distressing, but to forbid the subject ever be brought up again was a bit much. Was he too embarrassed about the way he had treated his own wife to talk about her? That couldn't be the reason considering he was now treating Bonnie the same way.

After a terrible night's sleep, I woke to find Zach had already left for work. When I walked into the kitchen, I found a handwritten note leaning against the vase of flowers on the table. It read, 'Thank you for everything you did last night. Love Zach.' I made a mental note to call my mother later and thank her for her motherly advice. I was quickly learning how she had made her marriage last so long.

Having Zach's father and Bonnie over the night before wasn't half as awful as I thought it would be. I had made a connection with Bonnie that I had never thought would be possible. I still wasn't completely sure if she had been playing me to see what I would say about Zach's mother and her death only to report it back to Zach and his father. I needed to talk to her again alone and see what else she was willing to tell me. How much if anything, did she know about the day Zach's mother died? Did she think it was an accident, a suicide, or a murder? I needed to find a way to get her to bring it up to me instead of the other way around.

The trickiest part about all of that was figuring out how I could get time alone with Bonnie without Zach or his father knowing about it. It got even trickier when I factored in that Bonnie didn't drive. It was going to take lots of planning and scheming. Talking over the phone wasn't an option. If Bonnie was in on something with Zach and his father, talking on the phone was too dangerous. How would I know if either of them would be listening in on a second phone? It would be impossible to deny saying something if they had heard it come out of my mouth.

Spaz was crying to go outside for his morning routine, so I let him out in the backyard while I fed the fish. For the first time in a while, I spotted lots of new babies swimming around. I watched while they followed who I assumed was their mother as she searched for her breakfast. I know this is going to sound strange, but while I was watching the babies follow their mother, I started wondering if I would be a good mother. I had gone through phases in my life when I thought I wanted to be a mother. I had also gone through phases when I thought I would be an awful mother. It's not like you could try out mothering and then return the baby if you decide it's not for you.

When Spaz had finished doing his thing, he joined me on the deck. I knew by the way he just sat there looking at me that he was ready for his breakfast. We went back into the house. I fed Spaz and made myself a cup of coffee. I had some planning to do with Zach out of the house.

First things first, I needed to do some work. I went into my home office/extra bedroom and started editing some of the stories I had been sent for the weekend edition. When you live in a place where there is not much going on the stories that would normally be on the back page become front-page news. 'Mother hen walks her ten chicks across busy street' was our biggest new story. I had to admit the photo that went along with it was adorable.

When I finished editing the mother hen story, I went into the living room and sat down in the recliner. I was sipping a cup of coffee waiting for an idea of how I could talk to Bonnie again to magically pop into my head. Considering Bonnie didn't drive, there was no way she would have been able to come to me by herself unless she took a taxi. That meant I would have to go to her. With that part figured out, I needed to work on the next part, figuring out how I would know when Bonnie would be home alone. How often did Zach's father go out of the house in his condition without Bonnie?

The more I thought about it, the more I realized I would not be able to figure that part out on my own. It wasn't like I was going to go sit in my car near their house just in case the opportunity presented itself. The only answer I could come up with was to somehow get Zach involved without him knowing it. If he caught onto what I was doing, I would be back in the doghouse with Spaz.

CHAPTER 14

Sometimes in life, good things happen to good people. More often, terrible things happen to good people, while good things happen to horrible people. That was one of the main reasons I had such a tough time believing in God. How many good people have died at an early age, while horrible people live into their eighties or nineties? Let me give you a perfect example, Joseph James DeAngelo, Jr. Most people know him better as the Golden State Killer. He killed at least thirteen innocent people, yet he is still alive at seventy-six years of age. How is that fair? Why does God let things like that happen?

I bring that up because I did consider myself a good person. I was always as honest as possible, and I treated people with the respect they deserved. Something good was coming my way. I could feel it. I was ready, willing, and eager to accept it.

When Zach came home from work, I asked him how he felt about ordering pizza for dinner. I had been so preoccupied with my scheming and planning; I had forgotten to take something out of the freezer for dinner. At first, he wasn't thrilled with the pizza idea until I reminded him that we had a few beers left in the fridge. Zach loved the pizza and beer combo.

The pizza arrived thirty-five minutes later. Zach always ordered pepperoni on his pizza. I didn't mind pepperoni, but I hated how greasy it made the pizza. I took a napkin and dabbed away at my slices soaking up all the grease. Zach always said I was soaking up all the flavor with the grease. I would rather have a tasteless pizza than have all that grease sitting in my stomach. About halfway through my first slice, my good thing made its presence.

"I talked to my father today. He hasn't been feeling good lately. He spoke to his doctor, and he wants him to go in for a check-up. He asked me if I could drive him to the hospital tomorrow in case he gives him something that would prevent him from driving back home." Was that opportunity I could hear knocking? "Of course, I said yes. It wasn't like I could say no. He is my father after all."

Knock, knock. Who's there? Opportunity.

"What time is his appointment?" I asked.

"Ten tomorrow morning. I had to put in for some personal time at work." I wasn't expecting my chance to talk to Bonnie alone to come so soon but I wasn't about to miss it.

"Will Bonnie be going with you to the hospital for moral support?" If he said she would be going with them I would have to put my plan on hold for now.

"No, Bonnie is staying at home. I think my father needs a little break from her. It sounds like she has been getting under his skin lately." If Zach wanted me to feel sorry for his father, he was crap out of luck.

For the rest of that night, I tried my hardest to hide my growing excitement about my upcoming talk with Bonnie the next morning. I was hopeful Bonnie knew more than she had already shared with me. If not, my surprise visit was going to be a waste of my time. There was a possibility that Bonnie, like me, held things back due to being unsure about where my loyalty would lie. I was married to Zach. She could have been worried I would've told Zach what she had told and asked me. Little did she know, my loyalty was wavering more and more every minute.

After another restless night, I crawled out of bed and put a pot of coffee on. Considering Zach wasn't going to work until after he brought his father to the hospital, he chose to sleep in. While I waited for the coffee machine to work its magic, I let Spaz out and fed the fish. A little over a week ago I felt like I was drowning. Now I felt like I was the queen of the pond. My adrenaline was pumping. Yes, I had talked to my mother about Zach's father and his mother's death, but being able to talk to someone who was living in the same house as Zach's father, seemed like a much better option. I couldn't wait to find out what she knew.

Zach finally got up, took a shower, drank a cup of coffee, and ate a bowl of cereal. A few minutes later he was out the door on his way to pick up his father. I waited five minutes before jumping in my car and heading over to see Bonnie. I saw Zach's car pulling out of his father's driveway just as I came around the corner. I had no idea how long they would be at the hospital, so I wasted no time. I pulled into the driveway, got out of the car, and made my way to their front door.

On the third knock, Bonnie opened the door. She was definitely surprised to see me standing there.

"Can I come in?" I asked. She stepped aside so I could walk past her into the house. She stuck her head out and looked both ways making sure Zach and his father were nowhere in sight, then she closed the door behind her.

"What are you doing here?" she asked. Before I got into my real reason for stopping by unannounced, I needed to feel her out. I needed to know if I could trust her not to repeat anything we were hopefully going to discuss.

"I was thinking about the things you had told me the other night while we were doing the dishes. Then this morning Zach mentioned that his father had told him that you were getting under his skin. I just wanted to check up on you while you were home alone and make sure you are alright." It wasn't exactly a lie. I was concerned about her, mostly about her safety considering who she was sharing a house with.

"Zach's father told him I am getting under his skin?" I was having a tough time reading her face though her tone sounded concerned.

"Not exactly in those words. Zach said it sounded like you were getting under his father's skin by the things he was saying about you. Zach didn't get into details about what his father had said about you. Either way, it concerned me after everything that has happened in the past." I may have gone too far that time.

"What do you mean after everything that has happened in the past? What else has happened?" I felt like I was stuck in a corner with nowhere to hide. I needed to decide right there and then if I was going to trust Bonnie or not. One slip of the tongue and I may have just buried myself in a pile of crap too deep to dig myself out of.

CHAPTER 15

When the time comes to make a big decision, a decision that could ruin your life, how do you go about making that decision? Do you leave it up to fate? Do you flip a coin, heads, or tails? Do you seek out a fortune teller? Do you ask your friends for their advice? Do you work your way through eeny, meeny, miny, moe? I take the easiest way out. I listen to my gut. If the thought of what I am about to do makes my stomach tie in a knot, I take that as a sign that it is the wrong thing for me to do. Don't get me wrong, I am not saying I don't sometimes still do it, but when I do still do it, I always live to regret it.

This was one of those times. I took a moment to clear my head and just focused on Bonnie's behavior the other night when she was telling me about how things had changed between her and Zach's father. Did she sound sincere and upset, or did she sound like she had practiced everything she had said in a mirror ahead of time?

I had no idea how long Zach and his father would be at the hospital. I knew it was a twelve-minute ride both ways. On average, you usually wait fifteen to twenty minutes in the waiting room before even going in to see the doctor. The length of the visit with the doctor would depend on how many tests they would be doing. I didn't want to risk still being with Bonnie when they made it back home. I looked at the clock. I had already been there for five minutes. That left me thirty more minutes to find out everything I could from Bonnie before I needed to leave.

"How much do you know about the way (in case you hadn't noticed, I never call Zach's father by his name. It makes me feel disgusting when I say his name aloud) Henry treated his wife?" I would've done anything for some mouthwash to wash the grossness off my tongue.

"I don't know much at all about his wife. Every time I tried to ask him about her, he shut me down. I assumed it was still too painful for him to talk about." That was not what I wanted to hear. She knew nothing that could help me. This was a complete waste of my time.

Then she got me right where I didn't want to be.

"What can you tell me about the way Henry treated his wife?" I could feel my stomach growling because I hadn't eaten breakfast, but I couldn't feel any knots tightening. I threw caution to the wind.

"I can only tell you what I witnessed myself. Any time I had asked Zach about things between his mother and father he always told me it was none of my business, which I guess it really wasn't." I took a deep breath and kept telling myself I was doing the right thing. Bonnie deserved to know as much as she could about the man she was living with.

I told Bonnie the same exact things I had told my mother. The darkness that would take over the minute Zach's father would walk through the door. The way nothing she ever did was good enough. The way he would belittle her right in front of me and Zach. It had been obvious she was afraid of her own husband. I could tell everything I was saying was resonating with Bonnie.

"Does he treat you like that? Are you afraid of the man you are living with?" It was clear she wasn't sure if she could trust me. She just sat there looking down at the floor. My heart ached for her. Nobody deserves to be treated that way.

"Can you tell me how his wife died?" Sweet Jesus! I had not planned to offer up that information. I was hoping she already knew so it wouldn't be me spilling the beans. What choice did I have at that point? It wasn't like I could tell her I didn't know.

"All I know for sure is that Zach found her dead at the bottom of the basement stairs." She instantly looked over at the door to the basement. Then she came at me strong.

"Was it an accident?" Was she playing me like a fiddle? Had I fallen into her trap? Did Zach or his father put her up to this? I played it as safely as I could.

"The police ruled it an accidental death. Though I have always wondered how she accidentally fell head first down the basement stairs with the basement door closed."

I was hoping that would be enough to satisfy her, but it wasn't. "Wait a minute. Are you saying you don't believe it was an accident? Do you think it was suicide? Do you think someone pushed her down the stairs?" It was feeling more and more like I had my head stuck in a guillotine just waiting for the blade to drop.

"I honestly don't know what I believe. I tried talking to Zach about it a couple of times, but he got upset with me every time. Like father, like son, I guess. Hey look, I have to run. I don't want to risk being here when they get back from the hospital. You can talk to me anytime."

With that, I got up from the dining room chair and walked over to the door. Bonnie followed right behind me.

"Thank you for telling me about Henry's wife and about how she died. It is nice to know I am not the only one he has no respect for." We said our goodbyes and I was on my way.

CHAPTER 16

I wasn't surprised to hear Zach's car pulling into the driveway fifteen minutes after I did. If I had stayed talking to Bonnie just a few minutes longer Zach and I would have probably driven right by each other. How would I have explained what I was doing in that area? Timing is everything in this game we call life.

I waited for Zach to come to tell me how his father made out at the doctor's office, but instead, he went straight to the bedroom to change his clothes. I had forgotten he needed to go to work. I didn't want him to think I didn't care about his father's health considering our marriage was on the mend, so I went to him instead of waiting any longer for him to come to me.

"How did things go for your father at the doctor's office?" I did my best to sound sincere and concerned, neither of which I was.

"Thank you for asking but I really don't want to talk about it right now. I need to get to work. Let's talk about it when I get home tonight." He walked over, gave me a kiss on the cheek, and left for work. I just stood there not knowing what to think. If he didn't want to talk about it, did that mean things didn't go well? Did the doctor find something else wrong with his father?

I spent most of the day working outside in the backyard. Spaz was running around like, well, like a spaz, while I was trying to spruce up the pond. The water lilies weren't looking too good and there was quite a bit of algae all over the rocks in the waterfall section. It would've been much easier if I just climbed into the pond, but with all the small babies swimming around, I was afraid I might step on one. Once I had done all I could in the pond I moved on to the garden which had been ignored for a few weeks. Most of the tomatoes had either been partially eaten by the squirrels or fallen to the ground and started rotting.

When I finished in the garden I went back into the house and started making spaghetti and meatballs for dinner once again. I could tell Zach had not been in the best of moods when he got back from taking his father to the doctor so I figured I would make him what he likes the most for dinner. I was trying my best to be a good wife. I didn't want my marriage to fail due to my lack of trying. For better or worse, for richer or poorer, in sickness and in health, till death do us part. Those were the vows I had made on our wedding day, and I intended to keep them.

When Zach got home from work, he seemed like he was in an even worse mood than he had been before he left. Something was definitely bothering him. I gave him time and space to relax. He didn't need me pestering him the minute he walked through the door. I kept our dinner warm while he took a long hot shower. When he came out of the bathroom, he was wearing a pair of pajama bottoms and a white T-shirt. I thought for a moment he was heading to bed, but he came into the kitchen and sat down at the table.

I made us both a plate of spaghetti and meatballs and grabbed us both a bottled water. We were out of wine, and I had forgotten to pick up a new bottle. I served Zach his dinner and then sat down in my usual chair. We still hadn't spoken one word to each other. For all I knew it could be something I said or did that put him in this worse mood. I started feeling uncomfortable, but I didn't want to be the one to break the silence.

About halfway through his dinner Zach finally spoke.

"Everything was good at the doctor's office this morning. The doctor reminded my pig-headed father that he shouldn't be drinking any alcohol while he is taking his medications. Mixing alcohol and his medications was what was making him sick." That wasn't what I had been expecting to hear. If everything was good at the doctor's office, then why was Zach in such a mood? I waited to see what he would say next.

"Sorry, I am in a lousy mood. I've been trying to snap out of it all day." Was he seriously not going to tell me why he was in such a lousy mood? I couldn't take it anymore. He had brought up the subject in the first place. Did he really expect me to let it go unexplained?

"Did something else happen when you were with your father this morning?" I was half expecting him to tell me it was none of my business but that's not what happened.

"While we were driving home from the doctor's office my father decided to have a man-to-man talk with me. He told me he is kicking Bonnie out of the house." Again, not what I was expecting.

"Why would he do that? I really enjoyed Bonnie's company the other night. She is a lot nicer than I gave her credit for." Zach finished his last meatball before answering. I offered to get him more, but he said he was too full.

"He said Bonnie has been driving him nuts by asking questions about my mom and how she died. He keeps telling her it is none of her business, but she still keeps asking. He's had enough. He wants her gone."

I had never realized how much Zach is like his father. 'It is none of your business' is a sentence they both like to throw around, especially to the people they live with and supposedly love. It didn't make any sense to me. Why was it such a horrible thing for Bonnie to ask the man she is living with about his dead wife? Horrible enough for him to want to throw her out of the house. That didn't sound anything like love to me.

"What did you say to your father when he told you that? Did you try to change his mind?"

The look Zach gave me after I asked him those questions answered my questions.

"Why would I try to change his mind? I would probably react the same way if you never listened to me when I told you to stop doing something." Did I just hear him right? If I didn't listen to him when he *told* me to stop doing something, he would probably throw me out of our house. Who was this man sitting across from me? I was starting to wonder if I knew my husband at all.

CHAPTER 17

Do we ever really know anyone? Everyone has secrets from their past that they hide away from everybody in their life. That includes the people they hold near and dear. We all build up walls to protect ourselves from getting hurt. Never letting anyone completely in. It is natural human behavior. We all tell little white lies when necessary to prevent one of our dirty little secrets from being revealed. We are the mama bears protecting our cubs.

While I lay in bed that night, I kept replaying what Zach had said about throwing me out of our house, over and over in my head. When he had said it earlier, right after he finished eating the meal I had made for him, I said nothing in response. I was completely flabbergasted. I just got up from the table, put the leftovers in the fridge, washed and dried all the dirty dishes, then went to read in bed. Zach went to the living room to watch television. When he came to bed later, I pretended to be asleep.

You know when you get a random thought that pops into your head and then in an instant, it's gone? No matter how hard you try, you just can't remember what the thought was. That is what happened while I was replaying Zach's semi-threat of throwing me out of the house. Typically, if I relax enough and clear my mind of all the white noise, I will remember what it was that had escaped my memory. The sound of Zach snoring was making it difficult for me to clear my mind. What he had said earlier had really thrown me for a loop. I didn't want to be in the same bed with him. Now I wanted him to go sleep on the couch.

When Zach turned over onto his side his snoring died down like it always did. I was able to just lie there in peace, but it wasn't helping me. I tried willing myself to remember. I even went as far as asking God to help me remember. Still nothing. I finally gave up. I tossed and turned until I got comfortable enough to drift off to sleep. My body felt lighter while my eyes felt heavier.

I had started to twitch a little like I always did right before I entered dreamland. Then just like that, the thought came back to me. I forced my eyelids open before the thought vanished into mid-air once again. While I had been replaying what Zach had said, something about it had seemed off. I had been too shocked when he first said it to even put much thought into it. My random thought that I had been chasing for the last thirty minutes was, if Zach agreed with his father's way of thinking, then why was he so upset in the first place? It would have made sense for him to be upset if he thought his father was in the wrong, but that wasn't the case.

The next morning, I woke up before Zach, but I stayed in bed. I had slept like crap once again, and I wasn't ready to face Zach just yet. When I heard him starting to get out of bed I pretended to still be sleeping. My mind instantly started working overtime trying to figure out what had caused Zach's bad mood the day before. I was tempted to get up when I smelled the coffee starting to brew. I would have done anything for a strong cup of coffee, but I fought my body to stay in bed until I could hear Zach walking out the door.

Zach took his shower and got dressed while the coffee maker did its thing. When I finally heard the front door open and close, I sat up in bed. I waited until I heard the car pulling out of the driveway to get out of bed. I went straight to the kitchen and filled the biggest coffee cup we had all the way to the top. The coffee was extraordinarily strong like it was every time Zach made it. The poor man couldn't even boil an egg correctly.

I grabbed a notepad and a pen before sitting down at the dining room table. After taking a gulp of my coffee I opened the notepad to an empty page and proceeded to write down exactly what Zach had told me his father had said to him. 'He told me he is kicking Bonnie out of the house. He said Bonnie has been driving him nuts asking questions about my mom and how she died. He keeps telling her it is none of her business, but she still keeps asking. He's had enough. He wants her gone.' If everything at the doctor's office regarding his father's health was good like Zach had told me it was, then whatever had put him in a bad mood had to be related to what his father had told him.

I read what I had written down several times trying to figure out what had caused Zach's bad mood. The only thing I kept coming up with was that Zach thought his father was making a mistake by throwing Bonnie out of the house, but I knew that wasn't the case after what he told me last night. I was missing something, but what?

I got up from the table and let Spaz out into the backyard while I fed the fish. Maybe some fresh air would help clear my mind. I watched the little babies follow their mother around the perimeter of the pond. Then just like that, I figured it out, or at least I thought I figured it out. The only way of being sure I was correct would be to ask Zach, but I knew if I did, I would hear his favorite saying: 'It's none of your business.' I found myself wondering if either of my parents had ever said that to each other. I would bet my life they had never even thought it, never mind actually said it aloud to one another.

Spaz and I went back into the house; he headed right for his water bowl, and I went right back to the table. After another big gulp of my semi-cool coffee, I reread what I had written one more time. Although it didn't really make sense to me, I was sure I had figured out the cause of Zach's bad mood. Zach, like his father, was upset because Bonnie had been asking questions about his mother and her death. Why either of them would be so upset about Bonnie asking questions had me extremely confused. Why was it such a big deal? Was there a secret they were both hiding from everyone else?

CHAPTER 18

As I tore the page I had written on out of the notepad, and then ripped it into tiny pieces, I found myself wondering if I was making a mountain out of a molehill. It was possible, no matter how small that possibility may be, that neither Zach nor his father had ever gotten over their loss and that was why they didn't want me or Bonnie asking about it. I put the ripped-up page into the trash can. Then I removed the trash bag, carried it outside, and put it in the trash bin. I didn't want Zach to find it when he got home from work.

Being suspicious of your father-in-law is one thing, but also being suspicious of your own husband is far worse. It was very difficult for me to stop thinking about what Zach had said to me for even ten minutes. Was it possible he could've been joking about throwing me out of the house? I wanted to talk to Bonnie again but that wasn't possible. I wondered if Zach's father had been serious about throwing Bonnie out of their house. Maybe he was exaggerating to impress Zach. Just blowing off some steam while Bonnie wasn't around.

I remember the first time I met Bonnie. Zach and I had stopped by his father's house to pick up some tools his father was letting us borrow when we were putting the addition on our backyard deck. My first impression of her was that she was a recovering addict of some sort. I would guess she was a good ten to fifteen years younger than Zach's father. I really didn't pay her much mind. I assumed she was only with Zach's father for whatever money he had left from his wife's life insurance. Once it was gone, she would be gone.

My impression of her never wavered, until the conversation we had in my kitchen. She may still be an addict in recovery, but she was also a woman who needed my help. When I think back to the first time I met her, I can't help but wonder if she was putting on a front for us. Was Zach's father already treating her the same way he had treated his wife? Did she want us to think everything was hunky-dory, when in fact, it was just the opposite? I wish I had known then what I know now.

Considering I couldn't talk to Bonnie again I did the next best thing: I called my mother. She answered the phone on the second ring like she always did. Her tone was cheerful and loving as it always was.

"Is this my Robin calling me?" she asked when she picked up the phone. She still called me *her Robin* after all these years. It made me smile every time.

"Hello Mom, are you busy?" I asked. I knew that was a silly question. She could be elbows deep in her garden and she would still tell me the same thing.

"I am never too busy to talk to you." Nailed it!

Over the next half hour, I filled her in on everything that had happened the last couple of days. For the most part, she didn't say a word, she just listened. I wish I was half as good a listener as she was. When I finished my two-day story, I asked her what she thought it all meant. The tone of her voice had changed dramatically.

"Why would he talk to his wife that way? Your father would never talk to me like that. He really said he would throw you out of your own house if you didn't listen to what he told you to do? Who does he think he is, your boss instead of your husband?"

Maybe this wasn't such a good idea after all. She was all worked up, which meant the second we got off the phone she would be telling my father everything I had just told her. They would never want to see Zach again, and if they did see him, it wouldn't be very pleasant. My father had always been, and always would be, overprotective of his only daughter. He wouldn't stand for Zach talking to me that way. Husbands are meant to respect their wives. Apparently, not all husbands felt the same way as my father did.

I did my best to calm my mother down before we hung up. The ironic thing about it all is that I was hoping she would tell me I was overreacting, and that Zach was a great guy. Instead, that was what I was telling her even though I wasn't sure anymore if it was the truth. I had three more hours before Zach would walk through the door again. I needed to get all the negative thoughts out of my head. Until I knew for sure what was really going on with my husband, I needed to play the part of June Cleaver, the perfect dutiful wife.

CHAPTER 19

I had been so distracted trying to figure out what was going on with my marriage, that I had completely forgotten about dinner yet again. It wasn't until I heard my stomach starting to rumble that I realized I had also missed eating lunch. Hopefully, Zach would be in a much better mood than he had been the day before when he got home from work. I stood in front of the mirror in the hallway practicing my fake smile and my fake laugh. I didn't want to have to deal with Zach asking me what was wrong with me. It wasn't like he would listen or try to understand. After all, whatever was going on between his father and Bonnie was none of my business.

I felt my entire body cringe and tighten up when I heard Zach's car pulling into the driveway. Just a couple of weeks ago I was conjuring up ideas to ruin my marriage. Then last week I was conjuring up ideas to save my marriage. This week I didn't even recognize the man I had married. Was he a lot more like his father than I had ever noticed? Had he been pretending all this time to be one of the good guys, when in fact he was one of the bad guys?

When I heard the car door close, I ran to the back door with Spaz right behind me. Spaz took off running into the backyard while I closed the door. I knelt on the bench and looked over the railing at the fish pond. There was a fifty-fifty chance Zach would come looking for me. The odds could be higher depending on how hungry he was. I had already fed the fish earlier in the morning but still, I grabbed a handful of food and started throwing the pellets one by one into the pond. Those fish would have eaten all day long if they could have fed themselves.

When I was about halfway done with the pellets, the back door opened, and Zach stuck his head out.

"There you are." His tone sounded friendlier than it was the day before. When Spaz heard Zach's voice, he came running onto the deck to see him. This may sound pathetic, but I hated that Zach was Spaz's *person* instead of me. I was the one who was home all day with him. I was the one who fed him and gave him water every day. I was the one who took him for walks and let him play in the backyard. Yet, the second Zach came home, it was like I didn't even exist anymore. Maybe it was a male bonding thing.

While Zach was bent down rubbing Spaz's head he asked, "What's for dinner? I'm starving." I threw the last of the pellets into the fish pond before turning around to face him. I plastered one of my practiced smiles on my face just in time as Zach looked up at me. I didn't want to admit that I had forgotten about dinner, so I told a little white lie.

"I was hoping we could go out for dinner, or order something to be delivered. If not, I could warm up the leftover spaghetti and meatballs from last night. I know how much you love leftover spaghetti and meatballs."

"I am kind of tired from working all day. You know I don't like going out to eat on workdays." His friendlier tone had changed in a matter of minutes. It was now somewhere between irritated and disappointed. I couldn't catch a break no matter what I tried. He turned and went back into the house with Spaz trailing right behind him. I sat down on the bench and for the first time in weeks, I felt like I was drowning. It was like I could feel a strong hand holding my head underwater, while I looked up into the eyes of the person who was waiting for me to blow out my last bubble of air.

When I snapped out of it, I took a few deep breaths before going back into the house. I had always thought burning to death would be the worst way to die, but now I was convinced it would be drowning. I found Zach and Spaz sitting on the couch watching a rerun of *Married with Children*. I had often found myself jealous of the life Peg Bundy lived. Although Al did a lot of whining and complaining, there wasn't anything he wouldn't do to keep Peg happy.

Since Zach had not answered me about dinner I tried again. "Considering going out to dinner is out of the question, do you want me to order something to be delivered, or would you prefer the leftovers?"

I was starting to feel like his mother or his servant, rather than his wife, and I didn't like it. We were equals after all. Unlike the situation with his father and Bonnie, this was my business. He took his time answering me. I couldn't tell whether he was actually thinking about what he wanted to eat, or if he was trying to stress me out by making me wait for an answer.

"I do love leftover spaghetti and meatballs. Plus, it's quicker, cheaper, and easier than ordering something else."

I would've bet my life he was going to say the leftovers. It did make the most sense. We were always tight on money. I did my best to not think about it, while Zach couldn't stop himself from thinking about it.

"Leftovers it is," I said, as I walked out of the living room and into the kitchen.

Ten minutes later we were sitting at the table eating our leftovers. I must admit I love any kind of pasta dish as a leftover. To me, it tastes even better as a leftover than it does when it is first cooked. One of the few things Zach and I would agree on lately. I was glad he hadn't asked me for a glass of wine because just like dinner, I had forgotten about buying a new bottle.

We spent our dinner in silence which was okay with me. I was still trying to adjust to Zach's new way of talking to me. It was like he had lost all his patience with me. I honestly had no idea what I had done that was so wrong that he thought I deserved to be treated so badly. Where was the man I had married? I wanted him back instead of the man who was sitting across from me.

After we finished eating, I started washing the dishes right away. I thought Zach was going to dry them as I washed them, but instead, he remained in his chair. He had said something but with the water running I couldn't make out what it was. Once there was enough water in the sink to wash the dishes, I turned the water off.

"I couldn't hear what you were saying with the water running," I said, in a voice that sounded to me like a wife who was interested in what her husband had to say. When in fact, I wasn't interested at all.

Zach walked over and stood on the side of me while I washed the dishes. I waited for him to grab the dish towel so he could start drying them, but instead, he left it hanging right behind him.

"I was saying I had something to tell you."

Sweet Jesus, please let it be something good this time. I didn't know how many more bad things I would be able to handle. I had a feeling I was about to find out.

"I talked to my father today. He told me Bonnie is gone."

Bonnie is gone. What was he telling me? What did he mean by gone?

I stopped washing the dishes and wiped my hands on the dish towel. The day after I visited Bonnie at her house she is gone.

"What do you mean she is gone?" I asked in a much more serious tone.

"Just what I said, she is gone."

I don't know about you, but when I hear someone say that someone is gone, it usually means they left where they were, or they died. Which of the two ways was Bonnie gone? A part of me was afraid to ask Zach any more questions. I knew it was only a matter of time before he told me it was none of my business, but it was my business. I had just seen her the day before. I was the one who had told her about how Zach's father had treated his mother. I was also the one that had told her about how his mother had died and about my suspicions. How could I not feel partly guilty? I needed to find out what had happened to Bonnie.

"Do you know where she has gone to?" I was trying my best to not sound overly worried or concerned, but I wasn't sure it was working. I was starting to sweat all over my body.

"That is all my father said. Bonnie is gone." Just the way he said it made me want to vomit in the sink with the rest of the dirty dishes. I couldn't allow myself to think about it anymore. I was seriously getting sick to my stomach.

"I am sorry to hear that," I said before turning back around and washing the rest of the dirty dishes. Instead of drying the dishes, Zach turned around and walked back into the living room, leaving me to finish everything on my own.

I had a new mission in life. I was going to find out where Bonnie was no matter what it took. Even if that meant destroying what was left of my marriage.

CHAPTER 20

Time changes everything, or at least it seemed that way to me. One day you are sleeping in a crib, then the next, you are a teenager in high school. One day you are married, then the next, you are divorced. One day you are a parent, then the next, you are a grandparent. One day you are collecting social security, then the next, you are buried six feet under. Life goes on, with or without us.

When I woke up the next morning and realized it was Friday, I couldn't help but feel a little sad. For the longest time, Friday night had been date night for me and Zach. Almost all of them had ended up being dinner and a movie or just a movie. After a few months of being married, it turned into every other Friday, then it turned into one Friday a month. Now I couldn't even remember the last time we saw a movie other than on Netflix.

By the time I was able to get myself out of bed and ready to face another day, Zach had already left for work. I had hoped to have a chance to ask him one more time about Bonnie being gone but it would have to wait until later. In the meantime, I needed to come up with a way to find out where Bonnie had gone in case Zach told me it was none of my business. I really didn't have too many options. I knew I couldn't ask Zach's father. I had no idea if Bonnie had any family in the area. Come to think of it, I didn't even know what Bonnie's last name was.

I started letting my imagination get the best of me. *Had Zach's father let her pack all her belongings before watching her walk out the front door? Had he thrown all of Bonnie's belongings out a window onto the sidewalk before escorting her out the front door? Had he pushed her down the basement stairs?* My thoughts were getting darker by the minute. I had to stop myself from thinking about it before I made an anonymous call to the police station for a wellness check.

Next came the guilt and blame thoughts. If I had tried harder to get to know Bonnie instead of just paying her no mind at all, I might've actually known her last name. If I had tried to talk to her more, maybe she would've confided in me sooner about the way Zach's father had been treating her. I might've been able to help her escape if that was what she wanted to do. I had known how Zach's father was with his wife. It only made sense that he would be the same way with Bonnie.

Thinking like that wasn't helping me in the slightest. I went into the kitchen and made a grocery list. I made sure to add a bottle of red and a bottle of white wine to the list and a six-pack of Zach's favorite beer. If things kept going the way they were, I was sure to become a full-fledged alcoholic in no time at all. I let Spaz out into the backyard to take care of his business before heading out to Stop & Shop.

I didn't usually get to the grocery store until later in the day. There were more employees in the store than there were shoppers which was fine with me. I had never been a fan of crowds. I always hated feeling like I couldn't get out of where I was quick enough if need be. That feeling intensified when I heard about the fire at the Station nightclub in West Warwick, Rhode Island, back in 2003. I was in high school back then, but I still remember it. At least a hundred people died, and another two hundred and thirty others were injured. I couldn't even imagine what had been going through their minds when they realized they were going to burn to death.

As I navigated my way through the aisles, I saw the back of a man's head that I thought looked familiar. He was gone from my view before I could be positive. I grabbed two jars of spaghetti sauce and dropped them in my cart before pushing the cart as quickly and quietly as I could down the rest of the aisle. When I got to the end of the aisle, I stuck my head out in hopes of catching another glimpse of the man. He was nowhere in sight. If it was who I thought it was, I didn't want him seeing me before I saw him.

I stopped my cart between the aisle I was in and the next aisle. Then I walked around the cart so I could sneak a peek down the aisle. The man wasn't in that aisle. Maybe he had gone in the opposite direction. I walked back around the cart and over to the next aisle. I peeked down that aisle and again he wasn't there. I was starting to think I had imagined seeing him. I grabbed onto my cart and pushed it into the next aisle. The next thing I knew, I had bumped my cart into Zach's father's cart.

I just stood there not knowing what to do. Should I say hello? Should I apologize and just keep shopping as if I didn't even know him? I really liked that option, but something about it felt wrong. What would Zach say if his father told him that I had bumped my cart into his at Stop & Shop and didn't even take the time to say hello? He just stood there looking at me. I wasn't even sure he had recognized me without having Zach on the side of me. Then he broke the awkward silence.

"Fancy meeting you here this early in the morning."

What choice did I have but to talk back to him now? That was the very first time we had been alone together, and I was feeling extremely uncomfortable.

"I have a bunch of errands to run today so I figured I would get the grocery shopping out of the way before it gets busy." By saying I had a bunch of errands to run, I was giving myself an excuse to get out of there as quickly as possible.

"I always come at this time. You do know this time of the morning is reserved for senior citizens, don't you?"

I looked up and down the aisle, and sure enough, every customer I could see was a silver top. How hadn't I noticed that earlier? Now I felt like everybody was looking at me weirdly. "I had no idea," I said, trying to not sound like a complete idiot. "I really should get going before I get yelled at by the manager." He backed his cart up so I could get around him then he said goodbye.

I started making my way down the aisle, then I stopped and turned around. We were the only two in the aisle now. In a hushed voice, I said, "I was sorry to hear about Bonnie." He stopped for a second, paused, and then went on his way without acknowledging what I had said. That one may come back and bite me in my behind.

CHAPTER 21

On the drive home from the supermarket, all I could think about was how long it was going to take Zach's father to tell Zach about bumping into me. Would he or wouldn't he mention that I had brought up Bonnie's name? I kept telling myself that I did the right thing. I had acknowledged that I knew Bonnie was gone, but I didn't ask any questions about what had happened. There was nothing for Zach to be upset with me about even if his father did tell him. So why did I have a bad feeling in the pit of my stomach?

When I got home, I put all the groceries away making sure Zach's beer would be the first thing he saw when he opened the refrigerator door. After I finished with the groceries, I let Spaz out into the backyard while I spent some quality time feeding and watching the fish. The little babies had already doubled in size and most of them had stopped following their mother around the pond. There was an all-black one with just one tiny orange spot on the top of his head. I named him Spot. He was very independent. Most times when I watched him, he stayed as far away from all the other fish as possible. He had become my favorite of them all.

When Spaz had had enough fun for the day, he joined me on the deck. He just sat there looking at me with his puppy dog eyes. I knew what that meant. He was ready to go back inside the house. He headed straight for his water bowl and then his bed. He had tired himself out. It was nap time. I had some thinking to do. I sat in my recliner and pushed it out as far as it would go so that I was almost lying flat. The more relaxed I am, the more clearly and easier I can think. I needed to have two plans ready to activate the minute Zach got home from work. One plan was for if Zach came home in a good mood. The other plan was for if Zach came home in a bad mood. The first thought that popped into my semi-relaxed mind was, *What the heck am I doing?*

How many wives sat at home while their husband was at work trying to come up with plans to match the mood their husband would be in when he got home from work? You know what? Let's make it even more interesting. How many spouses (husbands or wives) sat at home while their spouse was at work trying to come up with plans to match the mood their spouse would be in when they got home from work?

That wasn't how a marriage was supposed to be. I shouldn't have to be walking around on eggshells worrying if my husband was going to be in a bad mood again, or if he was going to be upset with me for some ridiculous reason. I didn't like the person I was becoming. I was trying to make sure Zach was happy at the expense of my own happiness. Who was looking out for my happiness?

I pushed the recliner back into the upright position. Thinking time was over at least for now. I got up and made my way over to my laptop. I opened Google and searched for the AMC movie theater closest to me. I had no idea what was playing but it was a Friday so there would be some new releases that had just come out. There weren't too many movies I was interested in, but they were showing an advanced screening of *A Star Is Born* with Bradley Cooper and Lady Gaga. They had a showing at 7:25 p.m. with extremely limited seating left. I bought two tickets online for the best seats they had left.

I wrapped two good-sized potatoes in aluminum foil and threw them in the oven. Zach and I both loved baked potatoes, but I hardly ever made them. They take forever to be just the right amount of baked. While the potatoes were baking, I jumped in the shower. I didn't want the two of us to have to take turns showering later. We wouldn't have enough time before the previews started at the movies. I loved watching all the previews. Zach and I would do a thumbs up or thumbs down after every preview. We were our own Siskel and Ebert.

By the time I was done showering and getting dressed, it was time to turn on the grill. I went out onto the deck and opened the lid to the grill. From the looks of it, Zach hadn't cleaned it after using it the last time. I grabbed the brush and scrubbed it down before lighting it. While the grill heated up, I went back inside to check on the potatoes and to grab the steaks that had been marinating in the fridge. My timing seemed to be right on. The potatoes were already starting to soften.

As I opened the back door, Spaz ran between my legs out into the backyard. I opened the lid to the grill and threw the steaks on before closing the lid again. I had watched Zach grill steaks so many times I knew exactly how he liked them. I went back inside and checked the time. Zach would be home in fifteen minutes and dinner would be ready five minutes later. While the steaks and potatoes cooked, I made us both a Caesar salad. A little extra dressing on mine and a few extra croutons on his.

When the salads were done, I put them in the fridge to stay cool before giving the potatoes another squeeze. I could tell by how deep my thumb went into the potato that they were almost ready. As I opened the back door again the smell of the steaks on the grill rushed in at me. I was suddenly starving. I loved the smell of meat cooking on a grill. I opened the lid and turned the steaks over. Spaz came up on the deck and laid down on the bench. He loved the smell and the taste of grilled meat too.

As I was going back into the house, I could hear Zach's car pulling into the driveway. He was home a few minutes earlier than I had expected. I grabbed a beer for Zach and a bottled water for myself and put them on the table. Then I grabbed two plates from the cabinet, shut the oven off, and took the potatoes out. When I walked out the back door with the plates in hand, I heard Zach coming in the front door. I held the back door open a couple of extra seconds to ensure some of the smell from the steaks cooking would make it to Zach's nose.

When the back door opened and Zach stuck his head out, I had just taken the steaks off the grill. Spaz ran over to Zach, almost tripping me up in the process. Zach held the door open so I could go back into the house.

"What is the special occasion?" he asked.

As I walked to the kitchen with the plates I replied, "It's date night." I put the plates down on the counter and plopped a baked potato onto each of them. Then I opened the fridge and grabbed the salads, the butter, and the sour cream.

From what I could tell Zach was in a good mood. I didn't know whether it was because I had grilled steaks for him or because I had finally remembered to buy him more beer. We made small talk while we ate. Everything was delicious. The potatoes were just the right amount of baked and the steaks were tender and juicy. After we ate everything on our plates, I told Zach about the movie tickets. I knew there was a fifty-fifty chance he would agree to go, but even if he decided to stay home, I was going.

"I heard good things about that movie. Let me go take a quick shower."

While Zach showered, I cleaned up in the kitchen. I was excited about finally going to the movies. Zach finished in the shower and got dressed while I gave the grill a good scrubbing. I could hear the phone ringing. Then I heard Zach saying 'Hello.' I came back inside and locked the back door just as Zach was hanging up the phone. He turned around and looked at me. Then he said, "That was my father."

I froze where I was standing. Why had Zach's father called him on a Friday night if it was not to tell him about seeing me in Stop & Shop? I tried to read Zach's face, but I was getting nothing. I threw caution to the wind.

"Is everything okay with him?" It was exceedingly difficult to sound concerned while I was on the verge of crapping in my pants.

"He's fine. I think he is just feeling lonely now that Bonnie is gone. We better get going before we miss the previews."

CHAPTER 22

The movie was even better than I thought it would be. Zach and I shared a large popcorn with extra butter and a medium Coke. We could've bought a third ticket for what it cost us. Zach used napkins to wipe the extra butter off his fingers while I used my tongue. It felt so good to be on a date with Zach again after all this time. I had even managed to not think about his father or Bonnie for a couple of hours. Things were looking up until they weren't.

The next morning, I got up bright and early. I made scrambled eggs and bacon with perfectly toasted English muffins. Zach made his way into the kitchen just as the toaster popped. He poured our coffees as I put everything on our plates. It was our first Saturday off together in a long time. We had nothing pressing that we needed to take care of, which meant we could just have a lazy Saturday all to ourselves.

It was a great day to do something outdoors. The sun was out but it was only in the low seventies, which was perfect for me. Once Spaz was taken care of, I asked Zach what he wanted to do.

"I thought we could go for a hike. It's been a long time since we did something fun together."

I guess he had not liked the movie as much as I had. A hike sounded like a good idea.

"Sounds like fun. What time do you want to head out?" A hike wouldn't have been at the top of my fun things-to-do list, but at least we would be doing something together.

Have you ever noticed there is always a catch to everything someone else wants you to do? Whenever something sounds too good to be true, that's because it probably is. You have to always be ready for the other shoe to drop. Do we ever really catch a break in this life with no strings attached?

"I told my dad we would pick him up around ten."

Hold up. He invited his father to go hiking with us without even asking me if I was okay with it. His father that had just suffered a mini-stroke not that long ago. Did he really think I would want to spend my Saturday off with his father? He must've noticed the disappointed look on my face.

"When he called last night, he asked me what we were doing this weekend. I told him I wanted to go hiking. He asked if he could join us. What was I supposed to do, say no?"

Every fiber in my body wanted to scream out 'Yes, you were supposed to say no!' It wasn't like I could ask him to call his father and tell him he couldn't go with us. Didn't he realize his father was going to slow us down dramatically? He may even have another stroke. What would we do then, carry him down the trail?

In my concerned daughter-in-law's voice, I asked, "Are you sure that is a good idea so soon after his stroke?" I knew it wouldn't work, but I had to at least give it a try.

"Relax, he isn't going to have another stroke. He's been feeling a lot better lately. It'll be fine." He has been feeling a lot better now that Bonnie is gone, is how I took what he had just said. There was no getting out of it. I was spending my Saturday off going hiking with Zach and his father. Could the day get any worse? Only time would tell.

We got dressed in jeans and old T-shirts. Spaz was running around in circles seeking attention. It was like he knew we were going to have fun without him. Having fun was definitely going to be questionable. Zach grabbed a backpack to hold some bottled waters, sunscreen, and a can of bug spray. I put some fresh water in Spaz's water bowl and gave him some of his favorite treats before heading out the door.

When we got to Zach's father's house, I wasn't sure if I was supposed to stay sitting in the passenger seat or if I was supposed to move to the back seat. I ended up moving into the back seat, which seemed to please Zach and his father. As we were driving to the hiking trails, I couldn't help but notice how much Zach was starting to look more and more like his father. They already had more than enough in common if you asked me.

"Did Robin tell you we bumped into each other at Stop & Shop yesterday?"

You have got to be kidding me. He waited until now to bring it up. I could see Zach looking back at me in the rear-view mirror. I just sat there without saying a word. Let them think I didn't hear what he had said.

"She didn't tell me about bumping into you yesterday." It was like they forgot I was in the car with them. I almost put my arm up in the air and waved it around as a reminder. I am right here! Instead, I played along with them.

"Sorry, I forgot all about it by the time you got home from work. Then we ate and rushed out to the movie." It sounded like a legitimate excuse to me.

CHAPTER 23

By the time we made it to the hiking trails, the mood in the car had lightened. I wanted so badly to bring up Bonnie's name, but I knew if I had it would've ruined the rest of the day for all of us. Bonnie now had one more thing in common with Zach's mother, she was another subject I needed to avoid, another subject that was clearly none of my business.

Once at the hiking trails, we looked at the map that showed all the trails. Due to Zach's father's latest health scare, we opted for the shortest trail just in case something happened during our hike. Zach and I had done the short trail once before when I wasn't sure how long I would be able to last in my new hiking boots. Not only was it the shortest trail, but it was also the flattest, and a part of it ran along a lake, which was a perfect spot to rest.

All three of us used the bug spray, mostly for the mosquitoes, and then we all applied a light coating of the sunscreen. I was grateful Zach had thought of bringing the bug spray, especially since we were taking the short trail. The mosquitoes near the lake could be a bit much that time of year.

Zach took three of the bottled waters out of the backpack and handed us each one, then we headed out for the trail.

Another good thing about the short trail is that not too many people used it. Most people who came to the trails were experienced hikers that preferred the longer, more challenging trails. The chances of getting stuck behind a slower hiker were slim. I had to admit the weather was perfect for hiking. The company could have been better, but you can't have everything. We walked in single file following the path into the woods. Zach took the lead, followed by his father, while I brought up the rear. It only made sense. If Zach's father was in the third position and something had happened to him, we might not have noticed right away. God forbid he be left behind while having a stroke on the trail.

The lake was about the halfway point of the trail. By the time we made it to the lake, Zach's father was drenched in sweat and having a tough time breathing. Zach headed to the bench closest to the lake and we all sat down. My hiking boots were hurting my feet a little, so I was fine with resting for a bit. Zach seemed a little off. He had barely spoken to me since we picked up his father. I couldn't tell whether he was upset with me for God knows what reason, or if he was irritated that his father had invited himself to come along with us.

After about ten minutes, I got up from the bench and walked over to the lake's edge. I could see a school of fish swimming around in circles. It reminded me of our fish pond. A bullfrog was croaking somewhere in the distance making his presence known. There were butterflies and all kinds of birds passing by. It was the perfect day to be spending in nature.

I sat down on the ground and put my hands in the water. It was a bit chillier than I had expected. Some of the fish came closer to where I was sitting, most likely looking for food, while others swam away. The next thing I knew, Zach came and sat down next to me. His father was still sitting on the bench. His breathing seemed to be almost back to normal. Then I heard Zach asking me a question, but I was having a difficult time registering what he had said. It sounded a bit distorted, almost slurred. Was he drunk? Was there alcohol in his bottle instead of water? I looked over at him, but with the sun in my eyes, his face looked blurry.

"What did you say?" I asked him, but my voice sounded as distorted as his did. Something was wrong but I couldn't tell what it was. Was I drunk too?

In a louder, slower voice, Zach repeated what he had said.

"Why did you have to stick your nose in where it didn't belong?"

What was he saying about my nose? I reached up and grabbed my nose with my hand. It felt normal to me. Was he telling me my nose was sunburned? It didn't feel sunburned. He must've known I was confused because he asked another question before I could answer his first one.

"Why did you go visit Bonnie while I was at the hospital with my father?" I couldn't believe my ears; he was talking about Bonnie with his father sitting right behind us. Was he trying to make his father upset?

I tried to turn around to look at his father, but I only made it halfway before falling over onto my side. Something was definitely wrong. The next thing I knew, Zach's father was on the other side of me helping me sit back up. I looked over at him only to realize his face was even more blurry than Zach's face had been. It looked like their faces were melting from the sun.

"It wasn't easy getting Bonnie to tell me you had paid her a visit. I knew you had because I smelled your perfume, the second I walked through the door." Zach's father's voice sounded like he was talking in slow motion.

Considering they had both mentioned Bonnie's name, did that mean I could ask them about where she was?

"Bonnie gone." That wasn't what I meant to say, but it was all that came out of my mouth. I could feel my body starting to sway. I felt like I was going to fall over again. I guess I wasn't in as good a shape as I thought I was. I needed my bottled water, but it was on the bench, which seemed so far away. I tried to stand up, but my legs felt like jelly.

Zach and his father both stood up. I looked up at them, but again, the sun was so bright I couldn't even make out who was whom. I put my arms up in the air so they could help me up. Why was I feeling too weak to stand up by myself? They each took one of my hands in theirs and pulled me to my feet. My body was swaying from side to side. I knew I wouldn't be able to walk over to the bench to get my water by myself.

"Water," I said, or at least I think that's what I said.

We started walking very slowly. One step at a time. It wasn't until I felt the water coming into my boots that I realized we were heading in the wrong direction. Did they think when I said water, I meant I wanted to go for a swim? Who goes swimming with all their clothes and boots on? I tried to stop walking, but it was like I had no control over my own body. We kept walking until the water was at my waist. It was even chillier that far out. Then I heard one of them say, "I told you it was none of your business."

One of them let go of my hand and then the other one let go too. I tried to turn around so I could follow them back to the shore, but I lost my balance. There wasn't much of a splash as my body slid under the chilly lake water. I could see lots of fish swimming around me. I tried to stand back up, but my legs wouldn't cooperate. I waited for Zach or his father to notice I was no longer behind them so they could come to help me, but the only thing I could hear was my fading heartbeat. I watched as the air bubbles slowly made their way to the surface. I tried to lift my arm so I could poke the bubbles and watch them pop, but I couldn't lift my arm. Something was definitely wrong.

Kari
2019

CHAPTER 1

I had given up on meeting anyone new. I was too old to be going out to bars, and I had no interest in joining any of the dating apps. Not that forty-six is old. They say forty is the new thirty. I am not so sure I agree with that. I had let myself go a bit recently, which was part of the reason I was feeling older and less desirable. My younger sister, Heather, talked me into joining a gym with her. I knew I needed to do something before my weight became a real issue. Heather was in perfect shape. I knew she only joined to get me to go. She was good like that.

At first, I didn't feel comfortable going to the gym at all. Heather would go dressed in a tank top and shorts, while I was in sweatpants and a loose T-shirt. There were people there that were in worse shape than I was, wearing less than Heather was. They had no shame in their game. A few of the times when we went, they had personal trainers there helping the newbies learn how to work out without hurting themselves.

One day I managed to get up the nerve to go to the gym without Heather. Cole, the personal trainer on duty that day, approached me. He could tell I was a bit uncomfortable being in the gym by myself. I am sure I must've looked completely out of place to him. He said all the right things like a typical salesperson. The next thing I knew, I had signed up for ten training sessions with him at twenty-five dollars a pop. The way I looked at it, there were a lot worse things I could spend twenty-five dollars on.

During our first workout session together, Cole was a bit more hands-on than I had expected him to be. It was nice to be touched, but it made me uncomfortable at the same time. I was covering most of my body because I didn't want anyone to see the extra weight I had put on, and here Cole was touching it. He never said anything to make me feel uncomfortable with myself, for which I was incredibly grateful. He was always positive and encouraging.

By our third workout together, we were spending more time talking about anything and everything, than we were working out. I thought it was all part of his plan to get me to sign up for more sessions with him. Once a salesperson, always a salesperson. I told him about my first marriage and how it ended. I told him all the places I had traveled to. I reluctantly even told him about when both of my parents died in a car accident. He was a great listener. He hung on every word I said. He would've made a great bartender.

On the day of our fifth workout, I wore a pair of loose-fitting shorts instead of my usual sweatpants. Cole accidentally touched my bare knee three times. Each time lingering longer and longer than the time before. I was trying to figure out what he was up to. Did he flirt with all the women he trained? Was he flirting with me or was I making more out of it than it actually was? The only things I knew about him were that his name was Cole Harper; he had lived in the area his whole life; he had lost his driver's license recently, and he rode his bike everywhere he went. He didn't own a house and he was only twenty-four years old.

By the time my tenth workout with Cole came, I was feeling comfortable enough with myself to wear tighter shorts and a form-fitting short-sleeved shirt. I wasn't ready to put on a tank top like Heather, but if I kept doing the same workouts I was doing with Cole, anything could be possible. When we finished my workout, Cole said he had something he wanted to ask me. I could hear his sales pitch in my head. He would start with a few compliments, then follow with some minor insults. Knock my confidence down a peg or two to get me to buy more workout sessions with him. It wouldn't take much to convince me.

I was certain I had heard him incorrectly when he asked me out on a date instead of asking me to sign up for more sessions. He knew I was old enough to be his mother. My age was in my folder that he carried around with him during our sessions. I didn't answer him at first. I couldn't understand why he would be asking me out on a date instead of one of the younger, prettier, more fit women he was surrounded by every day. He just kept looking at me waiting for an answer. I thought to myself, 'What the hell, one date can't hurt.'

CHAPTER 2

I hadn't been out on a date in a really long time. After my very contentious divorce, I had sworn off men. My ex-husband was a piece of work, to put it mildly. For some reason, he thought because I married him, he owned me. I was his live-in maid. I was his personal chef. I was his sex slave. I was anything and everything he wanted and needed me to be. Ask me what I got in return. Over the course of our four-year marriage what I got was three broken ribs, a dozen black eyes, twenty-something scars from cigarette burns, and more bruises than I could've possibly kept track of.

I had talked myself out of showing up for my date with Cole several times, but Heather wasn't having it. Heather knew everything my ex-husband put me through. With both of our parents gone, we were all that was left of our once-happy family. We weren't only sisters; we were also best friends. I would be lost without her in my life. Considering Cole didn't own a car, picking me up for our date wasn't an option. We decided to go to Olive Garden. It was close to where Cole lived so we agreed to just meet there.

It took me longer to get ready for our date than I had planned. What does a forty-six-year-old woman wear on a first date with a man who is young enough to be her son? I thought I had the perfect outfit picked out until I factored in that the date was a lunch date at Olive Garden. I wanted to look my best, but how many women do up their hair and make-up to go to Olive Garden while they are serving their lunch menu? I settled on a fairly loose-fitting fuchsia jumpsuit and white sandals.

I arrived at the restaurant ten minutes early. I didn't want to seem too eager, so I sat in my car watching the minutes slowly creep by. I nearly peed my pants when Cole knocked on my car window. I want to say the first thing I noticed was the big smile on his face, but that would be a lie. His smile was the second thing I noticed, right after his bicycling helmet. What the hell was a forty-six-year-old woman driving a Mercedes, doing at Olive Garden, with a twenty-four-year-old boy riding a bike?

Luckily, the restaurant wasn't very busy. We were led to our table right away. It wasn't until the waiter handed us our menus that I realized I had not planned well for this date. I was starving. I should've eaten a light snack before leaving the house. Although I had lost some of my extra weight, I was by no means fit. I wanted one of almost everything on the menu, especially the black-tie mousse cake. While I was taking my time reading the menu, I noticed Cole hadn't even looked at his. There was only one way to play this.

When the waiter came back to fill our water glasses and drop off a basket of their delicious breadsticks fresh out of the oven, he asked if we were ready to order. Cole looked over at me and asked me if I knew what I wanted.

"You order first. I need a few more seconds," I replied. After hearing Cole tell the waiter he was having the all-you-can-eat soup, salad, and breadsticks, I said, "Make that two please." I wondered if he had ordered what he did because it was the cheapest thing on the menu, or because it was the healthiest thing on the menu.

Anytime Heather and I go to places where there are a lot of people, we always try to figure out how people who are there together know each other. The word 'affair' gets thrown around a lot. Other frequent guesses are usually, first date, married, friends, co-workers, and sugar daddy. If anyone in the restaurant was playing the same game and they looked at Cole and me, would they guess first date, or mother and son? I know for sure Heather would've put her money on mother and son.

The entire time we were in the restaurant I felt like everyone was looking at us. Cole was an attractive, extremely fit young man, emphasis on young. I was an average-looking, out-of-shape, middle-aged woman, emphasis on middle-aged. With his darker complexion and slightly slanted eyes, it would be difficult to pass him off as my son. Cole didn't seem to notice or care if anyone was looking at us. He was probably used to having people look at him. Maybe it was all in my head. Maybe nobody even noticed us at all.

CHAPTER 3

Two bowls of soup, three bowls of salad, and two baskets of breadsticks later the awkward moment of who was paying the bill reared its ugly head. It was Cole who had asked me out on the date. Did that mean he should pay? I was the one driving around in a Mercedes while Cole was riding a bike. Did that mean I should pay? When the waiter came back to our table to pick up the check neither of us had even looked at it. To my relief, Cole reached for his wallet before I went for mine. While I watched him sign the receipt, I couldn't help thinking in a way I was paying for our lunch. He was using the money I paid him to train me to pay the bill. Some would say we went Dutch.

Cole walked me to my car. We both stood there like idiots just looking at each other. A couple of times I thought he was going to lean in for a kiss, but he never followed through.

Instead, he said, "I am glad we did this. I will see you tomorrow at the gym." I got into my car and drove away. He stayed where he was just watching me as I pulled out of the parking lot. I had so many thoughts going around in my head I was getting dizzy. Was I crazy for going on a date with Cole? What did he want from me?

In the middle of my racing thoughts, my phone rang. I could see from the caller ID that it was Heather. I knew what she wanted before I even answered the call, but I did anyway.

"So, how did it go?" she asked.

"I felt like I was having lunch with a son I never had," I replied.

To which she replied, "That doesn't sound like a fun date. Did you at least kiss him or feel him up?" I kid you not, she went there.

"It wasn't a bad date, just a bit awkward," I answered.

Did you notice I did not respond to her question?

She wasn't done yet.

"Are you going to see him again?" I wasn't enjoying our game of a thousand questions.

"I haven't decided yet," I told her. Then I went through a tunnel and the call dropped.

I came extremely close to skipping my training session the next day. I had no idea how I should act when I saw Cole again. I decided I would just go with the flow, something new for me, and see what happens. I showed up a few minutes early for my session. I wanted to do some stretching on my own before we started my workout. I spotted Cole as soon as I walked through the door. He was helping a twenty-something blonde bimbo on the chest press machine. I watched as she kept giggling and flexing her breast between sets. Almost every man who walked by them gave her a once-over.

Fifteen minutes later it was my turn. A cute boyish smile was on Cole's face as he approached me. I had one foot on the floor and the other foot up on a bar about three feet off the floor. When I tried to turn a little, so I could be more comfortable, I managed to get my foot under the bar. I was stuck with my legs spread apart for all to see. I could feel my face starting to turn red. All I needed now was for my shorts to split. I was trying my best to pretend nothing was wrong. I didn't want to have to ask Cole to rescue me. I tried twisting and turning my ankle to free my foot, but all I was doing was chafing my ankle.

In the end, Cole had to lift me off the ground so I could push my leg further under the pole allowing me to turn my ankle enough to free my foot. To my surprise, he didn't laugh or make fun of me. He carried me over to a chair so I could sit down while he examined the damage I did to my ankle. There were red friction marks on both sides of my ankle, which would most likely turn into nasty bruises later. Luckily, I didn't do any major damage. Nothing was broken or sprained. The poor guy went from a giggly busty blonde bimbo to an out-of-shape mother figure who managed to get her foot stuck under a bar while stretching.

Instead of working out, we sat at one of the little tables they had in their lounge area. My ankle was too sore for me to even think about working out. I wanted to be home sitting in my recliner with my foot up and ice on my ankle.

"Are you sure you are, okay?" Cole asked. Okay wasn't the first word that came to mind.

"I'm fine," I said. I felt like an old fool, but I kept that to myself.

Then he asked, "When can I see you again?" Talk about a loaded question.

I decided to continue playing it cool. "That all depends on what you mean by *see me* again," I said.

His response threw me for a loop.

"*See you, see you,*" he said.

CHAPTER 4

When I told Heather about getting my foot stuck under the bar, she had a good old laugh. She was curious if anyone had videotaped it and posted it on the internet. I thanked her for putting the dreadful thought in my head. I then made the mistake of telling her that Cole had asked me out again. She asked me if he would be picking me up on his bike. At least one of us was enjoying our conversation.

I didn't give Cole a definite answer when he asked if he could see me again. Don't get me wrong, I was flattered that a handsome, fit, young man was showing interest in me. I just felt like there was more to it. Pretty much every female that went to the gym would have said yes if he had asked them out. Why was it me that he was after? Did he have some kind of mommy issues? I hope that didn't sound as disturbing to you as it did to me.

When I woke up the next morning, my ankle was feeling much better. It was also many different colors. I considered wrapping it with an Ace bandage, but instead, I just put on a comfortable pair of socks. Out of sight, out of mind. I thought it would be best to stay away from the gym for a few days in case Heather was onto something about a video of me stuck with my legs spread wide open making it to the internet. I called the gym and canceled my scheduled sessions with Cole for the coming week. I was relieved he hadn't answered the phone when I called.

This seems like as good a time as any to fill you in a little more about myself. My sister Heather and I had been raised by amazing parents. Our father was one of the most prestigious cardiologists in New England. He had patients that would travel from all over to see him. Our mother was an extremely renowned defense attorney. They were a power couple if ever there was one. We all lived in a huge, beautiful house near the water. Our parents loved to throw parties for their friends and our extended family. Christmas in our house was spectacular.

When we lost them both in a horrible car accident, we were left with a huge hole that could never be filled. The family home had been left to me and Heather in our parents' wills. We agreed to sell it. To continue living in that house without our parents was more than either of us could bear. Between the proceeds from the house, our parents' savings, other assets, and the payouts from both of their life insurance policies, Heather and I ended up with almost three million dollars each. Having all that money was nice, but both of us would have rather been poor and had our parents back.

Heather and I both bought houses with part of our inheritances. We lived less than a block away from each other. Heather worked part-time as a receptionist in a dentist's office. She didn't need the money. She just needed something to look forward to when she got out of bed in the morning. A reason to leave her house a few days a week. As for me, I haven't worked a single day since we lost our parents. We were both still working through our grief. I found it easier to do that alone in my house. I wasn't ready to be around people every day again. Going to the gym for an hour, two or three times a week, was sufficient away time for me.

Now that you know about that part of my life, hopefully, you can understand more easily why I was so hesitant about going on a second date with Cole. I didn't feel emotionally ready for the possibility of letting someone new into my life. After my disaster of a first marriage, and the loss of my parents, I didn't know if I would ever be ready.

CHAPTER 5

When Cole called me unexpectedly, a few days later, I hadn't been sure if I should answer his call or let it go to voicemail. If I had let it go to voicemail, it would've then been up to me to call him back. That seemed like too much unwanted pressure, so I took his call. He sounded genuinely concerned when he asked me how my ankle was feeling. I told him except for some funky coloring it was as good as new. He sounded relieved to hear about my recovery. He then asked me if I had decided about our second date.

As I sat there in the parking lot of the gym in my Mercedes waiting for Cole to finish his shift, I was second-guessing my decision to go on a second date with him. I didn't tell Heather I was seeing Cole again that day. If it went better than our first date did, I would tell her about it later. Until then, it was on a need-to-know basis. When he walked out of the gym, I could see his hair was still wet from his shower. He spotted my car and walked over to my driver's side window.

"Should I hop in or follow you on my bike?" he asked.

My second-guessing had gone to third-guessing.

He put his bike in the trunk of my car and hopped in. I drove us to a low-key Chinese restaurant that I had been to several times before. It was pretty empty when we arrived. We sat in one of the corner booths. He sat directly across from me. As he looked at the menu, I looked at him. It was the first time I noticed how long his eyelashes were. He must've felt me looking at him. Without moving his head, he looked right at me. I looked down at the menu avoiding making eye contact.

I ordered my usual shrimp lo mein and Cole ordered honey chicken with brown rice. Our conversation was light and easy. We joked about my foot incident. Seems I wasn't the first person to get their foot stuck while stretching. I found myself feeling very relaxed with him. He made me feel like I was the only other person in the restaurant. He didn't seem to pass judgment, or if he did, he kept it to himself. I did notice that once again he didn't share much about himself. That time when the bill came, I handed my credit card to the waiter before Cole had a chance to even look at the bill.

Another one of those awkward moments happened when we left the restaurant. Cole's bike was in the trunk of my car. We hadn't planned the date out enough. *Should I offer to drive him home? Should I offer to drive him back to the gym? Did he think I was bringing him back to my house?* I was totally out of practice with the dating thing. I walked as slowly as I could toward my car. I wanted to see if Cole would head for the trunk or the passenger's door. When he noticed I wasn't walking at his pace he slowed down so I could catch up. Normally that would be a good thing, but not in that circumstance.

As we made it closer to my car, it dawned on Cole that we hadn't finished our date plan. He stopped walking when we made it to the front of my car. I stopped right on the side of him. He said, "My bike is in your trunk. Would you mind driving me back to the gym? If it is out of your way, I can just ride my bike back from here." I couldn't help but wonder why he hadn't asked me to drive him home instead of back to the gym. Was there a reason he didn't want me to know where he lived? I contemplated asking him if he would rather I take him home, but I decided against it.

Fifteen minutes later we were sitting in my car in the gym parking lot once again.

"Would it be okay if I kissed you?" he asked me.

"On one condition," I replied.

"Name it," he said.

"On our next date, we will only talk about you."

I couldn't believe the words had come out of my mouth. I had just asked a twenty-four-year-old boy out on a third date. He leaned over and kissed me on the lips for the first time. Electricity ran through every vein in my body. I hadn't been kissed in years. My ex-husband was an awful kisser. Cole, on the other hand, was not. I was so lost in the kiss I kept my eyes closed long after he had pulled away from me. I only realized the kiss had ended when I heard him say, "Deal."

I popped my trunk so he could get his bike. That time it was me sitting there watching him as he rode away on his bike. I could still feel his lips on mine. I knew at once I was in trouble.

CHAPTER 6

When I left the gym parking lot, I went over to Heather's house. I had to tell someone about my second date with Cole. I really didn't have anyone else in my life that I was close to anymore. Your life changes when you go through a difficult marriage and an even more difficult divorce, and then the deaths of both your parents. Things that were once important, now seem irrelevant. You learn, or hopefully, you learn, to put yourself first. No one should be more important to you than yourself. People with children may not agree with me on that one.

Heather wasn't overly excited when I showed up on her doorstep uninvited. She was having one of her, stay in bed all day, kind of days. I knew those days all too well. The days when you wished you had been in the car with your parents when the drunk driver decided it would be okay to get behind the wheel of his car while being intoxicated, and then collide head-on with your parents' car. They both died and he lived. His family can visit him in prison, while Heather and I get to go visit a headstone. Please explain to me how that is fair.

I saw a hint of a smile when Heather spotted the bottle of wine I was carrying. There isn't much a nice glass of wine can't fix. Though some things do require two or three glasses. That day was looking like a two-glass kind of day. Heather hadn't even bothered to shower or get dressed. She was most likely in bed when I rang the doorbell. Her hair was a mess, and she was still in her pajamas. Grieving the loss of someone you love can make you feel like you are on an emotional rollercoaster. Some days are good. Some days are okay. Then there are days that are so bad you scream at God and blame him for allowing your loved one to be taken from you.

I thought it would be best if I didn't tell Heather about my date right away. She needed some cheering up first. I opened the bottle of wine and poured us both a glass. I took a sip of mine. Heather chugged her whole glass at once. I may have underestimated her grief level. She held out her glass for me to fill again. The second time, I only filled it halfway.

Heather gave me a disappointed look and said, "Really?"

I filled the glass three-quarters of the way and put the bottle down on the table between us.

As I looked around her house, I noticed all her plants were either dying or dead. There was a nice even layer of dust on every surface I looked at.

In the center of the dining room table, there was a pile of mail. From the size of the pile, I would guess she hadn't opened any of her mail in weeks. By the time I was halfway done with my glass of wine, Heather had polished off her second glass. I chose that as the time to fill her in on my second date with Cole. If I had waited any longer, she would've been too drunk to pay attention to me.

I told her everything that happened and everything that was said. The only part she had any interest in was the part about the goodbye kiss. I could tell how much the wine had affected her when she started making out with the back of her hand. She wanted all the details. Was it a long kiss, or a short kiss? Was his mouth open, or was it closed? Did he try to stick his tongue in my mouth? Did he close his eyes, or did he keep them open? She continued using the back of her hand to demonstrate all the different questions she had. Normally I would've stopped her, but I knew she needed it. She needed to have something to laugh about and make fun of. I would rather hear her laughing at my expense than see her sad and depressed.

I stayed with Heather for most of that night. I could tell she didn't want me to leave, and honestly, there was no other place I would've rather been. She was there for me when I needed her most. I had no intention of deserting her when she needed me. A few hours later, I tucked her into bed and headed home. When I got home, I noticed I had a message on my answering machine. I pressed the button and let it play while I took my shoes off.

"I had a wonderful time today. Hope to see you again soon. You have great lips. This is Cole by the way." I hit rewind and let it play again.

CHAPTER 7

To be honest, I listened to Cole's voicemail five times. I had it saved on my answering machine for future pick-me-ups. I would be needing a pick-me-up when I got home that day. Our parents died on October twenty-fourth. On the twenty-fourth of every month, since they died, I have picked Heather up and then headed to the local flower shop. We usually spent about twenty minutes picking out just the right bouquets. Our mother loved peach roses, so we got those for her when they had some. Our father loved the smell of lilies, so we usually got them for him. If they didn't have either of those, we let the florist make up a bouquet of mixed flowers to match the season.

The drive to the cemetery was always a silent one. The grief we were both still dealing with seemed to intensify the closer we got to the cemetery. At least one if not both of us started crying as we made our way down the aisle that led to our family's burial plot. Hopefully, someday it will get easier. Our burial plot is right on the corner of two intersecting aisles. I turned the corner onto the side aisle so other cars could pass us easily. We each took one of the bouquets and walked over to our parents' resting place.

It was both unsettling and comforting at the same time seeing our own names on the tombstone. Our parents had decided years ago that the four of us would be buried together. I guess they had no hope for either of us to have a successful marriage. We gathered the bouquets we had left the month before and replaced them with the new ones. Then we cleaned whatever debris there was off of the tombstone the best we could. Lastly, we both had quiet conversations with our parents, followed by prayers we said aloud together. I dropped the dead bouquets in the barrel at the end of the aisle and then started heading back home. We had been doing that for over two years and it was still as traumatizing that day as it was the first time.

On our drive back to Heather's house, she asked me how things were going with Cole. I hadn't told her about the voicemail he had left me. I was waiting until she was having another really difficult day to tell her about my great lips. I couldn't tell if she was really interested in hearing about things with Cole or if she was just trying to keep her mind busy. I told her that I was going back to the gym the next morning for one of my training sessions with Cole. I hadn't been since I got my foot stuck. All the funky colors had faded away on my ankle. To my surprise, she asked me what time I was going. She hadn't been to the gym in almost two weeks. I thought she had quit as soon as she heard I had started going without her. I had a feeling she only wanted to go so she could meet Cole. That was going to be interesting.

The first thing I did when I got back home was listen to my saved voicemail from Cole. Going to visit our parents took an emotional toll on both of us. When we first started going to the cemetery I would stay and visit with Heather for a while afterwards. Turned out to not be such a great idea. We would spend most of the visit crying. When one of us would finally stop crying the other one would start again. We were keeping Kleenex in business. Recently, I would just drop her off at her house and then come back home to my empty house. I usually shut my phone off, closed all the blinds, and just moped around the house until I drowned myself in sorrow.

After listening to how great my lips were two more times, moping seemed silly. Instead, I opened all the blinds and let the sunshine in. I found myself wondering if Cole would kiss me again on our next date. It would've been unprofessional of him to kiss me in the gym considering I was paying him to train me. What if he didn't ask me out again? Would I be brave enough to ask him out with Heather there? Would Heather cause a scene and embarrass me in front of Cole, or worse yet, in front of everyone at the gym?

CHAPTER 8

When I picked Heather up that morning, she was in much better spirits than she was when I dropped her off the day before. She practically skipped down the walk to my car. I noticed right away that she looked much skinnier in her shorts and a tank top than she did two weeks prior. *Had she been eating? Did I need to worry about her? If I asked her about it, she would tell me I was crazy. She had always been self-conscious about her weight. I was fairly certain she suffered from one of the many eating disorders. I had always been heavier than she was. If she was fat, what was I?*

I started getting a little nervous as I pulled into the parking lot for the gym. I wasn't exactly sure what was making me nervous. It could've been just the idea of seeing Cole again. It could've been the fear of hearing people laugh at me if they recognized me as the spread-eagle stretcher. It could've been the thought of Heather causing a scene when she met Cole. The list was endless those days. Heather was out of the car before I even got the key out of the ignition. She held the gym door open as she waited for me to catch up.

We headed to the locker room to put our phones and keys in a locker. I told God I owed him one when Heather said she needed to pee. That would give me a chance to say hello to Cole alone and warn him about Heather. When I walked out of the locker room, I saw him leaning against the customer service desk. It was probably my imagination, but I could've sworn I saw a twinkle in his eyes when he spotted me walking toward him. He grabbed my folder and met me in the dreaded stretching area. I looked at the bar that entrapped my foot and silently cursed it.

"You must be Cole. I'm Heather, Kari's much younger sister," I heard Heather say. How in the world had she peed so fast? I hadn't even had a chance to warn Cole that she was there with me. Much younger sister? I was forty-six and she was knocking so loudly on the forty door it was deafening.

"Pleasure to meet you," Cole said, as he stuck out his hand for Heather to shake.

"The pleasure is all mine, or in this case, I guess it's all Kari's," Heather replied, as she shook his hand. They both let out a little laugh while I started turning red. I threw Heather a not-so-friendly look after her comment, and she politely excused herself.

With Heather far enough away on a treadmill, I apologized to Cole for what she had said about the pleasure being all mine. The look on his face left me wondering whether he missed the meaning of what she said or if I took it the wrong way. After five minutes of stretching, we worked our way through an intense leg and butt workout. Cole was even more hands-on than usual. He was making it difficult for me to focus on my form. My breathing was all over the place. There were mirrors on almost every inch of the gym walls. If I looked at just the right angle, I could see Heather on her treadmill. I was expecting to see her looking right back at me, but she was watching one of the huge televisions they had hanging from the ceiling.

I had been waiting for Cole to ask me out again. With only five minutes left of my session, I took the bull by the horns and asked him out instead. He tilted his head a little to the side, let a half smile take over his face, and said, "You took the words right out of my mouth."

You may not follow the connection, but I was suddenly in the mood to go to The Cheesecake Factory. They have the best meatloaf I had ever tasted. We agreed our third date would be on the coming Friday night. That was going to be our first night-time date.

Cole and I walked over to the treadmill that Heather was using. How she had managed to stay on a treadmill for an hour was beyond me. I would've been passed out on the floor. She shut down the treadmill just as we made it to her. I silently prayed she wouldn't embarrass me again. Luckily, Cole had someone else waiting for him, so he rushed off after a quick goodbye. Heather and I got our stuff out of the locker and headed to my car. On the drive back to Heather's house, I told her Cole, and I were going on a date Friday night.

She looked at me and asked, "Does he have a curfew?"

CHAPTER 9

Cole didn't have an official curfew, but he did want to be home before ten p.m. He had to be up early that Saturday for a training session at seven in the morning. I was fine with that. I am usually half asleep, if not out like a light, by ten anyway. Cole was freshly showered when I picked him up at the gym. I was starting to wonder if he lived there.

We had decided we would do something besides eat for our third date. I had read the *Gone Girl* book by Gillian Flynn and loved it like pretty much everyone else who read it. They had made it into a movie, and it was playing at the movie theater not too far from the gym. Cole hadn't read the book, which is probably why he liked the movie as much as he did. Movies that are based on books are never as good as the books. We shared a medium popcorn and a large Coke that had way too much syrup in it. Cole kept his hand on my knee the entire time.

My mind seemed to wander more and more those days. According to the all-powerful internet, minds wander due to being sad or depressed, or from being under the influence of alcohol. I wasn't a big drinker. My grandfather on my mother's side was a major alcoholic. Not a life I would wish on anyone. Being sad or depressed sounded about right.

Let me give you a perfect example of my wandering mind. About halfway through the movie, my mind went back to when I was picking Cole up at the gym earlier. It was like I was sitting in my car again looking out the windshield. I could see Cole coming out of the gym and walking toward my car. Seems normal right? So why was my mind fixated on it? Then it came to me. Where was Cole's bike? Was it there in the parking lot chained to one of the bike stands like it always was, or was it not there? If it wasn't in the gym parking lot, what did that mean?

As we were walking out of the movie theater hand in hand, Cole asked me what I thought of the movie. I didn't want to admit that I had been too busy overthinking where his bike was to have paid attention to the movie. I simply said, "The book was better," which was the truth. When we got to my car Cole followed me to the driver's side door. I was a bit confused why he was on the wrong side of the car. As I turned to face him, he put one hand on each side of my head, his elbows were against my shoulders. He gently pushed me up against the side of my car.

In a low, seductive voice, he said, "I can't wait another minute." Then he kissed me right there in the middle of the movie theater parking lot where anyone could have seen us. That boy certainly knew how to kiss a woman.

The tingling I had felt from head to toe ended much later than the kiss. Cole opened my door for me before walking around the car and getting into the passenger's seat. He still hadn't mentioned his bike.

I threw him a sideway glance and asked, "Am I taking you home?" I realized later as I replayed it in my head, that I didn't phrase it how I meant to. Cole, being the gentleman or rather the gentle boy that he was, replied, "Although I am really looking forward to spending the night with you, I do have to get home so I can get some sleep. It is getting late."

I thought about explaining to him that what I meant was, was I taking him home to his house, not mine, but I liked his response too much to ruin the moment. Cole gave me step-by-step directions to his house. As we drove, I asked him about his bike. Turned out he only lived four blocks from the gym. He had walked to the gym that day because his bike had a flat tire. He apologized for making me go out of my way to take him home. At least then I knew he didn't live at the gym.

When Cole told me to pull over in front of the yellow house, I was surprised to see it wasn't a dump. I don't know what I had been expecting, but it certainly wasn't a house like the one I pulled up in front of. Granted it wasn't as nice as the house I lived in, but it looked a lot nicer than a house a twenty-four-year-old trainer at a gym with no car could afford to live in. Cole must've seen the confusion I was feeling on my face.

He said, "Now you know my secret. I still live with my dad."

After I watched Cole walk into his house, I remembered that we had made a deal. We were supposed to talk about him on our next date. I wondered if he had suggested we go see a movie to avoid talking about himself. Was there something he was hiding from me?

CHAPTER 10

Over the next few weeks, Cole and I started spending more and more time together. I was still paying him to train me in the gym, which was starting to feel a bit awkward. We did our best to keep our budding relationship under wraps. Some of Cole's co-workers had caught on, but luckily, they never spread it around the gym. Can you imagine how embarrassing it would have been to have people pointing at us and snickering during my training sessions?

Almost everything between us was perfect at that time. I say almost because after dating Cole for over a month, I still knew very little about him. Getting him to tell me anything about himself was like pulling teeth. Most guys that are as handsome and in as good a shape as he was, are usually very egotistical. They love talking about themselves more than anything else. Cole was the complete opposite.

He did tell me he was born in Fall River, Massachusetts. He never went to college. He bounced around from job to job until he got his personal trainer certificate and landed a job at the gym he is still working at now. He lived alone with his father in the house that I still had not been invited into. He never talked about his parents at all. I asked him about his mother a few times, but he refused to talk about her at all. The biggest shock came when we had a conversation—let me rephrase that, when we had a brief chat about past relationships. Cole did have a few girlfriends through his high school years, which I was not surprised to hear. I was, however, surprised to hear that he had got married when he was twenty years old. The marriage lasted a little over a year. It didn't end well, is all he would say about it.

I know you must be wondering about the sexual part of our relationship. I had never been one to talk about my private life, especially my sexual experiences. I will say that when I saw Cole naked for the first time on our fifth date, I completely lost my breath. All men are definitely not created equal. Sex with Cole was like nothing I had ever experienced before. He was a very attentive and passionate lover. That is all you are getting out of me on that subject.

My sister Heather started out as a fan of Cole. She was happy that I had met someone to spend time with. The fact that he was hot, as she put it, was a major plus. Over the weeks she started changing her mind about him. She didn't like that Cole was so secretive.

"He must be hiding something," she had told me over and over. She also didn't understand why I hadn't met his father yet. Did his father even exist? Never mind that he wouldn't talk about his mother at all. Who doesn't talk about their own mother?

I started feeling like I was being forced to choose between the two of them and I didn't like it. I have never had many close friends, not even back in my school days. Most times it was just me and Heather against the world, especially after our parents died. I couldn't figure out whether Heather had become a bit jealous of the time I was spending with Cole instead of her, or if she really did think he was hiding some deep, dark secret. Was she purposely trying to plant doubts in my head, or was she simply looking out for me?

A few times Cole and I made a point of inviting Heather to join us for a movie or a dinner out. She did join us a couple of those times, but as her suspicions grew, it became hard for her to hide the way she was feeling toward Cole. It was like there was a chill in the air being there together with the two of them. Cole started noticing it. He asked me if Heather had a problem with me dating him after we had dropped her off the second time she had joined us. I lied. I told him it wasn't him and that Heather was just going through a tough time, and she didn't know how to channel her feelings. He may have believed me, or he may not.

After that second time, Heather started always saying no when we asked her to join us. Eventually, we stopped asking. That was one of the many mistakes I made in my life. I knew I was going to regret it. I just didn't realize how much, until it was too late.

CHAPTER 11

As time went on, my relationship with Cole grew closer, while my relationship with Heather grew more distant. For the first time in our lives, we weren't talking to each other every day. Heather had completely stopped going to the gym. If you ask me, she stopped going because she didn't want to chance running into Cole. The only times we spoke was when I called her and she actually answered my call, which wasn't often at all.

Cole had stopped asking me about Heather. He knew how much it had been bothering me that we had become so distant. What good would talking about it do? One day when I was home alone relaxing in my recliner, a thought popped into my head. At that moment in time, Cole was the only person in my life that I could count on. He was also the only person in my life that I was spending any time with. I had not seen or talked to any of my so-called friends in weeks. I looked up to the ceiling and thanked God for letting me find Cole.

I don't want to mislead you in any way. Yes, I was thankful that I had found Cole, but that doesn't mean that everything was perfect between us. We had been dating for almost three months and I had still not stepped one foot into his house. I also hadn't spoken one word to his father. The only friends of his I had met were his work colleagues at the gym. I often wondered if he was embarrassed to introduce me to anyone in his life because of our age difference. Was *I* his deep, dark secret?

I had one more training session left that I had already paid for. It was going to be my last one. I had learned everything I needed to know. After that last session I would, or rather I should, be able to stay fit and in shape without Cole holding my hand anymore. When I walked into the gym, Cole was finishing up with the same busty blonde I had seen him with before. She smiled too much, twirled her hair around her finger too much, and flexed her breast too much. As I stood in front of the mirror in the ladies changing room, I couldn't help but wonder why Cole had chosen me over someone like the busty blonde. It was more than obvious he could have had her in a heartbeat.

Considering it was our last session, Cole decided it would be an entire body workout. It was the first time we would be hitting every body part in one session. I knew I was going to be sore from head to toe the next day. I gave the bar an evil look during our five-minute warmup. Is stretching really that important? We started with upper body exercises and then worked our way down. By the time we had made it to legs, I was ready to call it quits but Cole wasn't having it.

After killing every muscle in my legs, we headed over to the stretching area again. Cole told me to lie down on the mat flat on my back with my arms stretched back behind my head. He grabbed hold of my feet and told me he wanted me to pull myself up on the count of ten and try to touch my toes. I casually checked out my surroundings. I knew there was no way in hell I was going to be able to pull myself up and touch my toes while he was holding my feet. I was relieved to see there was nobody in close proximity to the stretching area.

I did my best to relax and clear my mind. I tried to convince myself if I just focused on Cole's voice there was a chance, a very slim chance, that I would be able to at least sit up straight. As Cole counted down from ten, I let his voice relax me. By the time he had made it to five, I was in the zone. I was going to rise to the occasion even if it killed me. I braced myself when he hit two. When I heard him say one, I put every ounce of energy I had left in my body into pulling myself off the mat without using my legs.

I surprised myself as my body rose off the mat. When I was halfway up, I could see Cole looking at me with a smile on his face. That was all I needed to motivate myself to keep going. When I made it all the way to a sitting position, I noticed Cole was holding a small box between my feet. As he opened the box, he said, "You got this."

CHAPTER 12

I sat in my car in the parking lot of the gym for what seemed like hours. In reality, it was much closer to ten minutes. What had just happened? I was in no way prepared for Cole to propose to me. We had only just met three months earlier. I don't know whether I surprised him or myself more when I said yes. I was so caught up in the moment and people had stopped to see what was going on. How could I have said no?

I tried calling Heather several times. Every call went straight to voicemail. She was either avoiding me or having one of her 'stay in bed all day' kind of days. That wasn't working for me. I needed her more than I had in a while. I left the gym parking lot and headed over to her house. It is much harder avoiding someone that is knocking on your door than it is when that someone is calling you on the phone.

When I pulled into her driveway, I saw her car parked in its usual spot. I got out of my car and approached her front door. I noticed all the blinds on her windows were closed tight. The chances of her being out of bed were getting slimmer by the minute. I knocked on the door lightly at first. There weren't many neighbors close by, but those that were tended to peek through their blinds if they heard anything out of the norm. The second time I knocked a little harder. I called out Heather's name to let her know it was me that was knocking on her door. Still no answer.

I knocked so hard the third time I hurt my knuckles.

"Open the door, Heather. I need to talk to you."

The only reaction I got was a glare from the neighbor to the right of Heather's house. I was starting to doubt whether she was home at all. Maybe she had gone out somewhere. With her car sitting in the driveway that didn't seem plausible. Her social life was as pathetic as mine had been.

Heather had given me a spare key to her house in case of an emergency. Was this an emergency? I walked over to the neighbor that had been watching me through her blind. I had seen her several times before when I had come to visit Heather but had never spoken to her. No time like the present. As I walked in the direction of her house, I saw the blind close. A few seconds later the front door opened, and the old lady came out onto her porch.

"Can I help you with something?" she asked.

"I hope so. My name is Kari. I am your neighbor's sister. Have you seen her today?"

By the expression on her face, I could tell she was deep in thought. "Come to think of it, I haven't seen her at all the last couple of days. She hasn't even bothered to open her blinds to let some sunshine in."

I thanked her and headed back to Heather's house. It may seem strange to anyone who doesn't know Heather the way I know her, that she leaves her blinds closed. Lord knows I have had my share of those days too since we lost our parents. I wanted to try one more thing before using my spare key. I walked around the side of the house until I reached the window in Heather's bedroom. With the blind closed I couldn't see anything. I knocked three times on the window. The old lady had come down off her porch and was slowly making her way over to me.

"Are you sure you haven't seen her at all in the last couple of days?" It was obvious the old lady had heard the slight tone of panic in my voice at the same time I had. She cowered away from me looking frailer than she did a minute earlier.

"You don't think she's dead in there do you?" she asked.

Without answering her, I walked back around to the front door. I wasn't surprised to see the old lady was only two steps behind me. I reached into my purse and took out my spare key. This was officially an emergency. The panic I had started to feel took off like a rocket when I tried to put the spare key into the lock on Heather's front door and it didn't go in. I checked the key to make sure it was the correct one before trying to jam it into the lock. It was definitely the right key, but it wasn't fitting into the lock. Had Heather changed the lock on her door so I couldn't get in? Was she that upset with me?

I dropped down to my knees and looked at the lock. What I saw put my panic into overdrive. I started shaking.

"Are you alright dear?" the old lady asked me.

I was not alright. I was far from alright. I took out my phone and dialed 911. I was having a difficult time standing up. I walked over to my car and leaned against it.

"911, what is your emergency?"

Ten minutes later, two police cruisers, an ambulance, and a fire engine all pulled up outside Heather's house. More neighbors had come out onto their porches. A police officer approached and asked me what was going on. I explained to him that I had tried calling my sister several times, but she didn't answer. Then I drove over and tried knocking on her door and her bedroom window but got no response.

"Is that her car over there?" he asked.

"Yes, that's her car. Her neighbor said she hasn't seen my sister at all in a couple of days."

The other police officers, firefighters, and medics started walking the perimeter of the house. I walked with the police officer over to the front door and told him what I had seen when I looked at the lock. He bent down to look for himself.

"Looks like someone tried to force it with a screwdriver," he said. That was exactly what I had thought. It didn't make sense. Why would someone try to force Heather's front door open? We didn't know people like that. We lived in what we considered a safe neighborhood. I gave him my spare key so he could try to get it into the lock, but like me, he was unsuccessful. The lock was too messed up.

One of the firefighters joined us at the front door. They had checked all the windows, but they were all locked.

The police officer looked at me and asked, "Window or door?"

At first, I was confused. I had never dealt with anything like this before. Then I realized what he was asking me. Did I want him to break in through a window or the front door? Considering the lock was already messed up and would need to be replaced anyway, I answered, "The door."

The firefighter ran over to the fire engine and returned with a crowbar. He jammed the crowbar into the tight space between the door and the door jamb. After a few pushes and pulls the door opened. An awful smell drifted in the breeze and smacked us right in our faces.

The police officer looked at me and said, "Stay here."

The old lady was standing right next to me. We both covered our noses and mouths with our hands. I heard her say something but with her hand covering her mouth I couldn't make out what she had said. I looked down at her and asked her what she had said.

"I know that smell. I smelled it the day my Nicholas died."

CHAPTER 13

Have you ever lost someone that you loved unconditionally? If so, multiply that feeling of loss by three. If you haven't, thank your lucky stars. Just as I was starting to accept the loss of my parents, Heather was taken from me too. I felt like my heart had just been ripped right out of my chest. What do you do when all the people in your life that you would have given your life for have all been taken away from you?

When the police officer walked back out of Heather's house, I knew what he was about to tell me before he even said a word by the look on his face. I had seen that look the day the police came knocking on our door to tell us about our parents' car accident. I fell to my knees and started crying as the words "I am so sorry" left his lips. The old lady dropped to her knees to comfort me. Bless her heart. She didn't know me or know anything about me, but she did know my pain. She wrapped her arms around me the way my mother would've if she were still alive.

I ended up having a slight panic attack. One of the medics helped me into the ambulance so I could lie down while they gave me a sedative. While I lay there on the stretcher, the nice police officer joined me in the ambulance. The old lady went to sit on one of the wooden chairs on her porch while she waited to be questioned after me. My head was spinning so much that it was hard for me to focus on what the police officer was asking me. I somehow got up the courage to ask him how Heather had died. They hadn't let me in the house at all. Her lifeless body was still somewhere in there.

The only thing the police officer had told me was that they had found Heather in her bed. I knew pretty much every inch of Heather's house. I could picture myself standing in the doorway to her bedroom looking down at her in her bed. The images became distorted. They initially started with her looking like an angel just sleeping. Then the skin on her face started changing to white, then yellow, then brown, and finally all that was left was her skull. I fought to get the image out of my head. That wasn't how I wanted to remember my best friend, my sister.

The police officer was still asking his routine questions, but I had no answers that could be of any help. Heather had no known enemies. There was no one with a grudge against her. I couldn't understand why he was asking me these kinds of questions in the first place. He was the one that had told me they found her in her bed. Was I wrong in assuming she had died in her sleep? What wasn't he telling me?

"Do you know how my sister died?" I asked him.

In a gentle tone, which I very much appreciated, he replied, "All I can tell you at this time is that we are treating it as a suspicious death."

A suspicious death. What did that even mean? Was my sister killed in her own bed? I looked at him with what I can only imagine must have been a puzzled face.

"What about it is suspicious to you?" I knew from watching *Dateline* that he wasn't supposed to tell me anything at this point, but I had to at least try.

The only thing he would tell me that day was that there were two things that concerned him. One of those things was the damage to the lock on the front door. With everything that was going on, I had completely forgotten about the lock not working. The second thing that concerned him was that there was an empty bottle of pills on Heather's bedside table. The second thing made no sense to me. Yes, I knew Heather occasionally took pills when she was feeling down or depressed, but never had I thought she would overdose on them.

My beautiful loving sister was gone from this world. I would never be able to see her, talk to her, or laugh with her ever again. How long had she been lying there dead in her own bed? How could this have happened? Why wasn't I there to save her? I had let down the most important person in the world to me, and now I would have to live with that for the rest of my life.

CHAPTER 14

It took all the strength I had to get myself out of bed on the morning of Heather's funeral. I still hadn't allowed myself to believe I would never be able to talk to her again. I had told Cole I needed some time to myself at least until after the funeral but he wouldn't listen. Instead, he camped out at my house. He made sure I ate at least a little something here and there. He listened to me cry for hours on end. He even volunteered to sleep on the couch. He gave me as much space as I needed.

When the time came, I wore the same black dress and heels I had worn to my parents' funeral. After putting mascara on, and then having to wash it off after crying three times, I ended up not wearing any makeup at all. I didn't know how many more tears I had left in me, but I knew that whatever was left was going to flow out of me at the funeral.

Cole rode with me in the limo right behind the hearse that carried my sister's coffin. The ride to the cemetery seemed longer than usual. I was practically hyperventilating the entire time. Cole held my hand to try to calm me down and comfort me. It wasn't working, but at least he was trying.

You never realize how depressing life can be, until you go to a funeral for the most important person in your life, and you don't recognize any of the pallbearers. They were all volunteers from the church. As I watched them carry my sister's coffin, I realized it would be the same thing when it was my turn. Neither of us had many friends, those that we did have, were all women our age or older. I don't think I had ever seen a woman as a pallbearer before.

The one and only good thing — if you can call it a good thing — was that Heather was with our parents again. I needed to believe that, even if I didn't. Luckily, the old lady from next door and a few other neighbors came for the funeral. If they hadn't come, it would've just been me, Cole, and the priest. The tears began to flow the second I saw the hole they had dug in the ground near my parents' tombstone. This was really happening. I felt completely empty inside. Before walking away, I told all three of them how much I loved and missed them.

When we turned around and started walking back to the limo, I spotted the nice police officer that had questioned me the day Heather died, standing behind a tree. I was happy he had taken the time to come to the funeral. He met up with us as we approached the limo. I assumed he was there to offer his condolences, which he did, but he also had some information for me too.

"I know this isn't the best time, but I wanted to let you know the outcome of the autopsy we did on your sister," he said, in a low, gentle tone. This definitely wasn't the best time, but was there really a best time to hear about how your sister died?

"Do we really have to do this now? She just buried her sister," Cole replied, in a bit of a defensive voice. The police officer turned and looked at Cole.

"If you wouldn't mind, could you please wait in the car? I would prefer to talk to Ms. Jacobs alone." This time his tone wasn't as low and gentle.

I asked Cole very nicely to go wait in the limo. The sooner we got this over with, the sooner I could get out of this cemetery. Cole wasn't too pleased that I had sided with the police officer. He stormed away like a spoiled little brat. It was embarrassing, to say the least. Once we were alone, I asked the police officer what they had found out from doing the autopsy. I had originally told him I didn't want them to do an autopsy. Just the thought of them cutting into Heather like an animal made me sick to my stomach.

Turns out, whenever a death is labeled a suspicious death, they automatically do an autopsy. I could've fought it in court, but like the police officer had told me, if I had fought it in court and then the death turned out to be murder, it would make me look like I had been trying to hide something.

"The autopsy showed a high level of alcohol in her system. But that alone is not what killed her. From what they found they are estimating she took at least half a dozen of her sleeping pills. The combination of the liquor and sleeping pills is what caused her death. I thought you would want to know sooner rather than later."

I just stood there looking at his kind face. Was he trying to tell me that Heather had committed suicide? Why would she take her own life? Why would she choose to leave me all alone in this cruel world? It didn't make sense to me.

"Are you still considering her death suspicious?" I followed his eyes as they fell from mine to the ground. I knew what was coming next.

"From the results of the autopsy, it looks like this was an intentional overdose."

No-no-no! Please don't say that.

"But what about the messed-up lock on her front door?" I asked in a hurried voice.

"We have no way of knowing when the lock was actually messed up. For all we know, your sister could've locked herself out of the house and messed up the lock herself trying to get back in, especially if she was drunk at the time. If anything changes, I will contact you at once." With that, he turned around and left me standing there all by myself.

I just stood there looking back at our family plot. How had Heather thought that taking her own life was the answer? I knew how much she missed our parents, and I knew things weren't great between us since I had started dating Cole seriously, but to take her own life, went against everything we believed in. It didn't make any kind of sense.

I walked over to the limo and climbed in. Cole started asking me right away what the police officer had told me. I couldn't bring myself to repeat the words.

"Can we please talk about it later? It is more than I can handle right now."

He reached over and took my hand in his. I leaned my head on his shoulder and silently started crying again. I don't know what I would've done if I didn't have Cole in my life.

CHAPTER 15

I barely left my house for a month after Heather died. I picked up my phone so many times to call her. I had left her phone service on just so I could hear her voice on her answering machine. I hoped it would make me feel better being able to hear her voice any time I wanted to, but it backfired on me. Hearing her answering machine come on every time I called was just another sad reminder that she was no longer here with me to answer the phone. My one and only source of comfort was believing she was up in heaven with our parents watching over me. My three guardian angels.

Cole had tried to see me more often than I allowed him to. I just wanted to be alone to drown in my sorrow. I needed time to grieve for Heather. Luckily, Cole understood that. We hadn't been intimate since before Heather passed away. I didn't want to be touched by anyone, not even Cole. I knew it was much easier for me to not be intimate than it was for Cole, but he never once tried anything. He had even started kissing me goodbye on my cheek instead of on my lips. He was my guardian angel here on Earth.

I also hadn't been to the gym in over a month. It felt strange for me to be missing going to a gym. I had no idea who knew about Heather's passing. I assumed Cole had told some of his co-workers, especially considering Heather had a membership at the gym. I didn't want to go to the gym and listen to strangers tell me how sorry they were about my loss. I asked Cole to cancel Heather's membership for me. One less thing for me to deal with. I had more than enough on my plate as it was.

The first time I left the house after the funeral was to go to our family lawyer, or rather, my lawyer. That was a hard pill to swallow. There was no more *our* family. It made me feel like an orphan left all by myself in this so-called life of mine. When I made it to the lawyer's office, he greeted me with heartfelt condolences. He had been with my family since before I was even born. A few tears trickled down my cheek as we shook hands. He gave me his handkerchief to dry my tears. He had always reminded me of my father. They were both good, honest men who worked hard for the money they made.

There were a bunch of papers for me to sign, but first, he read Heather's will. None of it came as a surprise. Right after our parents had died Heather and I went to our lawyer and had our wills drawn up. We left everything we had to each other. By the time I walked out of his office, I was the new owner of Heather's house, and every penny she had to her name was also now mine. The only two things I had left to deal with were selling Heather's house and collecting her life insurance. It was a huge payday for me, but without Heather there, it seemed pointless.

When I was back in my car heading to the safety of my house a ray of sunshine bounced off my engagement ring. I had been so busy dealing with my grief that I had forgotten I never had a chance to tell Heather I was engaged to Cole. Then a very morbid thought entered my mind. *If Cole hadn't proposed to me that awful day, how long would Heather have stayed lying there dead in her bed? Who else would've gone knocking on her door? I suddenly felt a rage building up inside of me. How had I let my relationship with Cole come between me and Heather? If she really did commit suicide, was I partly to blame? How could I live with myself if that was even remotely true?*

When I made it back home, I closed all the blinds, took the phone off the hook, and climbed back into bed. I let my sorrow overcome me. *Please, God, don't let my selfish stupidity be a part of the reason Heather took her own life. How would I ever know if I was or wasn't part of the reason?* I was going to have to live with the guilt, without ever knowing if I had anything to feel guilty about, until my own pathetic excuse of a life ended.

CHAPTER 16

They say time heals all wounds; I say that is bollocks. Time may let you come to grips with all the poop life may throw at you, but you are left with the scars. I have three scars, one from my mother's death, one from my father's death, and one from Heather's death. They all serve as permanent reminders of the family I once had and then lost.

Over the next few months, I fell into my new norm. I started going back to the gym on a semi-regular basis. More so as a reason to get out of the house than to get in better shape. I had put back on most of the weight I had lost, and I didn't even care. I was sure Cole had noticed my weight gain, especially when we were intimate, but he never said anything about it. He was simply happy we were back to seeing each other pretty much every day.

One night, while we were snuggling in my bed, Cole took my left hand into his and asked, "How much longer are you going to make me wait?" To be honest, I hadn't given our wedding much thought since Heather died. The day Cole proposed to me, I had played out our wedding in my head during my drive to Heather's house. She of course was to be my maid of honor. Without her here I didn't have a plan. In case you are wondering, I still hadn't met Cole's father or any of his friends other than his co-workers at the gym. I know it's messed up. Would I finally meet them at our wedding, or would it just be me, Cole, and the priest? Maybe we should just go to Vegas and get married by an Elvis impersonator.

I had a flashback to the last conversation I had with Heather. She was insistent that Cole was hiding something from me. 'Why else wouldn't he let you meet his father?' she asked. She had grown to not trust Cole. She was certain he was going to hurt me one way or another. I knew in my heart of hearts that she was wrong about Cole, even though I had no idea why he wouldn't introduce his fiancée to his father or friends. We had always ended our conversations, whether in person or over the phone, by saying 'I love you' to each other, but we didn't that day. Another huge regret I now had to live with.

I turned my head so I could look Cole in his eyes and asked, "Are you sure you still want to marry me?"

I knew it was a silly question to ask after he had just asked me how much longer I was going to make him wait, but I wanted to offer him an out if he wanted one.

Instead of taking the offered out, he took my face into both of his hands, leaned forward, and said, "Absolutely!" before kissing me. It was times like that that I had no other choice but to believe in God.

Speaking of believing in God, it wasn't until we started talking about our wedding that I found out Cole was an atheist. It didn't matter much to me until Cole said he refused to get married in a Catholic church. What did that mean for our wedding? I had no idea where atheists got married.

"We could elope," Cole said in a questioning tone. At first, the thought of eloping sounded like an awful idea. Isn't eloping what teenagers did when they wanted to rebel against their parents who had forbidden them to get married?

The more I thought about it, the more it started sounding like an okay option. Without my father there to walk me down the aisle, or Heather there as my maid of honor, was there really a need for a church wedding? I had no close relatives or real friends. My side of the church would've been empty pew after empty pew. How sad and depressing would that be? If I were lucky, maybe the old lady that lived next door to Heather would show up if I sent her an invitation.

We agreed that night that we would elope. The next day we searched on Google for a local justice of the peace and applied for a marriage license. When all was said and done, we would be husband and wife for $250. My mother would never have approved of me eloping, not even at my age. She loved big fancy weddings. Instead of a three-tier wedding cake, we would each be eating a cupcake. Instead of listening to a church organ playing 'Here Comes the Bride', we would be listening to it on a worn-out cassette tape, or a CD if we were lucky enough.

When the day finally came two weeks later, I got dressed in an off-white dress I had bought for our special day. Considering Cole still didn't own a car, I drove over to his house to pick him up. Having him ride his bike to City Hall on our wedding day would have been pushing it a little too far. While I sat in my car waiting for Cole to come out of his house, I couldn't help but wonder if his father would be joining us. Would I finally be allowed to meet the mystery man?

When the house door opened, I saw Cole standing there. He was dressed in an outdated black suit that looked a little big for him. I assumed it was actually his father's suit. Most likely the one he had worn to his own wedding. Cole closed the house door behind him before walking over to my car. His father was not going to his own son's wedding. What kind of father was he?

We made it to City Hall with ten minutes to spare before our marriage appointment. I wanted to feel happy and excited. I was marrying the man I loved, but it was hard to be excited with none of our family members there to support us. It was even more depressing when we stood in front of the justice of the peace. He looked behind us before asking where our witnesses were. I felt my face turn red with embarrassment as Cole told him we didn't have any. He left the room and came back a couple of minutes later with two older women that looked like they were office clerks and had been office clerks for many years.

Ten minutes later, we were back in my car as husband and wife. Cole looked down at his left hand and smiled the biggest smile I had ever seen. It made my heart smile along with him. When we got to my place, we fed each other a cupcake. I half thought he would shove it in my face at the last moment, but instead, he fed it to me more gently than I fed his to him. Then we opened a bottle of wine and made a toast to the beginning of our lives together.

Cole took out his phone and started playing with it, so I headed to the bedroom. I wanted to change out of my dress. I never felt comfortable wearing a dress. Before I made it to the bedroom, I heard the beginning of one of my favorite songs playing on Cole's phone. I had only told him one time how much I loved the song. I couldn't believe he remembered what it was.

I turned around and saw Cole standing there with his hand out waiting for me to join him. I walked over and put my hand in his. He pulled me into his embrace, and we danced our first dance as husband and wife, listening to Sheena Easton telling me I am the wind beneath her wings. It was my favorite part of our wedding day. Well, that and what happened in our marital bed once our dance ended.

CHAPTER 17

Over the next few days, Cole moved all his belongings into my — or rather our — house. For a man in his mid-twenties, he had even less to his name than I imagined. I had offered to help him move his stuff, but he wouldn't allow it. I wasn't sure if it was because I was his older wife or because he didn't want to chance me meeting his father. I had a new father-in-law whom I had never met.

It had been four months since Heather died, and I still hadn't done anything with her house. It was the last part of her that I still had. I would occasionally go over to the house and just sit on her bed and have myself a really good cry. A part of me had still not accepted that she was gone. I would've done anything to see her walk through the door. The new door that had replaced the one with the busted lock.

I never accepted the police officer's assumption that Heather had damaged the lock herself. She knew I had a spare key. If she were locked out, she could have easily asked me for the spare key to get in the house without damaging the lock.

During month five after Heather's death, I called the local real estate company and asked them to list the house for sale. I knew it would sell quickly given the neighborhood and the condition it was in. I met the realtor at the house to give her a tour and to sign all the papers she needed me to sign. After the realtor left, I went through every room and collected all the things I wanted to keep as a memory of the sister I had lost. I purposely ended in her bedroom. I wanted to say one last goodbye to her in the place she had died.

When I was done collecting everything and saying goodbye, I walked out of the house for the last time. As I made my way toward my car, I saw the *For Sale* sign sticking out of the ground at the end of the driveway. It was really happening. I was letting go of Heather. The only place I would have to visit her now was in the cemetery with my parents. Although I was a married woman, I felt completely alone.

While I was putting all the things I had collected into the back seat of the car, the old lady next door came out onto her porch. She was just standing there looking at me. When she saw me looking back at her she made a hand movement. I thought she had waved hello, so I waved back at her. Then she did it again and I realized she was actually trying to get me to go over to her. I wasn't in the mood to talk to anyone, but I didn't want to be rude.

I closed the car doors and walked over to the old lady's porch.

"I see you put the house up for sale. That must've been a tough thing to do. When I lost my Nicholas, I thought about selling our house, but there are too many memories here that I want to hold onto for as long as I can." I hadn't noticed how frail she looked before. At least she still had enough of her mind left to remember the memories they had made in their house.

She noticed I was on the verge of crying again.

"I'm sorry dear. I didn't mean to upset you. I just wanted to ask if you had heard anything new about how your sister had died. I know they said it was a suicide, but what about the messed-up lock? How did they explain that?"

Seemed I wasn't the only one that didn't believe Heather had taken her own life.

"I haven't heard anything new from the police in a few months. The last I heard; they ruled it a suicide. They think Heather messed up the lock herself after locking herself out of the house." I could see by the expression on the old lady's face that she didn't believe the police's assumption any more than I did.

"You know what I think?" she asked. "I think they are too lazy to actually do their job and investigate it as a possible murder. It is much easier for them to call it a suicide and be done with it."

I couldn't have agreed any more than I already did. This old lady had more common sense than the police.

I promised her I would let her know if I heard anything new from the police before walking back over to my car. She stayed on her porch and waved goodbye as I pulled out of the driveway. I had forgotten the *For Sale* sign was there and almost ran it over. As I drove away, I couldn't help but wonder if I had just made a huge mistake. Maybe there was something in the house that could help prove that Heather didn't take her own life.

CHAPTER 18

I have heard it said many times that money rules the world. Money can buy happiness. The one with the most toys at the end wins. Fact or fiction? I don't know about you, but for me, I say fiction. You can have as much money as Oprah does and still be sad, lonely, and depressed. You can own a huge mansion, have a bunch of cars and your own private jet, and still have no one in your life whom you love and who loves you back. I say having love in your life is much more important than having money. Lucky for me, I had both.

It took less than a week to sell Heather's house. Between the proceeds from the house, her savings, and her life insurance, I was now 2.3 million dollars richer. Once you add that to what I already had, I was a very rich woman. I had more money than I would ever be able to spend in my lifetime. You would think that would also make me an incredibly happy woman, but truth be told, that wasn't the case. I missed Heather and my parents every day. I would've gladly given every penny I had to have just one of them back in my life.

Don't get me wrong, I wasn't completely miserable every second of every day. I was married to a man I loved and who loved me back. Cole was a great husband. He was very attentive and supportive. He knew I was still feeling depressed about losing Heather. He gave me space any time I needed it. He held me and let me cry for as long as it took without ever complaining. I honestly don't know what I would've done without him.

Then one day, things started to change. That may not be completely true. Things may have started to change before I even realized they were changing. Love can make us blind. That is a fact, not fiction. I had started feeling like something with Cole was off. He had never asked me how much money I had. He had never even asked me how much Heather's house sold for. I was his wife; he had a right to ask me questions like that, but he never did. It was like he didn't care. Was that normal? Was he just trying to prove to me that he didn't marry me for my money?

He was still riding around on the same bike he was riding when I first met him. I had offered to buy him a car several times, but he didn't want one. He was still working as a personal trainer at the gym. He didn't need to work if he didn't want to. He said he wanted to work. He needed to feel like he was contributing to the household. I occasionally found myself thinking back to what Heather had said about Cole hiding something. Had she been right all along?

A couple of months after our one-year anniversary, I noticed Cole had started acting differently. He was volunteering for more shifts at the gym, thus being home less often. He also started touching me less and less. Something was going on with him, but I had no idea what it was. I asked him a few times if something was wrong, but he always said everything was fine. Business at the gym had picked up so he was helping out as much as he could. By the time he got home from work, all he wanted to do was relax and sleep.

At that point, I couldn't even remember the last time we had been intimate. For a woman my age that had only been married a little over a year to not be able to remember the last time she had been intimate with her husband, spelled concern. For a man Cole's age to not want to be intimate with his wife after only being married a little over a year, spelled trouble.

Then one day while Cole was at work, I did something that I had thought about doing for quite some time. I got in my car and drove over to the house Cole had lived in with his father. I had no idea what I was going to do when I got there. Cole wouldn't even talk about his father to me, never mind let me meet him. What would he do if he knew I was sitting outside his father's house right then in my car?

I parked my car directly across the street. Then I just sat there looking over at the house. All the blinds were closed even though it was the middle of the afternoon. There was no car in the driveway. Maybe his father was out of town on a vacation. It was obvious the lawn had not been mowed for quite some time. Perhaps his father was too old to keep up with the yard work. I was trying to find a reason or an excuse for everything that didn't seem right.

After sitting there for a half hour, I finally mustered up the nerve to get out of my car and approach the house. I still didn't know what I was about to do. Should I just ring the doorbell? Should I make my way around the house to see if any of the blinds were open? Should I get back in my car and head back home? As I got closer to the front door, I noticed there was a storm door with a mail slot in it before the actual front door. I tried the handle on the storm door, but it was locked. The top half of the storm door was a pane of glass. When I looked down between the storm door and the front door, I noticed the mail was almost as high as the window. Nobody had been home for quite some time. I wasn't sure what that meant, but I was going to find out one way or another.

CHAPTER 19

I knew it was against the law to take a piece of someone else's mail, but I think that only counts if you get caught. I made sure to check my surroundings as I stood outside Cole's father's front door. There was no one around. I lifted the cover to the mail slot and did my best to work my hand through the slot. Thanks to my man-sized knuckles, I couldn't get my hand in far enough to grab one of the envelopes. Trust me, I tried every angle possible. I finally gave up when I scraped one of my knuckles hard enough to start bleeding.

On my way back home, I made sure to drive by the gym. It is embarrassing to admit aloud that I was checking up on my husband, but that was exactly what I was doing. I had seen the way most of the women in the gym looked at Cole when I was there with him. Who knew how far they would go to get his attention when I wasn't there? I slowed down as I approached the entrance to the gym parking lot. I could see Cole's bike chained to the bike rack. At least I knew he hadn't lied to me about working another long shift. Then again, just because his bike was there, didn't mean he hadn't driven off in some women's car like he had in mine.

I was starting to drive myself crazy. I had always dealt with many insecurities in my life. Heather had always been the one to tell me how absurd they all were. With her gone, I had no one to tell me I was wrong for feeling old, out of shape, and undesirable. When you add being shy and an introvert into the mix, it can become almost impossible to want to leave the safety of your own house. For a while, I'd had Cole telling me how beautiful I was and wanting to be intimate with me all the time. Over the past two to three months, both of those occurrences had become less and less frequent. Things were changing between us and not in a good way. Was he getting bored with me already?

I checked the time on my car stereo and realized it was ten minutes before Cole's lunch break. I knew he would be hopping on his bike and riding to the Subway a few blocks away. He loved their tuna fish sub. I offered to make him tuna fish sandwiches for his lunches, but he preferred to go to Subway. It gave him a reason to leave the gym for an hour instead of just eating in their employee break room. I decided I would join him for lunch considering I was so close by.

I wanted it to be a surprise, so I drove to the Subway and parked toward the back of their parking lot. After I saw him ride into the parking lot on his bike, I would pull up close to where he left his bike and join him inside. I sat in my car watching out the windshield for Cole to ride into the parking lot. It started getting busy a few minutes after I arrived. The *lunch rush* I think they call it. I watched as car after car pulled into the parking lot. One man on a bike pulled into the parking lot but I knew right away it wasn't Cole.

I checked the clock again. I had been sitting in the parking lot for fifteen minutes. Cole should've been there by then. Maybe he had decided to go somewhere else for lunch and I was wasting my time sitting in the Subway parking lot. I started my car and just as I was about to head for the exit, I noticed a car pulling into the parking lot that I had seen before. I wasn't sure who owned it, but I was certain I had seen it parked in the gym parking lot a few times. It isn't every day you see a white car with pink trim and a pink interior. I shut my car off again and waited. From where I was parked, I had a perfect view of the entrance to Subway.

I didn't have to wait very long. A car had pulled out of one of the parking spots right in front of the entrance. The white car pulled into the spot right after the other car had pulled out. I leaned forward in my car trying to block the sun that was shining in my eyes. When the driver's side door opened, I recognized the driver right away. I should've been able to guess without even seeing her. I watched as the busty blonde got out of the car. As I started to lean back, I noticed the passenger's door was opening as well. I leaned forward again only to watch my husband getting out of the busty blonde's car.

I immediately crouched down in my car just in case Cole or his lunch date happened to look in my direction. With my eyes just over the steering wheel, I watched as Cole held the door open for his invited lunch guest. I had a feeling I wasn't invited to join them. I couldn't help but wonder how many other times they had gone to lunch together. My insecurities were definitely getting the best of me. Just because they went to lunch that day, didn't mean it was a regular thing. It also didn't mean there was anything going on between the two of them. It could all be completely innocent.

Once they were inside the restaurant, I couldn't really see what was happening anymore. I waited a few minutes to make sure they weren't getting their lunches to go, although that was exactly what I was hoping they were going to do. An innocent ride to Subway to pick up their lunches. No harm in that right? When enough time had passed, I moved my car to a closer parking spot. I was two rows behind the white car. I was tempted to get out and drag my key up and down the side of it, but I was too afraid one of them would look out the window and see me doing it.

105

From my new parking spot, I could see right into the restaurant. I scanned the windows looking for where Cole had sat down. I finally spotted him and the busty blonde sitting at the far corner table. There were a few empty tables right in front of the windows, but they had chosen the table furthest from the windows with no one else around them. It wasn't easy to see what they were doing considering I was three rows away from the building. I suddenly wished I owned a pair of binoculars.

From what I could tell they had just finished eating. They were putting their empty wrappers and cups on the tray. Cole stood up first with the tray in his hand. He walked over to the trash receptacle and dumped its contents into the trash can before dropping the tray on the shelf above it. Then he walked to the door and once again held it open for his lunch date before exiting himself.

Then I watched as Cole, my husband, took the busty blonde's hand into his, as they walked toward the white car. He walked with her over to the driver's side door. He opened the door for her just like he had done for me. Before getting into the car, she turned around and he kissed her on the lips, just like he had done to me. If he had looked in my direction when he walked to the passenger's side door, he would've been looking right at me. I just sat there as they drove out of the parking lot. Everything was starting to make a lot more sense. Now I had to decide what I was going to do about it.

CHAPTER 20

Have you ever tried to unsee something that you had seen in real life, with your own two eyes? It is hard enough to unsee something you saw on the news, or something you saw in a movie that you found extremely disturbing, never mind when it happened in real life right before your eyes. If you are like me, instead of unseeing it, you end up watching it replay over and over in your mind. You might even try closing your eyes as tightly as possible while praying to God to make it stop. It may even stop for a minute, an hour, or even a day, but at some point, something will happen to make you remember it, and you will find yourself stuck in the same routine as before. Replay. Stop. Replay. Stop.

I have no idea how long I sat in the Subway parking lot after the white car had left. My head was spinning so fast after what I had just seen. I needed the spinning to stop before I felt okay enough to drive home. I kept seeing Cole kissing the busty blonde up against her car in the parking lot of a restaurant. The same exact thing he had done to me in the parking lot of the movie theater. I lowered all the windows in the car to let whatever breeze there was that day blow in on me. I scanned through the radio stations until I found a song I really liked and turned it all the way up. A few people walking by my car stopped to see where the music was coming from, but I didn't care. I needed to clear my mind at least enough to be able to drive myself home. I could feel a migraine coming on. I needed my bed.

When I finally made it home, I closed all the blinds in the house to keep as much sunlight out as possible. Climbing the staircase made me feel dizzy. Then I took two extra strength Excedrin and climbed into bed. I wished myself to fall asleep, but instead, I was flooded with new thoughts and questions. Most of the questions involved the busty blonde. How long had Cole been sticking his tongue in her mouth as well as in mine? Had Cole already been involved with her before he even met me? Why had Cole married me instead of her?

Then I started thinking about Heather. Why wasn't she there with me when I really needed her? I would have given anything to have her loving arms wrapped around me. I started crying while I heard her words repeating in my head, 'Cole is hiding something.' She had been right about him all along. Not only was he possibly hiding something about his father, but he was also hiding an affair. I felt like such a fool for not listening to her. I had assumed she was just jealous because I had found a man to spend time with while she hadn't. I should've known better. If she hadn't believed Cole was hiding something from me, she would've been happy for me, not jealous of me.

I just lay there in bed as still as I could. When you have a migraine even the slightest turn of your body can make you nauseous. My head was pounding. I squinted my eyes to look at the alarm clock. I wanted to see how much time was left before Cole would be home from work. The light from the alarm clock made my eyes burn. I shut them tight again as I cursed myself for opening them. I needed the migraine to pass before Cole got home. I wanted time to think about how I was going to handle being cheated on. Should I pretend I didn't know? Should I confront him about it? What would Heather or my mother tell me to do?

Over the next few hours, the pounding in my head subsided. I could open my eyes and look around the room without wanting to vomit. I slowly got out of bed and walked over to the bathroom. I splashed water on my face to hopefully make myself feel somewhat refreshed. Then I walked around the house and opened some of the blinds. It would be getting dark again soon, so I left some of them closed. I checked the time on the clock hanging on the living room wall. Cole should be home in less than half an hour. I sat down in my favorite recliner and waited for the answers to my questions to magically come to me.

Have you ever been to a magic show? I don't mean one of the magic shows at a circus or a carnival. I mean a real magic show like the ones in Las Vegas. Our parents had taken us to a few when Heather and I were teenagers. While everyone else there was oohing and aahing, I spent the entire show trying to figure out the magician's secrets. I wasn't happy enough just watching the show. I had to know how they were really doing the tricks they wanted us to believe were magic.

Just like at the magic show, I wanted to know what was going on with Cole and his mistress. I would never be happy just pretending I didn't know about it. That wasn't the way my parents made me. Amid my thoughts, I heard the front door open. That was another thing about Cole riding his bike everywhere. I could never hear him coming home until he was at the front door.

I grabbed the remote for the television and turned it on. Seconds later, Cole came walking into the living room and found me laughing at one of the jokes Rose had said on an episode of *The Golden Girls*. Heather and I had watched every episode at least two or three times over the years. I would pretend to be Dorothy, while Heather would pretend to be Blanche. I really missed those days.

Cole walked over and kissed me on the cheek. I swore I could smell a woman's perfume on his neck.

"How was your day?" I asked with a slight tremble in my voice. He stood behind me gently rubbing my stiff shoulders. I didn't want his hands on me after being on his mistress. It was making my skin crawl.

"It was okay. Not as busy as it has been lately. How was your day? Did you do anything exciting?"

It was now or never. If I didn't ask him about it now the chances of me finding the nerve to bring it up later were very slim. I had to know. I didn't want it festering in the back of my mind for any longer than it already had.

"I wouldn't call it exciting, but I did go out for lunch today." I instantly felt his hands stop rubbing my shoulders. He came out from behind the recliner and stood in front of me.

"You did? Where did you go?" he asked in a curious tone.

I made him wait about thirty seconds before answering him. "I went to your favorite Subway. I thought I might bump into you while I was there, but I didn't see your bike. I guess you went somewhere different for lunch today."

I let my words just hang there in the air as I watched Cole's face turn a light shade of red. Was he angry with me for trying to meet up with him for lunch, or was he embarrassed because he was thinking that maybe I had seen him after all?

CHAPTER 21

If you are ever caught in a lie, what do you do? Wait, let me try that again. If you are ever caught in a lie when you are face-to-face with the person you are lying to, what do you do? There is an enormous difference when you are lying to someone face-to-face as opposed to over the phone, in an email, or in a text message. Most people, me included, always tell the truth with their facial expressions, even when we are telling lies with our words. The exception to this rule is a pathological liar.

Even if I hadn't seen Cole with his lunch date at the Subway, I would've known something was wrong as he told me to my face that he had skipped lunch that day. The guilt was plastered all over his face. How many other lies had I missed? Love makes us blind to so many things. Trusting someone had not been an easy task for me after the hell my ex-husband had put me through. For some unknown reason, it was different with Cole. I started trusting him almost immediately. I should've listened to Heather. I should've known it was too good to be true.

I used the 'I have a headache' excuse when Cole tried getting frisky that night in bed. Just the thought of his hands on me after what I witnessed in the Subway parking lot made me sick to my stomach. How had I allowed this to happen? Had I been so desperate for a man's attention that I ignored every single red flag that had been swaying right in front of my eyes? I felt like a fool. Now that I knew I was married to a liar and a cheater, I needed to decide what I was going to do with what I knew. If I just asked him straight out about his relationship with the busty blonde, he would just lie right to my face again. I needed a plan. I needed Heather.

I waited until I heard Cole close the door on his way to work before I got out of bed. Now that I knew he had cheated on me and was more than capable of lying right to my face before trying to have sex with me, it felt like I had no clue at all about the man I had married. I decided to go with the assumption that everything he had ever told me was a lie. He had played me from day one. I had been too blinded by his charms to realize it until now. That was all stopping immediately. My eyes were wide open, and they were staying wide open.

The way I saw it, I had one huge decision to make. Was my marriage worth fighting for, or was it past that point? Would I ever be able to trust

Cole again? If I confronted him about his affair, would he end it to stay with me, or would he end our marriage to stay with her? If he told me he had ended it, would it be the truth or just another lie? I needed someone to talk to about this. Sadly, there was no one I was close enough to that I could trust not to repeat it to Cole before I had a chance to make my decision.

I got dressed, jumped in my car, and headed to the flower shop. I bought three bouquets of flowers and then headed to the cemetery. The trip was harder than it had been when I had Heather with me. When I made it to my future resting place, I did everything Heather and I used to do together. I removed the old flowers and dropped them in the garbage can at the end of the aisle. I placed the three new bouquets in the holders. I removed the leaves and debris that had landed on the headstone. Then I dropped to my knees and had a conversation with the family I had lost. They all listened to everything I had to say without passing judgment. Though I could swear I heard Heather say, 'I told you so.' My mother and father had nothing to say to me. I hope that didn't mean they were disappointed in me. When I was done telling them everything that was going on between me and Cole, I said separate prayers for all three of them before having myself a really good cry.

After I shed my last tear, I got in my car and drove back home. I knew what I had to do. There was no way I was going to live a lie. When Cole got home from work, I was going to tell him that I knew about his affair. I was going to make him choose between me and his mistress. For better or worse. For richer or poorer. Which would he choose?

CHAPTER 22

Have you ever been the victim of a womanizer? You meet a man who seems to have all the qualities you look for in a potential husband, only to find out it was all part of a game he was playing just to get you to sleep with him, or worse yet, to marry him. By the time you figure out what he is really like, you have devoted your life to him. You have changed things about yourself just to make him happy because you didn't want to lose him. He consumes your mind and gets all your attention, while he is doing the same thing to another woman. What did you do when you finally saw the real him?

When I got home, I opened a nice bottle of wine. If I was going to confront Cole about his lunch date, I was going to need a little liquid courage. With all the long shifts Cole had been working (if that was even true), I never knew when he was going to be walking through the door. I couldn't remember the last time he had worked a regular shift. Then again, I had never seen even one of Cole's paychecks. It was very possible that all the overtime he had been putting in, was not taking place in the gym. Had I really been that big a fool?

I pulled one of the kitchen chairs over to the window that faced the driveway. I knew I wouldn't be able to hear Cole's bike coming up the driveway and I wanted to be ready for him as soon as he walked through the door. I sat in that chair for over two hours before I saw Cole riding his bike up the driveway. He had worked an extra-long day. I knew he was going to be tired and grumpy once again, but it wasn't going to deter our conversation from happening. I had to do it that night for my own sanity.

Before Cole had a chance to walk through the door, I moved the chair back into the kitchen. He didn't need to know I had been sitting there waiting and watching for him to get home. By the time he walked through the front door, I was sitting down in front of the television watching the local news. I waited a few minutes to see if he was going to join me, but he didn't. Instead, he went straight to the bathroom to take a shower. Was he washing off sweat from the gym, or was he washing off the scent of his mistress?

Dressed in pajama bottoms and an old white T-shirt with yellowish-brown stains in the armpits, Cole walked into the living room and sat down on the sofa. We hadn't said one single word to each other since he got home. My liquid courage wasn't enough that I couldn't walk a straight line if need be, but it was enough for me to ask the questions I needed answers to. The lies needed to stop.

I didn't want to just start bombarding him with questions and accusations right away, so I started out normal.

"How was your day today?" Simple easy question that he should be able to answer honestly.

"It was okay. Another long one. How was your day?" A man of many words he was not.

I was going to have to play dentist to get anything out of him.

"My day was okay too. Nothing to write home about. Did you at least have time for lunch today?"

He looked at me with questioning eyes. Like one does when they are overthinking their answer before saying it aloud. Did he forget he had lied to me the day before about not taking a lunch, or did he feel a trap being set in place?

Suddenly, the look on his face changed to almost a smirk. He had just remembered the lie he had told me. He thought he had escaped the trap.

"Luckily, today there was enough help scheduled so I got to take my lunch. Speaking of lunch, what are we having for dinner? I'm starving." Seems he had worked up an appetite during his overtime hours.

"I made a reservation for us at your favorite steak house. They only had one opening available for our favorite table, so we have to wait a bit." I know I shouldn't have lied to him, but considering he was continuing to lie to me, I figured why not. What's good for the goose…

"Did you go to Subway for their tuna fish sub like usual, or did you go somewhere else?" Again, the look on his face changed. He was starting to feel the trap tightening around him just a tiny bit.

"Why are you suddenly so interested in what I do for lunch? You asked me about Subway yesterday too." He knew something was up. There was no turning back even if I wanted to. Instead of answering his question, I came at him with another of my own.

"Do you always go to lunch on your own, or do you bring co-workers with you sometimes?" The trap closed another notch. Was he going to tell me the truth, or at least part of the truth, or was he going to boldly lie to me while sitting less than three feet away from me?

"More questions about my lunches? What's up with you lately?" So, he was going to try to deflect instead of answering. Was he catching on that I knew what he had been up to, or did he think I was losing my mind?

"Is it wrong for a wife to ask her husband questions about his day? It seems like we don't talk much anymore. I am just trying to fix that. To get us back on track." It sounded reasonable to me as I played it back in my head. His face grew less leery as the trap prepared to tighten once again.

"I guess not. I always go to lunch by myself. We never have enough coverage for two of us to go to lunch at the same time."

Okay, so part of that could actually be true. I had asked about his co-workers, not any of his clients, but do not fret, that is next in line.

"That must make for lonely lunches, always being by yourself. Unless of course, you bring one of your clients with you. I think that would be unprofessional and frowned upon at the gym, even though you used to do it with me when I was one of your clients." The trap was so close to closing and he knew it. He started fidgeting and little beads of sweat started forming on his forehead.

"There is a fraternization policy at the gym. Trainers are not supposed to hang out with any of their clients. I broke that policy when you joined the gym." He gave me a quick wink and a cute boyish smile. Did he really think that was going to work on me?

It was time to close the trap before I lost my liquid courage. "So, when I saw you with your busty blonde client at Subway yesterday, was that you breaking the policy again?" I stared at him as his jaw dropped open. He was in trouble, and he knew it. Was he going to try to tell me I was crazy, that I was imagining things, or was he going to try something new and tell me the truth?

Instead, he turned what I had just said around and played the victim. "Have you been following me?" Did he seriously think I would cave that easily? He may have fooled me once, but I was by no means a fool.

"Thank you for not denying it. How long have you been sleeping with her?" The gloves were off. The chips were going to land wherever they landed.

"I can't believe you followed me. Don't you trust me?"

What did he just ask me? Was he serious? Had he not realized the game was over?

"To be honest, something you clearly know nothing about, I didn't follow you. I was there before you. I wanted to surprise you for lunch, but you had other plans that definitely didn't include your wife."

I could hear my own voice getting louder and angrier. He had hurt me and that hurt was busting out of me in my words.

"Whatever you think you saw, was not what really happened. Your insecurities are getting the better of you." He seemed to think he was good at playing the victim, using my own insecurities against me, but I was seeing right through all his smokescreens.

"Is that a fact? So, when I saw you sticking your tongue down her throat with my own two eyes, that's not what really happened?" Trap closed! The look on his face was one of complete shock. Either he thought I had left after seeing them arrive in her car, thus missing their make-out scene in the parking lot, or he didn't think I had the nerve to call him out about it as I had. Either way, I had him right where I wanted him, trapped.

Full steam ahead. "I think you missed one of my questions earlier. How long have you been sleeping with her?" His eyes dropped to the floor. He knew I knew, and that I was not backing down anytime soon. He tried to change the subject.

"What time is our reservation? I need to get dressed."

I don't know whether it was my liquid courage or not, but I jumped up out of my chair. I wanted to wrap my hands tightly around his neck and squeeze as hard as I could until his eyes popped out of his head, but that wasn't the kind of person I was.

I stood right there in front of him waiting for his eyes to meet mine. When they finally did, I tried a third time.

"How long have you been sleeping with her? Please do not make me ask you again." I was losing the little bit of patience I had left.

"For a few months now. It just sort of happened. You shut down when Heather died. I couldn't reach you no matter what I tried."

I could feel my face turning red. I was about to boil over with rage. Was he really blaming his affair on how I dealt with Heather's death? How dare he. It took all the strength I had in me to not slap him across the face.

Then I started to cry. What if what he was saying was the truth? I had tried my best to not shut him out while I grieved for Heather, but it wasn't always an easy thing to do, especially when a part of me wanted to die like the rest of my family had. Was I partly to blame for Cole's affair? Did that even make sense? Cole got up from the sofa and wrapped his arms around me. I tried to fight him at first, but he didn't give up. I gave in and buried my head against his neck while he held me tightly.

Then he whispered in my ear, "I am so sorry I hurt you. You know how much I love you. I will tell her it's over. Please forgive me."

I gently pushed away from him a bit unsteady on my feet.

"I am going to lie down for a bit. Maybe you should order some takeout for dinner. We will go to the steak house another night."

He pulled me close to him again and kissed me on the forehead. When he let me go, I headed up the stairs to the bedroom, while he headed to the drawer in the kitchen with the takeout menus in it.

CHAPTER 23

Over the next few weeks, I started going to the gym more often. I had started feeling much better about my marriage after learning that the busty blonde had suddenly stopped coming to the gym. Rumors had been circulating around the gym that she and Cole caused quite a scene in the parking lot the day after I had confronted him about their affair. Seems he had kept his word about ending things with her. Maybe he really did love me after all.

On a few of the days that I went to the gym, I drove past Cole's father's house before heading home. Each time I snuck up to the front door and checked to see if the mail was still piling up. If it got just a little bit higher, I would be able to grab an envelope through the mail slot. This was one of those days.

After seeing no nosy neighbors lurking around, I casually made my way from my car to the front door. When I looked down into the space between the two doors, I couldn't believe my eyes. All the mail that had been piling up for God knows how long was gone. Did that mean Cole's father had finally come home from wherever he had been all this time? Was this the day I finally got to meet my father-in-law?

I tried the handle on the storm door expecting it to be unlocked, but it was still locked. Was it normal for people to lock their storm doors? I could see if you were away on a long vacation or something similar, but what were the chances he would be gone again after just coming home? I knocked on the door and rang the doorbell several times. I got no answer. After checking the windows of neighboring houses, I made my way around the perimeter of the house. Nothing had changed since the last time. All the windows were locked, and all the blinds were closed. He had come home, collected all his mail, left again, and I had missed him.

For the first time in about a month, I could hear Heather telling me that Cole was hiding something from me. I really wish she would've just come out and told me what it was she thought he was hiding. Was he having another affair? Had he been seeing someone else when we first met? Was that what Heather had caught onto, or was she just being suspicious, overprotective? I always thought she meant he was hiding something about his father, but maybe I had been wrong all along. How many other wives out there had never met their father-in-law? I was sure there were lots that wished they had never met theirs once they had, but I had never even been given the chance.

Another thing had changed since Cole and I had our talk: he was back to working his normal hours. No more long shifts keeping him away from home. He was trying hard to earn my trust again. I had no intention of making it easy for him.

When Cole came home that night, I had a nice glass of his favorite wine chilled, poured, and waiting for him. I had asked him several times to quit his job at the gym so we could do some traveling, but he refused. There were enough people calling him a gold digger as it was, never mind if he quit his job and just lived off my money. With the amount of money I had, it wouldn't have mattered to me, but he had his pride, and he wasn't about to give it up.

After Cole finished his shower, we relaxed on the sofa with our glasses of wine. I was starting to get used to being his wife again. His great foot massages were definitely a plus. He knew his way around every inch of a woman's body, head to toe.

"You know what I was thinking about today?" I asked him in a very casual tone. He was working his magic on my stubby little toe. At first, I thought he was so invested in my massage that he hadn't heard me.

After a couple of minutes, he moved onto my other foot and asked, "What were you thinking about today?"

His magic hands had me so relaxed I had almost forgotten what I was going to say.

"You haven't mentioned your father in quite some time. Have you seen him lately?"

It never hurts to show interest in your spouse's life. Just because I had never met the man, didn't mean I couldn't ask about him. I would've done anything to spend just one more minute with my father or my mother. Cole didn't know how lucky he was to still have his father in his life. He had no idea how envious I was of him. I think that is the main reason I had been passing by his father's house. If I couldn't spend time with my own father, at least I could spend time with Cole's father.

With only my big toe rubbed on my left foot, Cole stopped the massage. He picked up his glass of wine and drank almost half of it in one big gulp.

"I would prefer to not talk about my father. I haven't seen him since I moved in here with you."

Hearing him say that made my heart hurt. Was his father really that horrible a person that he didn't care if he had not seen him in months? They must've gone through some really dark times in the past.

"I'm sorry I brought him up. I didn't mean to upset you." After placing his wine glass back down on the table, he picked up the massage right where he had left off. I didn't say another word. I just let him finish spoiling me. I was, however, contemplating if there was any way I could help fix whatever was wrong between Cole and his father. Maybe if I could manage to track his father down, I could talk to him and hopefully get him to reach out to Cole. What harm could it do? They were family after all.

CHAPTER 24

Some secrets are better left kept as secrets. Sometimes it really is best to let sleeping dogs lie. It is not always easy to accept that not everything is our business, especially when it comes to our families. Every family has its own share of secrets for one reason or another. Have you ever been part of a family secret that you have been sworn to keep to yourself? Were you able to keep it, or did it slip out accidentally, or on purpose? Keeping secrets can lead to an unnecessary lack of trust once the secret rears its ugly head.

I'm not sure if it was out of boredom or out of curiosity, but my new goal in life had become getting Cole and his father to at least be on speaking terms. I had no real plan for how I was going to accomplish this goal considering his father was most likely away again. With Cole working full-time at the gym, I was left with enough extra time on my hands to figure something out. I didn't want to involve Cole in case the whole thing backfired, and his father blatantly refused to talk to him.

I had to pick a place to start. After much consideration, I decided that my best bet for getting any information, whether it be bad or good, would be from the people I had been trying so hard to evade, his neighbors. I waited for thirty minutes after Cole left for work before jumping in my car and heading over to his father's house once again. When I drove past the gym, I took a quick glance to make sure Cole's bike was chained in its usual spot, which it was.

One of the reasons we liked living where we did was because the houses weren't stacked one on top of another. You couldn't look out your window and see your next-door neighbor staring back at you from less than ten feet away. We all had our fair share of privacy. I mention this because although my plan was to talk to Cole's father's neighbors, there were only five other houses on his street. There was one on both sides of his property and three others on the opposite side of the street. From the way the houses were spaced out, his closest neighbor was easily seventy-five feet away from him. This may not have been such a clever idea after all.

Considering I was trying to attract attention this time, I parked my car in the driveway, instead of across the street. Just like all my other visits, there wasn't a single person in sight. I just sat there in my car looking up and down the street waiting to see or hear someone that I could talk to. I thought I would've had the courage to go knock on the neighbors' doors, but when push came to shove, I couldn't get myself to do it. As I sat there, I started second-guessing my plan. Suppose I started talking to one of the neighbors about Cole's father only to find out that the neighbor was friends with Cole.

I had just about convinced myself that my plan wasn't going to work when I heard a small dog barking. I sat up and leaned closer to the windshield. I couldn't tell which direction the barking had come from. I sat there turning my head from side to side waiting to see if there was a human to go along with the dog. I wanted to spot them as soon as I could to ensure I would have enough time to get out of my car and approach them before they had a chance to pass me by. Then I heard the barking again. It was definitely coming from farther down the street. I got out of my car and casually made my way over to the sidewalk to get a better view.

About fifty feet down the street, I spotted them. The barking dog was a dachshund. The human holding its leash was an older woman. They were slowly making their way in my direction. I didn't want to startle either of them, so I just remained where I was. It would be impossible for them to pass me without seeing me first. I felt safer knowing it was an older woman. The chances she would even know who Cole is, never mind being friends with him, was very unlikely.

The dachshund saw me first. It gave a few barks in my direction and then the older woman saw me and told the dachshund to be quiet. To my surprise, it worked like a charm. The barking ended immediately. I walked a few steps to close the gap between us a little quicker. My nerves were starting to get the best of me. When we were finally side by side, I bent down to pet the dachshund, but it backed up and hid behind the older woman. Luckily, the older woman was much more friendly than her dog.

I wasn't sure what I should ask her to get the answers I was looking for without making her feel uncomfortable. I was originally going to say I was looking for a house to buy in the neighborhood and was hoping to get some insight on the neighbors, but I didn't want to lie to her or mislead her. She reminded me of my mother.

I stuck my hand out and introduced myself.

"Hello, my name is Kari. You have a beautiful dog there."

It never hurts to compliment someone's dog even if it's a lie. It usually helps build a bond of sorts.

"Why, thank you, for saying that. He is all bark and no bite as you can see. I protect him, instead of him protecting me. My name is Doris."

I instantly liked Doris. Occasionally in your life, you meet people that you just know are good people. You can feel their kindness generating off of them. Doris was one of those people.

"Do you live on this street, Doris, or are you just out for a walk?" Always use someone's name when talking to them, especially if they have just told you what it is. It lets them know you are listening and paying attention to them. Things we all want for ourselves. Why not give it to others when the opportunity arises?

"My house is the last one on this side of the street. Been living on this street for forty-seven years." If she had been living on that street for that long, there was no way she didn't know who Cole's father was.

"Wow, that's a long time to live on the same street. Do you mind if I ask you a few questions about one of your neighbors?"

I didn't know how long she would be happy to stand talking to a stranger, so I didn't want to waste any more time.

"I was wondering what you were doing just standing there on the sidewalk. Which neighbor is it that you want to talk about?"

I guess she hadn't put two and two together yet. My car was parked in the driveway with me standing not too far away from it.

I turned halfway around and pointed to Cole's father's house.

"This is my father-in-law's house. I have been trying to visit him lately, but he never seems to be home. I was wondering if you had seen him recently?"

She was looking at me as if I had asked her a trick question. "Are you saying you married Henry's son?"

CHAPTER 25

We stood there on the sidewalk just looking at each other. From the tone of her voice when she had asked if I had married Henry's son, I could tell she seemed uneasy at just the thought of it. I, on the other hand, felt like I was almost in a trance. For the first time since I met Cole, I had heard his father's name, Henry. Was I really one step closer to helping them bridge the gap that had been between them all this time?

I put on my best smile and replied, "Yes, we met a year and a half ago and got married not too long after. Do you remember Henry's son from when he lived here?" Doris was looking at me as if she didn't believe a word I was saying.

"I don't remember him being old enough to marry someone of your age." Now it was making sense. It was the age thing all over again.

"To be honest, he really isn't old enough to be married to a woman of my age. It was sort of a whirlwind romance that came out of nowhere."

Now she had a little smirk on her face. What would I see behind that smirk if I could read her mind?

"Good for you snagging a man who is so much younger. I bet he is good in the sack." Source of the smirk revealed. Doris may be old enough to be my mother, but she still had a dirty mind. She had caught me so off guard with her remark, I couldn't help but let a little chuckle out.

"I plead the Fifth," I said in a girlish voice.

"So, what do you want to know about Henry, not that I know too much?" If there is anything I know about women Doris's age, it is that they are often widowed and living with a pet to help them deal with their loneliness. They hardly ever have company, so when they do, they love to tell stories and gossip. I was getting closer to that age than I would care to admit.

"Do you remember the last time you saw him?"

Doris took her time answering my question. I could almost picture her flipping through the pages of a hanging calendar trying to find the exact date she had last seen Henry.

"I can't say for sure, but it has to have been almost two years ago." How could that be right? She hadn't seen Cole's father since before Cole and I ever met. She must be remembering incorrectly. Maybe she wasn't as right in the mind as she seemed. I didn't want to insult or embarrass her in any way considering she didn't have to talk to me at all, but I needed the truth, not what her mind was allowing her to remember.

I turned to face the house. It was easy to see that the lawn had not been mowed for quite some time. The paint on the house was starting to chip and some of the shingles from the roof had blown off and were now sitting on the overgrown lawn. Then add into the mix that all the windows had been locked and all the blinds had been drawn every time I had stopped by, and let's not forget about the stacked-up mail between the two front doors. Was what Doris was saying true? If it was true, what happened to all the mail that was now gone?

"Where do you think he has been for the last two years?" The dachshund had finally worked up the nerve to come out from behind Doris. He moseyed on over to a patch of the overgrown lawn and laid down.

"To be honest I have no idea. Henry was not one of the friendliest neighbors. I know he went through a rough patch when he started drinking too much. His wife had died a while back. I can vaguely remember he moved another woman in with him, but that didn't last very long. She was here one day and then gone the next."

My mind was all over the place. Cole had never told me that his father had moved another woman into their house after his mother had died. How many other secrets was he keeping from me? He also never told me his father had a problem fighting the bottle. Was that why he never wanted me to meet his father? I had always assumed it was me he was embarrassed about due to our age difference. Maybe he was actually too embarrassed of his father being a drunk.

Have you ever experienced a pivotal moment in your life? If so, did you know it was going to be a pivotal moment before it even happened, or did you realize it later in life? Just the idea that a single moment in time could change someone's life dramatically seemed preposterous.

"When I came by here a couple of days ago, I noticed there was a lot of mail stacked up between the two front doors. Yet, when I came by here yesterday, all the mail was gone. What do you think happened to it if it wasn't Henry that took it into the house?"

I noticed Doris's eyes move from me to the recyclable bin that was on the side of the house. I had walked right past it a few times but had never thought to open it.

"I saw your husband here yesterday. He was going through all the mail. Most of it he put in that bin over there."

My head was spinning so fast I thought for sure I was going to pass out. Doris had seen Cole here at his father's house the day before, going through his father's mail and then throwing it away in a recyclable bin, without even showing it to his father first. Why would he do that? Where was his father? What the heck was going on?

I tried to sound as unshocked and as calm as I possibly could when I asked Doris my next questions.

"You saw Cole here yesterday going through his father's mail? Are you sure it was him?" There was a slight hint of confusion that ran across Doris's face. Maybe she had been mixing up distant memories and only now was she realizing it.

"Are you okay, Doris? I didn't mean to confuse you."

I was starting to feel bad. The poor sweet older woman was just going about her business, taking her dog for a walk, until I came along and started asking her questions about one of her neighbors that had clearly stressed her out. That had not been my intent at all. That was when it happened. The pivotal moment that I had not seen coming at all.

"I thought you said you married Henry's son?" It was my time to look confused. "Henry's son's name isn't Cole."

As I stood there dazed and confused, Doris pulled on the dachshund's leash and continued their walk. There had to be a reasonable explanation for the confusion about Cole's name. I was certain Doris was also confused about seeing Cole the day before going through his father's mail. Once Doris was far enough away from me, I made my way over to the recyclable bin. I lifted the lid secretly hoping to not see all of Henry's mail piled in it. My hopes were short-lived.

It was obvious that someone with a key to the storm door had been here the day before and put all the mail that had been between the two doors into the bin. From what I could see, none of the envelopes had been opened. I reached into the bin and grabbed one of the envelopes. Sure enough, it had been addressed to Henry. I put the envelope in my pocket, closed the lid to the bin, and headed for my car. I had come here to get answers, yet I was leaving with even more questions.

CHAPTER 26

During my drive home from Henry's house, I swear I could feel the envelope burning a hole in my pants pocket. I knew I was not going to be able to keep what I had found out from Doris to myself. Cole was still keeping secrets from me. I needed him to come clean with me about everything from his past, especially everything to do with his father. If Doris had been right about seeing Cole at his father's house getting rid of the mail, what was his reason for doing so?

I must have paced every inch of the house that day waiting for Cole to get home. I even stopped by the Subway hoping to meet him for lunch, but he didn't show up. I instantly started wondering if he was off somewhere with another woman. What is that old saying, 'Once a cheat, always a cheat.' Five minutes after he should've been home from work, I started calling his cell phone. It went to voicemail every time. I knew he would be able to see all my missed calls, but I didn't care. On my fourth attempt of reaching him, I left a voicemail asking him to please come home as soon as he could.

I had a good pattern of pacing going on. I was walking the perimeter of the entire downstairs. Every time I made it back to the front door, I would look outside in hopes of seeing Cole coming up the driveway. Just as I was about to call Cole's cell phone again my phone rang.

"What's up with all the calls? Is something wrong?" He sounded totally normal. No hint of guilt in his voice at all.

"Where have you been? I need to talk to you about something. When will you be home?" I hadn't meant to sound as crazed as I could tell I did.

"I stopped for a coffee after work at the coffee house a few blocks away. I am heading home now." The dial tone after he hung up on me was deafening. Since when did Cole drink coffee after work? That was news to me. What else didn't I know about the man I had married? I put the phone away and headed for the front door. If the coffee house was only a few blocks away, he should be home any minute.

Our neighborhood had always been quiet and safe. You never heard of anything bad happening on the news. I guess that was why I found it so odd when I saw a woman crouching down behind a car across the street from our neighbor's house. I couldn't tell what she was doing. Hopefully, she had just stopped to tie the laces on her shoes. Out of the corner of my eye,

I spotted Cole. I opened the door for him as he put his bike away. I snuck a peek across the street again, but I couldn't see the woman anymore. She must have finished tying her shoes and continued on her way.

Cole went straight to the bathroom and jumped in the shower leaving me to wonder once again if he had been with another woman. Was 'coffee house' code for another woman's bed? I had a feeling it was going to be a rough night but to be completely honest, I didn't really care. There was no way we were going to bed that night without all my questions being answered. I took the envelope out of my pants pocket and put it on the dining room table before sitting down on the sofa.

My heart started to race a little when I heard the shower shut off. Was I doing the right thing? I had to stop myself from getting up and grabbing the envelope before Cole had a chance to see it. I turned the television on just to have some background noise. The silence of the house was adding to my nervousness. I took a deep breath as Cole walked out of the bathroom and into the kitchen. There was no turning back now.

Without saying a word, he walked into the living room and sat down on the recliner. I could see the envelope was in his hand. He leaned forward with his elbows on his knees.

"Where did you get this from?"

It was obvious by his tone that he wasn't happy with me. I could feel the weight of his stare on me. I started feeling like I was a little girl again about to be punished by my father. Come on Kari you can do this, pull yourself together. Nothing is ever as bad as it seems.

"I stopped by your father's house today. While I was there, I ran into one of your old neighbors. We had an interesting conversation." Only then did I muster up the courage to look over at Cole. His entire body was tensing up and he was crushing the envelope in his hand. I may have told him too much too soon.

"Why did you stop by my father's house?" I had never heard him use that tone of voice before. From where I was sitting, it looked like his pupils were dilating.

"I stopped by because I was hoping to talk to your father. It bothers me that the two of you are estranged. I wanted to try to mend things between the two of you." He may not have liked what I was telling him, but at least it was the truth. Would he answer my questions honestly, or would he tell me more lies?

"I really wish you hadn't done that. My relationship with my father, estranged or not, is none of your business." I didn't know whether he was trying to be rude or not, but he certainly was, and I didn't like it.

"I was just trying to help." Okay, so that part may not have been entirely true.

Cole got up out of his seat. He was now pacing back and forth in front of the television. He looked like a caged animal. Why was he so upset with me for trying to patch things up between him and his father? What could have happened that would cause this reaction? Cole finally stopped pacing and stood right in front of me.

He straightened out the envelope the best he could before asking, "Where did you get this?" He was making me extremely nervous standing that close to me.

"Like I already told you, I met one of your old neighbors while I was there. She may have been a bit confused. She told me your name isn't Cole. She also told me she saw you at your father's house yesterday. She said you were going through his mail before throwing it away in his recyclable bin. I didn't believe her of course, until I checked the bin. That is where I got the envelope from." As I was saying all of that, he had crumbled the envelope into a tight ball. I half expected him to throw it at me.

"What else did this old neighbor of mine have to say?" He was really starting to scare me now. This had been a huge mistake. My chances of being forgiven were in the red.

"The only other thing she told me was that she hasn't seen your father in almost two years."

What was I doing? Why was I still telling him things to anger him even more? I should've stopped two questions ago. Was I digging my own grave?

CHAPTER 27

The change that came over Cole was quick and very unexpected. It caught me so off guard I thought maybe I had fallen asleep while he had been in the shower and was just now waking up from a bad dream. A switch had been flipped, which had me feeling both relieved and terrified at the same time. He went from the darkest of night skies to the brightest of sunny days.

"Sounds like you met up with the loony old lady who puts her nose into everyone else's business. Did she also tell you she still sees her husband even though he died twenty years ago?" All the tension had left his body. His eyes were back to normal, and his face had lost its reddish complexion. It was quite amazing to see.

He started making his way to the kitchen with a little pep in his step when he said, "I could sure use a beer after that story. Would you like a glass of wine?"

I had no idea what had happened to completely change his demeanor, but I wasn't about to question it.

"I would love a glass of wine."

Have you ever felt like you were having an out-of-body experience? I have had many instances of déjà vu in my lifetime, but this was something different. It was like I was floating, looking down on the real me just sitting there on the sofa waiting for Cole to bring me a glass of my favorite wine. I was trying so hard to scream 'RUN', but nothing came out.

Cole came back into the living room and handed me my glass of wine. It was a bit fuller than usual, which was greatly appreciated. I thought he might sit down on the sofa with me, but he went and sat right where he was earlier. I had no idea what was going on. I had more questions I wanted answers to, but Cole seemed to have moved on from that conversation. If I brought it back up again, how would he react? The next thing I knew, the television was on, and we were watching a rerun of *The Golden Girls*.

I must've been drinking my wine like it was Kool-Aid. I had finished my glass before Cole had even finished his first beer. For some reason, it tasted a little sweeter than usual. The sweeter the better for me. Cole looked over at me with a cute little smile on his face. Maybe he was better at forgiveness than I had thought. When I looked back at the television, I was having a tough time getting it to come into focus. The wine was hitting me, and it was hitting me hard. Served me right for downing a glass of wine that full on an empty stomach.

I was starting to feel drowsier by the second. My head kept bopping up and down. My eyelids wanted to close in the worst way.

Cole looked over at me again and asked, "Are you feeling okay?" My loving, caring, thoughtful husband was back.

I was ashamed of myself for thinking such terrible things about him yet again. He was a good man; he was *my* good man. I was the lucky one after all.

I tried to stand up. I wanted to go over and tell Cole that I loved him and give him a kiss. I missed the way he kissed me. However, I could barely get my butt off the sofa. It felt like I was being weighed down. I had never been that drunk before. Thank God Cole was home with me. I knew no matter what, he wouldn't let anything bad happen to me.

"I think I'm going to go take a nap." Possibly the longest nap I had ever taken. The hangover that would definitely follow would be life-changing.

Ever the loving husband, Cole got up from where he was sitting and came over to help me get up from the sofa. He picked me up in his arms and carried me over to the staircase. I wasn't heavy, but I also wasn't light. Carrying me up the stairs wouldn't be an easy task for any man.

"Do you think you can manage going up the stairs if you wrap one arm across my shoulders?"

By then I was so drunk, I could barely even see the stairs. They seemed to go on forever.

I did my best to pick my feet up and climb one stair at a time. Cole was doing most of the work. I was moving my left foot up a stair, then Cole would lift me by the arm I had around his shoulders and move my right foot up to the same stair. He was being very patient with me. I would never have been able to climb those stairs alone. It took us about five minutes to get to the top of the stairs.

I could see our bed from the landing. How I wished I were Dorothy at that moment in time. Three little clicks of my red slippers and I would've been fast asleep in our comfortable bed. That was when I realized Cole was taking my arm off his shoulders. I was waiting for him to pick me up again and carry me over the bedroom threshold like he did the day we got married. He could be quite the romantic charmer when he wanted to be.

Cole leaned over and put his lips to my ear. Couldn't he tell how drunk I was? The last thing I wanted was for him to be kissing my ear or whispering sweet nothings into it. I just wanted to be in my bed, alone, asleep.

In a low sweet voice, he whispered, "Tell Doris's husband she misses him."

The words floated around in my head as I felt my body starting to fall over backward. I tried to reach my arm out to grab onto Cole, but for some reason, he had backed away from me. Couldn't he see I was in trouble? The first time my head smashed into one of the stairs, it felt like it was going to explode. I tried looking around for Cole, but I had blood dripping into my eyes. Then my legs were flipping over my head. It was like I was doing a backward flip down the stairs but without hands. Freeform acrobatics were not intended for a staircase. The second time my head smashed into one of the stairs, I heard something inside my head crack.

That was the last thing I remember except lying at the bottom of the staircase and sensing that someone was standing over me. I couldn't see anything. I wasn't even sure if my eyes were open.

Then out of nowhere, I heard Heather's voice saying, 'I told you he was hiding something.'

Magen
2021

CHAPTER 1

One of the worst things a girl can do is watch any of the Disney Princess movies. All they do is give false hopes and bring major disappointments. There is no enchanted rose that can turn a beast into a hunk. There is no prince that will put a glass slipper on your foot or kiss you back to life after being poisoned. Fairy tales and reality are two vastly different things. Some people call me a pessimist. Some people call me cynical. Some people call me a negative Nellie. I call myself a realist.

The day started out just like every other day. My internal alarm clock woke me up bright and early. I have never been a good sleeper. No matter what type of sleep aid I try, none of them seem to do me any good. I yawn my way through most days. I set out for my morning run before the sun had even finished rising. There was a slight chill in the air, which was to be expected this time of year. I love autumn in New England. The leaves were all starting to change their colors. The greens were slowly turning into bright yellows, oranges, and reds.

I did the same run every morning rain or shine. In the winter months, I had to settle for my older-than-dirt treadmill. Ten minutes after leaving my front door, I was bending down to make sure my sneakers were tied nice and tight. It only took me one hard fall face-first to learn that lesson. Then I started my run on the community trail. It had taken me a while to plan out just the right route. I knew I wanted a five-mile run. I also knew I wanted my resting point to be at the waterfall. Sometimes watching the waterfall felt like being in one of the Princess movies. If the sun reflected off the water just right, it could be a magical thing to see.

Most mornings I was the only person out running that early, which was perfectly fine with me. I had Lady Gaga blasting through my earbuds and sweat dripping in places it shouldn't have been. I tended to watch the ground while I ran more than I watched ahead of myself. They allowed dogs on the trail. The last thing I needed was to be running through some disgusting dog shit that the owner decided to leave behind. I always knew when I was getting close to my resting place because I could start to feel dampness in the air from the water crashing off the rocks. I started to slow my pace down to a jog as I got closer and closer to the waterfall.

As I went around the last bend in the trail before the waterfall, I looked up to appreciate the beauty Mother Nature had created. I suddenly realized something was different that morning than every other morning. There was a man sitting on my resting bench. It wasn't really mine, but I called it mine because I had never seen anyone else sitting on it. I slowed my pace from a jog to a brisk walk. The man heard me approaching and glanced in my direction.

I found myself in a conundrum. Should I pretend I didn't see him and sit on a different bench? Should I pick up my pace and continue my run without resting? Before I could decide what to do, I was close enough to him to see that his lips were moving. Instead of hearing what he was saying to me, I heard, 'I'm on the right track baby.' I took that as a sign. I stopped approximately two feet away from him and took my earbuds out of my ears. In the friendliest voice I could manage while I was winded from my run and irritated that there was a man sitting on my bench, I said, "Sorry, I couldn't hear you with my earbuds in."

Forty-five minutes later, I was watching him dry off after using my shower. Don't get the wrong idea. I had never done anything like that before. I couldn't even remember the last time I had sex. Never mind, sex with someone I had just met less than an hour earlier. I knew I was going to hate myself the minute he walked out the door. He caught me watching him and he liked it. He ran his hands through his hair and let it fall right into place. Then he turned from the mirror and walked right toward me. He had my favorite towel wrapped around his waist. I knew he had nothing on under the towel. His clothes were still in a pile on the floor at the foot of my bed. Round two.

When I finished taking my shower, I was surprised to find I was alone in my house. It wasn't until I was about to call out his name that I realized I had no idea what his name was. How was that possible? I don't do things like that. I looked on my dresser, on my kitchen table, on every possible surface hoping to find a note with at least a name and number on it. Finding no note, I suddenly felt like I needed another shower.

CHAPTER 2

If you stand around the water cooler long enough on any given Monday, you will hear at least one person talking about their latest anonymous tryst. Was I going to be the subject of this Monday's water cooler talk? Just the thought of it made me want to vomit. I know I probably sound like a prude. People these days hook up with strangers all the time. Sometimes more than one in a single day. With all the dating apps available these days, anonymous sex is literally at your fingertips. I am not passing judgment on anyone, but for me, I want to at least know your name before you walk out my door.

I may have overreacted when I stripped my bed and washed my sheets and my favorite towel twice. I was sure I could still smell the scent of him on my sheets after the first wash. I spent the rest of the day lounging around the house feeling disgusted and sorry for myself. I started second-guessing my abilities in bed. Granted I was out of practice, but it is kind of like riding a bike. Once you learn how to ride it, you never forget. Maybe I just wasn't up to his standards. There had to be some reason he thought I wasn't worthy of at least saying goodbye before leaving.

When my internal alarm clock woke me up again the next morning, I tried hitting snooze, but it rejected my efforts. My self-pity was exhausting. All I wanted to do was stay crawled up in a ball under my nice clean sheets forever. I was not used to feeling that way about myself. I am a good girl. I have never even teetered on the brink of breaking the law. Was I really going to let some nameless man ruin my own self-perception? Absolutely not!

I got out of bed, got dressed in my usual running attire, and headed out the door. My musical choice for that morning's run seemed quite appropriate. Hearing 'Say my name', felt like a jab to my wounded pride. By the time I could hear 'I'm gonna make it', I was feeling a new batch of adrenaline running through my veins. I was running at my top speed. Sweat was dripping down into my eyes making them burn but it didn't faze me. I'm a survivor after all.

I was so into the music that was blasting into my ears that I hadn't even noticed I was nearing the waterfall. When I made it around the bend just before the waterfall, I couldn't believe my eyes when I saw the same nameless man sitting on my bench again. What the hell was he doing there? This was my resting spot, at my time of the morning. I started feeling so many different emotions at the same time. I was furious. I was embarrassed. I was irritated. I wanted to keep running. I wanted to stop and hit him. I wanted to ask him why he just left the way he did.

As I got closer to him, he stood up. He had a mischievous smirk on his face. Was this a game to him? Was I his new toy to play with? I could see his lips moving, but once again, I couldn't hear a word he was saying to me. Did I want to hear what he was saying? I made up my mind, I picked up my pace and ran right past him. Not the most mature decision I had ever made, but it felt right at the time. Part of me wanted him to run after me. The other part of me wanted him to feel how I felt when I walked out of my bathroom yesterday only to find he had left.

After about a minute, I turned the volume down on my earbuds. I wanted to be able to hear him running after me or calling out to me. Had he realized he had no idea what my name was? The only thing I could hear was my own heavy breathing. I hadn't run at my full speed for some time. I knew I needed to stop and rest but turning around and running back to the waterfall seemed like a ridiculous idea. How foolish would I look if I went back there now after just running past it? Was he right behind me but I couldn't hear him? Was he back at the waterfall waiting for me? Would he be outside my door when I made it back home?

CHAPTER 3

The only way for me to get back home without running past the waterfall and possibly seeing the nameless man again was to take the longer route. I stopped to rest for a few minutes at the first bench I came across. There was a random bike chained to one of the light posts close to the bench. The sun was about halfway done with its morning routine. A couple of people started running past me in the opposite direction. I stretched my legs for a bit then started on my way again gradually working my way up to my full speed.

By the time I made it back to my place, I was drenched in sweat and breathing very heavily. My hair was sticking to the back of my neck. I felt disgusting. I had temporarily forgotten about the nameless man during the rest of my run. That was until I saw him leaning against my front door. He was saying something but with my earbuds in I missed it. I pulled up short right in front of him and took my earbuds out. This time I heard him when he asked, "What took you so long?"

After a quick shower, by myself, we were sitting at my dining room table. The nameless man, AKA Trent, apologized profusely for just leaving the prior morning. He said he had looked around for something to write his number on, but he couldn't find anything. He hadn't felt comfortable enough to go looking through my drawers for paper and a pen. He thought of opening the bathroom door and sticking his head in to say goodbye, but he figured if I had closed the door in the first place, that was my way of saying, 'You can go now.' I half believed him.

We sat and talked for about half an hour, mostly about me. He didn't seem comfortable talking about himself. Every time I tried to stir the conversation in his direction, he found a way to turn it right back to me. I started hearing Adele singing Turning Tables in my head. He got a text message and then quickly stood up to leave. As I walked him to the door I asked if everything was okay. He said he needed to head to work for a bit. I less-than-half believed him.

Then he said, "See you tomorrow, same place and time." Before I could answer him, he was gone.

It was right after Trent left that I had an epiphany. I knew something seemed off the previous morning, but after our extracurricular morning activities, it slipped my mind. Then it started kicking around again inside my head as soon as I saw him leaning against my door. You know when you have a random thought, but you can't focus enough to make sense of it and then suddenly poof, there it is. I could see myself sitting on my bed yesterday morning looking down at Trent's clothes in a pile on my floor. I remember thinking, 'That's odd.'

In all the times I had gone running I had never seen anyone running in jeans. If you are a serious enough runner to be out running before the sun has a chance to rise, you don't do it in jeans. The more I thought about it, the more it started bothering me. Not only was Trent wearing jeans yesterday morning and again this morning, but he was also not sweating at all either time. In fact, he was just sitting on a bench, my bench, both times. I guess he could just find listening to the waterfall a peaceful way to start his day.

I tried to not think about it for the rest of the day. Easier said than done. I couldn't shake the feeling that something just wasn't right. Was I making something out of nothing? I do have a habit of doing that. Just because I would never go running in jeans, doesn't mean no one else would either. I was sure there was a perfectly good explanation. Maybe when I saw him again, he would be in shorts or sweatpants. Maybe he was behind with his laundry. I would ask him when I saw him the next morning.

I am a little embarrassed to tell you this, but I spent a good chunk of the day Google stalking Trent. What else was I supposed to do? He hadn't offered up much information about himself. Was there something about him that he didn't want me to know? It's amazing the things your mind can conjure up when you have little to nothing to go on. Had he done time in prison? Was he on the run from something? Was he married? When I finished my Google stalking, I was even more sure something wasn't right. Although there were several people with the name Trent Harper, none of them matched the Trent Harper I had plans to meet the next morning.

CHAPTER 4

I had the toughest time falling asleep that night. My racing mind with its random thoughts kept me tossing and turning for hours. I kept seeing Trent sitting on my bench in front of the waterfall with nothing but his jeans on. For some reason, I was fixated on his jeans. Was my mind trying to tell me something? I do have a tendency to ignore red flags. I look at a man's flaws as challenges for me to fix. No one is perfect after all. Including myself.

I thought about going for my run earlier than usual considering I was up so early, but if I made it to the waterfall too early, I would miss Trent. Let me pause for a minute. I was doing it again. I had only met this Trent guy two days earlier and I was already putting him before myself. Why do I always do that? Let me explain what I mean. If I hadn't met Trent and I was up that early, I would have already been out the door. Instead, I was putting off starting my run until later just because Trent said he would see me at the same time in the same place.

I used to make fun of people who would change things about themselves just so they could be a better fit in someone else's life. I had this friend a few years back. She wanted to be married so badly that she would date any guy who asked her out. Some of the guys she introduced me to were lucky if they were a four on a scale of one to ten. When I first met her, she hated all sports. When she started dating a guy who loved watching baseball, she suddenly became obsessed with baseball. The next guy was a football junkie. One time when she invited me over to her house, they were both wearing football jerseys and watching a game. Baseball was out and football was in.

I put my hair in a ponytail and headed out the door. Sometimes you just have to leave things up to fate. In the spirit of full disclosure, I was running a bit slower than I usually did. I wanted to see Trent again. I wanted to see if he was wearing jeans again instead of shorts or sweatpants. I didn't want to waste any more energy trying to rationalize his running attire. I was so distracted when I left the house, I forgot my earbuds. I had nothing to occupy my mind, which wasn't a good thing.

When I started feeling the moisture in the air from the waterfall, I started getting butterflies in my stomach. I have a tough time telling the difference between being nervous, anxious, or excited sometimes. That was one of those times. I started fighting with myself. Part of me wanted to run faster around the bend so I could see if Trent was sitting on my bench again waiting for me to show up. Another part of me wanted to turn around and run right back home.

I slowed down to a jog. As I made it around the bend, I was a little relieved and a little disappointed when I saw my bench was empty for the first time in three days. I didn't know whether I was too early, or Trent had no intention of showing up in the first place. Would he have been sitting there waiting for me if I had put out the morning before? I sat down on my bench and watched the water as it poured down onto the rocks. If the water came down at just the right angle, it would crash against the bigger rock and splash me on its way back up. The water was chilly, but it felt refreshing.

When my ten-minute resting period was over, I bent down to check my laces again. As I sat back up, I saw Trent walking toward me. He was coming from the opposite direction. It was then that I realized I had no idea where he lived. It was also then that I noticed he was wearing jeans again.

We both sat on my bench facing the waterfall. I made sure to sit down first. I wanted to see how close or how far away from me he would sit. I was pleasantly surprised when he sat down, and his leg was against mine. His hand was on my knee in a matter of seconds. I don't know whether you are anything like me or completely opposite, but when I get a thought in my head it sticks there nagging at me until I find a way to squash it. I bring this up because right then while Trent's hand was on my knee, the only thing I could focus on was the feeling of his jeans against my leg. I really need to learn how to control my mind. It likes to run away on me all the time.

Trent could tell something was amiss. I couldn't take my eyes off our touching legs. I could hear him talking to me, but it sounded like gibberish. I couldn't take it. I moved my leg away from his. I didn't want him to think I wasn't interested so I turned my body until I was facing him instead of facing the waterfall. He put his hand back on my knee. Then I heard him ask, "Are you okay? You seem jumpy today."

I know honesty is the best policy. I hate when people lie to me, so I try to never lie to anyone. Well, maybe a little white lie occasionally. In my innocent girl voice, I said, "I would be better if I knew more about you." If I know anything about men, it is that they love getting their egos stroked. He tried to match my not-so-convincing innocent voice.

"There isn't much to tell. What would you like to know?"

Not much to tell, or not much he wanted to tell me?

My mind started working overtime again. I was remembering the Google stalking I did. I had come up empty. No matter what I asked him, I had no way of knowing if the answer he would give me was the truth or a lie. Having no results from a Google search is one of the biggest red flags there is. I decided to start with the million-dollar question.

"Why do you wear jeans to go running?" He looked at me with his head tilted to one side as if he misunderstood the question. I didn't know whether he was stalling, or he was totally confused, but he repeated my question.

"Why do I wear jeans to go running?"

I nodded in agreement and waited for his answer.

"Whoever said I go running? I found this spot last week. I like coming here to relax. Why do you think I didn't run after you yesterday when you ran right past me?" As I said, a perfectly good explanation. One crazy thought squashed.

I was just about to ask Trent if he wanted to go for a walk, not a run, when I heard my alarm going off on my cell phone. I had set an alarm in case I needed an excuse to have to cut our meeting short.

"Seems we both have somewhere else to be this morning. Can we continue this later?"

I didn't really have someplace else to be, but considering he did, I decided to let him think I did as well.

"Sorry, I forgot I have an appointment today. What time later are you thinking?"

CHAPTER 5

Ten minutes before our meeting time I headed out to meet Trent. I was wearing jeans and a T-shirt instead of my running attire. Trent and I made it to the waterfall within seconds of each other. After a quick hello, we started walking in the direction he had come from. I assumed we were heading to his place. You know what they say about assuming. When we made it to the bench I had stopped at the day before, the same bike was still chained to the light post. Before I knew what was happening Trent was bending down and unlocking the lock on the chain.

It was a little bit weird walking with Trent while he walked his bike along with us. After a few blocks, we ended up at a quaint little coffee shop that I had never seen before. I am not a huge coffee drinker. It makes me jittery. It was obvious that it hadn't been Trent's first time in the coffee shop. He knew exactly what he wanted without even looking at the handwritten menus on the huge blackboards covering the walls behind the counter. I opted for a freshly squeezed orange juice.

We were the only customers in the place, so we had our pick of which table to sit at. I wasn't sure if Trent had a favorite table, so I let him lead the way. He headed for the one closest to the window, which was the same one I would've picked. I am an avid people watcher, not that there were any other people to watch besides the barista.

"So, do you live around here?" I asked.

He seemed a bit caught off guard by my question. He had been taking a drink of his coffee and ended up spitting most of it back into his cup. He was the one who had asked me earlier what I wanted to know. I wanted to know where he lived, so I asked him.

After he wiped the coffee that was dripping from his lip he said, "I guess you could say I live around here."

What the hell kind of answer was that? What is it with this guy? It was like pulling teeth trying to get anything personal out of him. He had been inside my house twice, inside me twice, yet he wouldn't even tell me where he lived. He was either married, or he was hiding something else he didn't want me to know about. I am not a fan of playing games unless they are played on a board.

I am a firm believer that everyone has secrets they take to the grave with them. Some secrets are formed in our childhoods that we carry with us for our entire lives. Some secrets are forced upon us by someone else in our life. There is another interesting thing about secrets. Some can be about good things that you would share with select people whom you are close to and trust. While others can be about terrible things that you would never tell another living soul. It had become quite obvious, that like me, Trent had some secrets of his own. My new mission in life was to find out if they were good or bad secrets.

I could tell I wasn't going to get anywhere by the way Trent was answering my questions. Instead of being an open book, he was a closed shell. I was going to have to pry him open slowly and gently. I had been planning to ask him why he was invisible on Google, but I wasn't ready to admit to him that I had been doing some online stalking just yet. That would be my little secret for now. We spent the rest of our potential first date talking about useless information. If he wasn't willing to share anything personal with me, why should I tell him my life story? We talked about the weather, our tastes in movies and music. All the usual small talk people do when they first meet a stranger.

As the sun continued setting more people started coming in for their after-work coffees. I couldn't help but notice a couple of women eyeing Trent as they walked past the window we were sitting in front of. I wondered if he sat at this same table every time he came in, like a piece of eye candy. He didn't seem to notice any of the women checking him out. I wondered how many of them had shared their bed with him. My mind was all over the place as usual. I only partially heard him when he said, "… get going. Would you like me to walk you home?"

I had been planning to take the long way home so I nicely told Trent I would be fine on my own. We left the coffee shop at the same time. He kissed me goodbye on the cheek, and we parted ways. Then my plan of taking the long way home suddenly changed. I stopped walking and turned around. If Trent knew where I lived it was only fair that I should know where he lived. If he wasn't going to tell me where he lived, and I couldn't find him anywhere on Google, then there was only one other way for me to find out his address. I was going to follow him home. Hopefully, home was where he was headed.

I looked both ways then I crossed the street. There weren't many people out and about or cars driving by. I made sure to stay one block behind Trent which was tougher than I had expected considering he was riding his bike. I could see him well enough to know he was doing something on his phone. From the looks of it, he didn't have a care in the world. After making it a few blocks, he stopped in the middle of the sidewalk. I thought he was at his house, but he was just reading something on his phone. I dropped down behind a parked car just in case he decided to look around. About a minute later he was on the move again.

I was starting to understand his response when I asked him if he lived around here. He lived a bit further than *around here*. I wasn't familiar with that part of the city. From what I could see, block by block, the houses were getting bigger and bigger. When he made it to the fifth block from the coffee shop, he turned the corner. I went into a full-on sprint. I needed to make it to the corner before he went into a house. They say the quickest way to get from point A to point B is to go in a straight line. Keeping that in mind, instead of sprinting from my location to the corner on my side of the street, I sprinted from my location to the corner on the other side of the street.

I made it to the corner in less than ten seconds. I stood as close as I could to the house on the corner and stuck my head out. I could see Trent. He was riding his bike nonchalantly down the sidewalk. I made a mad dash across the street. It was easier for me to see exactly how far down he was from the other side of the street. I started counting the houses he had passed so far. He was at the fourth house on his side of the street. There was a car parked in front of the third house on my side of the street. I moved as stealthily as I could down the sidewalk, keeping my eyes on Trent the entire time. The last thing I needed was for him to turn around and see me following him. By the time I made it to the car, Trent was closing in on the fifth house. The next thing I saw and heard stopped me in my tracks.

A door opened on the fifth house. A woman stood in the doorway holding the door. I could faintly hear her say, "Where have you been? I have been calling you on your cell phone." Trent entered the house with the woman right behind him.

CHAPTER 6

I just stood there in a daze. My emotions were jumping all over the place. I wanted to know what the hell was going on. What kind of game was Trent playing? Who was that woman who had just followed him into that house? I wanted to walk right up to the door, ring the doorbell, and let the chips fall where they may. From where I was standing, I hadn't seen the woman very clearly. I couldn't tell whether she was young or old. She could be his mother for all I knew. Instead of confronting him and possibly embarrassing myself, I decided to head home.

There was one thing I wanted to do before leaving. I crossed the street, so I was on the same side of the street as Trent's house. I made my way along the hedge that separated his house from the previous house. When I made it to the end of the hedge, I stuck my head around the corner. At first, I couldn't see what I was looking for. My nerves were starting to get the best of me. I was half expecting to hear a neighbor yelling that they were calling the police. Then I spotted it above the door. House number eighty-two.

I ran all the way back to the waterfall. After resting and stretching a bit, I ran back home. By the time I made it home, I was covered in sweat. I tore my clothes off and jumped in the shower. The number eighty-two kept flashing before my eyes. I tried remembering everything Trent had told me about himself, which wasn't that difficult. Most of what had been said between us was about me. He had made sure of that. None of the tidbits he had shared with me made me believe he was a married man.

When I finished in the shower, I grabbed a glass of water and sat down at my desk. I turned my laptop on and waited for it to do its thing. When it was awake, I opened Google. I entered 'reverse address lookup' in the search bar. When the website opened, I entered Trent's address and hit enter. The house has 2,432 square feet of living space. There are four bedrooms and three bathrooms. It was valued at $749,000. It didn't list the current property owners. I tried as many different websites as I could find, trying to find out if Trent, or the woman who had opened the door for him, owned the house. I was unsuccessful. Everything about this Trent guy was a mystery.

I finally gave up. I shut my laptop down and finished the rest of my water. I did my best to stop thinking about Trent, about the woman who had been calling him, and about the number eighty-two. I was getting angry with myself for allowing any of this to affect my life the way it was. People hook up with strangers every day and just move on. They don't Google stalk them or follow them to their houses. I was better than that. After arguing with myself back and forth I made myself a promise. The next time I saw Trent, if there was a next time, I was going to ask him very direct questions. For instance, where exactly does he live? I wanted to see if he would tell me what I already knew. Was he then or had he ever been married? What did he do for a living? If he refused to answer, or if the answers he gave sounded like lies, I was putting an end to whatever could have been between us.

I refused to be the other woman. There were too many available men out there to be shacking up with an unavailable one. I was perfectly happy and content on my own. I didn't need a man to make me feel complete. Men are dogs. Men are pigs. Finding one that is neither of those is like finding a needle in a haystack.

CHAPTER 7

It wasn't until I woke up the next morning that I realized Trent and I had not discussed when we would see each other again. I wondered if that had been intentional on his part. There was a light drizzle coming down. I got dressed in my usual running attire. When it rains, I like to wear my light hooded jacket. I don't care about getting my hair wet, the hood covers my earbuds. I thought it would be appropriate to start my run listening to Mother Nature being praised for letting it rain men.

I had tried to convince myself that it didn't bother me when I made it to my resting bench only to see that it was empty. We had not agreed to meet up again and it was drizzling. Why I had expected, hoped, and *thought* Trent would be sitting there on my bench waiting for me was beyond me. I am not even sure if I wanted him to be waiting there for me so I could drill him with questions, or just because I wanted to see him again. How messed up is that?

By the time the drizzling had stopped, I was sitting at the table in the coffee shop window. Please don't ask me to explain why I headed to the coffee shop instead of heading home after resting. There was no rationale for it that made any kind of sense, not even to me. I don't even remember making the decision yet there I was.

There were even fewer people out walking that day probably due to the wet weather. There was no one else in the coffee shop except me and the same barista that was there the previous day. She looked at me kind of funny when I asked her if Trent had been in yet. She said she didn't know anyone named Trent. I took it one step further and asked her if she remembered the guy I was with when I came in the day before. Not only did she not remember the guy I was with, but she also didn't even remember seeing me ever before. Way to make an impression Magen.

As I continued sitting there looking out the window half expecting Trent to show up or walk by, a couple of other customers came in and placed their orders. When the barista called out their first names letting them know their drinks were ready, I flashed back to the day before. Trent had definitely been in that coffee shop before. He knew exactly what he wanted without looking at the menu. Which meant he also knew the barista would've called out his name when his fancy coffee was ready. If that was so, why had we stood there waiting for it for almost five minutes?

Was my imagination running wild again? Was I once again making something out of nothing? Why did I even care? I finished my orange juice and left the coffee shop. The sky was clearing up. I stood there on the sidewalk looking both ways. To my right was the way back to the waterfall, thus the way back to my house. To my left was the way to Trent's house or at least the house he went to yesterday that a woman lives in. Why was I doing this to myself? I needed to get a grip. I checked my laces and headed to the waterfall.

By now you are probably wondering why I am never at work. When you are born with a silver spoon in your mouth you look at life much differently than those that aren't. I went to all the best schools with all the other privileged brats. I even have a degree from Harvard. I did try working for a living like most of my friends when we got our college degrees, but once I turned twenty-one and started getting payments from the trust fund my grandfather had set up for me, working for a living became boring. My monthly payments from the trust fund were more than any of my college friends were making at their jobs.

The first few years of living off my trust fund were probably the best years of my life. I did a lot of traveling and tried a lot of things most people only talk about trying. I went on an African safari. I visited the Leaning Tower of Pisa. I was blinded by the beauty of the Eiffel Tower at night. I was temporarily lost in a Costa Rican rainforest. After all my amazing adventures, I started missing home. By *home,* I don't mean a physical place. I mean a feeling of belonging somewhere. Figuring out where I actually belonged, had become my next adventure.

CHAPTER 8

During my search for a place to call home, I had quickly ruled out my mother's offer to live with her. Money does strange things to people. My mother's father was the grandfather that set up the trust fund for me. Our money is what people refer to as *old money*. Not everyone who has more money than they can spend in their lifetime deserves to have it. My mother is one of those people. She thinks she can do whatever she pleases without consequences. She can buy herself out of any trouble she might get herself into. That didn't go over so well with my grandfather. They butted heads all the time.

I know this is going to sound insane, especially after hearing about all the money my family has, but I hated my childhood. I was, as my mother so nicely puts it, the product of a drunken one-night stand. She was too drunk to even get the guy's name or number. To this day I have no idea who my father is. Thinking back on that was helping me understand why I was so disappointed with myself for bringing Trent back to my place the first time I met him. The last thing I ever wanted was to be anything like my mother.

My mother lived — or rather lives — her life as if she is one of those crazy bitches from that show *Dynasty*. She spends more time lounging around making her staff, as she calls them, wait on her hand and foot. She has been married and divorced three times. All three of her husbands were way too good for her. They treated her like a queen, and she treated all three of them like a member of her staff. If I remember correctly, the longest of her marriages lasted less than three years. Not exactly a role model for her only daughter.

I knew I wanted to live somewhere in New England. I love the different seasons. Having the same weather all year long gets too monotonous. I knew I wanted to be near a bike path or a trail I could run on. My morning runs have been a part of my daily routine since I was in high school. When I heard about the bike path with a waterfall at the center of it, I rented an Airbnb near it for a week. I wanted to test out the bike path and the neighborhood at different times of the day.

It was late September when I went for my first run on the bike path. All the leaves were assorted colors. The water splashing off the rocks at the bottom of the waterfall was chilly. I never left. I ended up buying the house

I had rented as an Airbnb. I had found a place that felt like home. Like my mother, I have never been lucky in love. After watching her go through three divorces, each with a prenup preventing any of her ex-husbands from getting even a dime from her, the idea of getting married seemed absurd.

These days I live a simple life. I haven't spoken to or seen my mother in years. I never even gave her my new address. She only knows where I live because I had to give my address to our family attorney. She sends me a birthday card every year with a blank check inside as my thoughtful birthday present. I shred the card and the blank check every year. I am not one of her staff, she can pay to love her.

That is the thing about having money. You can never tell who wants to be part of your life because of the person you are or because of the money you have that you might spend on them. It makes trusting people extremely difficult. Imagine if you woke up one morning and checked the Megabucks numbers and realized you were a millionaire. How many relatives that have not bothered with you in twenty-odd years do you think would suddenly crawl out of the woodwork? How many neighbors that never bothered to even introduce themselves do you think would be knocking on your door with a nice casserole or a delicious Bundt cake they just took out of the oven?

I never tell anyone new that I meet about my financial situation. It can be a lonely life when you aren't able to trust the people around you. I guess that was why I was acting a bit crazy regarding Trent. I hadn't let anyone get too close to me for a long time. I kept everyone at arm's length. For some reason unknown to me, I felt a connection to Trent. I needed to find out more about him one way or another.

CHAPTER 9

The next morning it was beautiful outside. It was seventy-two degrees and dry. I got dressed, tied my laces nice and tight, and headed out the door. I left my music choice up to fate. There are ten different playlists I have saved on my phone. I clicked on my 'You Got This' playlist and hit shuffle. When I heard the chorus, I remembered the very first time I watched the video with Channing Tatum. About halfway through the video Pink opens her closet door and finds Channing dressed in her clothes. A man dressed in a woman's clothes in the closet, pure genius.

I had been trying my hardest to not think about Trent. Playing it cool was not easy for me, especially if I felt like I was the one being played. I had questions that I needed answers to, but how could I get them without admitting that I had Google stalked him and followed him to his house? I promise you I am not a wackadoodle even though I had been acting like one. As the mist started hitting my face my anxiety heightened. The waterfall, thus my bench, was close by.

I started slowing down as I went around the bend. I could see the first bench, and then the second. My bench was the next one. It too was empty. It wasn't until I had made it all the way around the bend that I saw Trent. He was leaning against the fence in front of the rocks that the water was bouncing off. He hadn't seen or heard me. I contemplated turning around or running right past him again, but instead, I slowed down and walked over to where he was standing. He was so entranced with the waterfall that I startled him when I tapped him on the shoulder.

I took my earbuds out and asked, "Are you afraid you might melt if you get rained on?" It wasn't until he turned his head sideways to look at me that I could see he had been crying. That wasn't part of the plan. Men aren't supposed to cry. I had no idea what to do or say. I just stood there looking at him. He used the sleeve of his shirt to wipe his eyes, then he turned to face the waterfall again. I couldn't tell whether he wanted me to stay or leave. He wasn't saying a word.

"Are you okay?" I asked.

It was a stupid question. It was obvious he wasn't okay, but I had no idea what else to do. His way of answering me was by shaking his head no.

I felt so uncomfortable standing there next to a man I didn't really know, watching him as he cried. I walked over and sat down on my bench.

Then I asked, "Do you want to talk about it?" He wiped his eyes on his wet sleeve before turning around and joining me on my bench. That time he didn't sit as close to me. I couldn't feel his jeans against my leg. He took a couple of minutes to pull himself together before telling me why he was crying. What he told me was also not part of the plan. I just sat there completely stunned while he told me that his wife, yes, his wife, had committed suicide two nights earlier.

I tried to pay attention to what he was saying. Most of it was hard to make out with all the changes his voice was making, and the sniffling in between crying. I kept hearing the word 'wife', over and over in my head. The woman I had seen hold the door open for him two days earlier, the woman who had been trying to call him while he was out meeting me, was indeed, his wife. It was two days earlier that I had seen her alive and well. It was two nights earlier that she had committed suicide. Was that just a coincidence?

CHAPTER 10

Contrary to what you might believe, I do try my best to be a good person. I may have had sex with a married man, but in my defense, I had no idea he was married. I had done the ring finger check and he was ring free. Yes, I could've asked him if he was married, but I assumed he would have mentioned it before or during our walk from the waterfall to my place that first morning. A good person, a really good person, would be feeling sympathetic while listening to a man telling you his wife had committed suicide two nights earlier. What does that say about me if all I was feeling was anger?

I missed most of what Trent had told me. I tried to suppress the anger that had taken over me at least for that moment. He noticed I was looking blankly at him. Had he asked me a question that he was waiting for me to answer?

"Did you hear what I just said?" he asked me.

The deer-in-the-headlights look on my face must've been a giveaway. Another part of being a good person is being honest whenever possible. "All I heard you say was the words 'my wife'," I told him. I didn't mean for it to sound as cold as it did. I am not heartless after all. What is that saying about a woman scorned?

I will not bore you with all the details Trent shared with me about his marriage. Mostly because I was still having a tough time focusing on what he was saying. This is some of what I did hear him tell me. He had only been married to his wife for about a year and a half. In the beginning, they had been incredibly happy together. Unfortunately, that didn't last long. According to Trent, his wife had insecurity issues, which caused her to not trust him. She started questioning him about everything he did. If he came home even a minute later than she expected him to, she would start in on him as soon as he walked through the door about where he had been. That fit in with exactly what I had seen happen when I followed him home. What he was saying seemed to ring true until it didn't.

He should have stopped talking while I was still believing him, but that wasn't how it played out. The next thing I heard him say was that his wife had been accusing him of cheating on her for over a year. He had the nerve to look me in the eyes and tell me that he had never cheated on his wife until the morning he met me. Did he expect me to believe him? Was I supposed to think I was *the lucky one*? I did start to feel sympathy, but it wasn't for Trent, it was for his poor dead wife.

I can't tell you the exact second the switch was flicked. I can't even tell you if it was something Trent had said or a look he had given, but something happened as we sat there on my bench that was about to change my life forever. I had no idea at the time if it was going to change for the better or the worse. What I did know was that it was time to put on a show, and that is exactly what I did. I reached out my hand and wiped the fake-ass tears from Trent's cheek.

"I am so sorry for your loss," I said to him with the taste of vomit in my mouth.

He took his time before saying, "I am sorry I didn't tell you I was married when we first met. I can tell you are upset with me. I wanted to tell you. The truth is my marriage had been over for a while. We hadn't had sex in months. My wife had threatened to kill herself every time I brought up getting a divorce. She said she couldn't live without me. I felt trapped."

None of this was part of the plan. Not that there really was a plan to begin with. All I wanted was answers to my questions. Instead, I was sitting there with a man who had cheated on his now-dead wife with me, trying to console him while not believing a single word he was telling me. I wish I were wrong. I wish every word he was telling me was the truth. But for some reason, I was positive it was all lies. He is a liar and a cheat. If he was lying about me being the first woman he had cheated on his wife with, what else was he lying about?

You might be asking yourself why I didn't just walk away right then and there. After all, I had only known Trent for less than a week. Yes, we did have sex twice, but that wasn't what kept me sitting there with him, telling him everything was going to be okay. It was my curious mind. I still had unanswered questions that I wanted answers to. That was certainly not the right time to ask him why I couldn't find him anywhere on Google.

What is the difference between being scorned or being betrayed? Is there a difference? If so, which one is worse than the other?

CHAPTER 11

I may or may not have handled what Trent told me in the best way possible. I suspect most people would have tried to be there for a man who had just lost his wife, but that wasn't the case for me. I don't even know if it was because I was angry that I had been played, or if it was because of my wounded pride. I just knew for me, it would be best to stay away from Trent, at least for a short while.

Over the next couple of days, I checked the local newspaper online several times. It wasn't that I didn't believe Trent that his wife had died. I just wanted to find out as much as I could about Trent, his wife, and most importantly, about how his wife had died. Being able to see it in print would make it much more believable than if I heard it from Trent himself.

As I played over our interactions, I came to realize that Trent hadn't exactly lied to me about being married. I never asked him, and he never offered up the information. Come to think of it, I never told him I wasn't married. But in my defense, he had been in my house, my shower, and my bed. If I were married, he most certainly would have seen some tell-tale signs of a man living in my house with me. Was it fair of me to be angry with him for lying to me if he never actually lied? Was I seriously making excuses for his bad behavior?

On the third day of checking the online newspaper, I found the death notice for his wife. There was a black-and-white photo of her. She was definitely a bit older than Trent was. She wasn't ugly, but she also wasn't what I would consider pretty. She was somewhere between the two. Maybe in her younger days, she had been pretty. As I read her obituary, I couldn't help but feel sad. Trent was her only living relative. No parents, no grandparents, no sisters, no brothers, and no children. She had been alone in the world except for a cheating husband. I did notice something interesting: her husband's name was listed as C. Trent Harper. Why was he going by his middle name?

This may sound crazy, but on the day of her funeral, I put on the only black dress and heels I owned. My curious mind needed to see what if any, emotional reaction Trent would have at his wife's funeral. I had contemplated going to the wake, but with no living relatives to attend, I was worried Trent would've noticed me there. I didn't want him to know I went. At least with the funeral being outside, I could always hide behind a tree.

I had seen in the death notice that the funeral was starting at noon. By the time they had the service at the church and then the travel time to get to the cemetery, I estimated I should arrive by about quarter to one. I made it to the gates of the cemetery just as the hearse was pulling in. It was perfect timing. If I had arrived any later, I would've had to drive through the cemetery trying to find where she was being buried. There were only six cars in the procession. I assumed Trent was in the limo right behind the hearse. I waited for all six cars to pass and then I followed behind them.

I waited in my car until everyone else, all ten people counting the priest, made their way to the gravesite. Once they were all standing around Trent's wife's final resting place, an eight feet by two and half feet hole in the ground, I got out of my car and made my way over to the closest tree. I was about ten feet behind the priest. Luckily, I have incredibly good vision. I could see everyone's faces. If I had to guess, Trent was the youngest person there. Everyone else looked to be around the age of his deceased wife or older. I couldn't help but notice none of the others were standing close to Trent. It could've been out of respect or out of disgust. I wondered how many of them knew about Trent's cheating ways. How many of them knew about me?

The priest made a short speech and said a few prayers. When the priest finished, he asked Trent if he had anything he wanted to say. Trent just shook his head no, walked over to the casket, and placed one single red rose on top of it. Then he hung his head and walked away leaving everyone else standing there in disbelief. I may be wrong, but from what I could make out, Trent was the only person at the gravesite that didn't shed one single tear.

CHAPTER 12

A few days later, I was and wasn't surprised to find Trent sitting on my bench. I knew it was just a matter of time before we bumped into each other again. He had been staring at the waterfall but when he heard me approaching, he turned around. I hadn't prepared myself mentally for being so close in proximity to him again. I felt more awkward and uncomfortable the closer I got. I popped my earbuds out of my ears and sat down on my bench. Playing it cool seemed like the right thing to do.

I made sure to leave as much space between us as I could without seeming rude when I sat down. I took a big swig from my water bottle trying to put off having to make small talk for as long as I possibly could. I was secretly cursing myself for not changing my running time.

"How have you been?" he asked. I was quite sure it should've been me asking him that same exact question. I looked him straight in his eyes trying to find even the slightest sign of sadness over the loss of his wife, but all I could see was a darkness I hadn't noticed before.

"Same shit, different day," I replied, followed by, "How about you?" It was like I could see the tiny little wheels inside his mind turning as he tried to figure out how to best answer my question. You would think his answer would've been on the tip of his tongue considering he had just become a widower. It might've been my imagination, but I could've sworn he was trying to force himself to cry. A few crocodile tears were all he could muster up before he finally answered my question.

"Some days are easier than others. I have missed seeing you" he said.

Was this guy for real? His wife had just died a week ago and yet there he was telling me he missed seeing me. Was he waiting for me to say I had missed him too? The hairs on the back of my neck were standing at attention. I was praying someone would come running down the path and rudely interrupt us. There was nothing I wanted more than to put my earbuds back in and be on my way. What were the chances Trent would just show up on my doorstep again if I did that? I should've never brought him home with me in the first place.

I couldn't believe how nonchalant he was being about his wife taking her own life. Had he ever cared about her at all?

"What will you do now?" I asked him. He looked back at the waterfall as if the answer to my question was written on one of the rocks. I found myself wondering if anything he had ever told me was the truth. Then a darker thought entered my mind. How much did Trent stand to gain from his wife's death? I wasn't sure why such a morbid thought had entered my mind but now that it had, I was sure it would stick like glue. I started wondering if that great big house they lived in had been bought by his wife. Was all of this about money?

"I was wondering if I could take you out to dinner?" he finally replied. Whatever the word is for feeling even more uncomfortable than you had already been feeling, was how I was feeling after he answered my question. Was he out of his mind? It was bad enough that he had cheated on his wife with me, now he was asking me out to dinner a week after she died. Who in their right mind would do such a thing? Maybe that was just the point. Maybe he *wasn't* in his right mind. Everybody grieves differently. Maybe being in denial about losing his wife was his way of dealing with his grief.

Was I being too judgmental? It wasn't like I knew him well enough to know how he dealt with his emotions. 'Never let them see you cry.' My mother had told me that so many times when I was a teenager. I found myself sitting there arguing with myself. Was he really a good guy that had shut down his emotions after finding his wife dead, or was he really a bad guy that never really loved his wife as much as he loved her money? Damn this curious mind of mine. I had no intention of saying yes to his question about dinner, but if I said no, how would I ever learn the answers to all my questions?

"Dinner would be nice. Let me know where and when."

With that, I got up from the bench, put my earbuds back in, and set off to finish my run.

CHAPTER 13

It had been a long time since I let someone other than myself influence my way of doing things. Maybe 'influence' wasn't the correct word. Maybe 'disrupt' was the word I was looking for. I have always been a very independent woman. I had found that any time I allowed myself to count on someone else for anything, no matter how big or small, it always left me feeling disappointed. Yet there I was, changing my running time the next morning just to avoid seeing Trent again so soon.

When I had left Trent sitting on my bench the morning before, I had told him to let me know where and when he wanted to go for dinner. Then I purposely put my earbuds back in before he had a chance to say anything else. The longer I could avoid running into him at the waterfall, the longer I had to do some digging into his wife and her death. Unless of course, he came knocking on my door.

Instead of heading out for my early morning run, I grabbed my laptop and sat down at the dining room table. I had already done a search trying to find the current owner of the house Trent and his wife lived in and came up empty. It was time to try something new. I remembered from reading his wife's death notice that they had different last names. I hadn't thought too much about it when I read it considering a lot of women these days keep their maiden names.

I opened Google, entered their address, and hit search. I could see all the links I had clicked on the last time I searched. I knew what I was looking for, but I was having a tough time finding it. I knew for some reason the recent owner wasn't listed, but if I could find the listing from when they bought the house, I would be able to see the name of the realtor the previous owner had used to sell it. It was possible this would get me nowhere, but it was worth a shot.

I kept scrolling and scanning the names of the links. Finally, on the fourth page of the results, I found what I was looking for. The previous owners were listed as Tom and Lucy Watkins. They had used Ruth Watkins (a relative perhaps) as their realtor. Ruth worked for the local Re/Max. I was finally getting somewhere. One small step at a time.

I entered 'Re/Max near me' in Google and hit search. Within seconds I had the office address and phone number. I clicked on the 'Agents' button and was taken to a page with pictures of all the agents working in that office.

I scrolled through the pictures until I found the one I was looking for. Lucky for me, Ruth Watkins was still working there. Under her photo was her direct phone number. I looked at the clock and realized it was only quarter past seven in the morning. I wrote the number down on a napkin with a reminder to call her at nine.

In the meantime, I tried doing a search for Trent's dead wife. Strangely, I couldn't find one single trace of her online except for her death notice. There was hardly anything about me online, but at least I had a Facebook page. It was like she never even existed. I found myself thinking back to her funeral. What a sad and lonely life she must have led. Let's not forget, on top of her having no friends, her husband was a liar and cheater. How could you not feel sorry for the woman?

After getting ready for my later-than-usual run, I called Ruth's direct number. It was earlier than nine, but the suspense was killing me. She answered on the second ring. I didn't want to sound like a crazy person, so I made up a little white lie.

"Hello Ruth, my name is Magen. I have been looking for a house to buy in the area for a while now. Yesterday I happened to drive by one that really caught my eye. Unfortunately, I don't think it's for sale. When I researched it online, I noticed you were the realtor that sold it last. This might be unethical, but I was curious if you could reach out to the owners and see if they would be interested in selling."

It sounded legit to me. Hopefully, she thought so too. The commission she would make off the price of that house would make for a great payday for her. "Which house is it you are referring to? There is a chance I know the owners personally" she replied. As I told her the address, I could swear I heard her say 'Ka-Ching.'

Instead, she said, "I know that house very well. My brother and his wife were the previous owners."

I had figured that was the case.

"Do you happen to know the current owners?" I asked. I could hear her working a keyboard. From the sound of it, she had really long fingernails. I never understood why women let their fingernails grow that long. Every time I tried to let mine grow, I would end up breaking one and then clipping all the rest. Finally, she had an answer for me, sort of.

"Funny you should be asking about that house. It is not for sale now, but I have a funny feeling it will be shortly," she said.

"Why is that?" I asked. I already knew the answer, but I wanted to see how much information I could get out of her.

She took her time answering me. I could almost picture her sitting there contemplating how much she could or should tell me. I was certain the dollar bills that were flashing before her eyes would convince her to disclose information.

"I guess I can tell you. It's not like it's a secret. The current owner passed away last week."

'Current owner' she said, not 'owners.' Did that mean I had been right? The house was only in Trent's wife's name, or did she just misspeak?

"I am so sorry to hear that. There was only one person living in the great big house?" I was getting close to answering one of the questions that had been bothering me.

"I believe she was married, but the house was only in her name. When she bought the house, she wasn't married yet. She never added her husband's name to the deed. I am assuming she left the house to him in her will."

I bet she did, and I also bet she was turning over in her grave because of it.

"Would you like me to reach out to the husband and see if he is interested in selling?" Time for another rehearsed lie.

"That won't be necessary. There is no way I could possibly live in a house where someone had died."

I apologized for wasting her time and hung up. One question answered. Next up, I needed to find out how Trent's wife died. Was it really suicide like he had told me it was, or was there more to it?

CHAPTER 14

The next day I was determined to find out more about the way Trent's wife had died. I wanted to have all my ducks in a row before going to dinner with a possible killer. I knew it was just a matter of time before Trent came knocking on my door. One of my distant relatives, a cousin twice removed, worked for the local police department. It was time to ask her for a favor. It had been about twenty years since we saw each other last so I figured it would be better to ask in person.

I called the police station first to make sure she was on duty before heading over. The police officer that answered the phone confirmed she was at the police station. Seems she had been promoted to running the evidence room. He offered to patch me through to her, but I told him it wasn't necessary. This wasn't a conversation to be held over the phone.

I finished my breakfast and hopped in my car. I had forgotten to ask what time her shift ended, and I didn't want to call again. If I had waited too long, I might have missed her. Ten minutes later, I was pulling into the police station parking lot. I tried to remember the last time I had stepped foot in a police station. Luckily, it was too long ago to remember.

I got out of my car and walked over to the entrance. The doors were made of glass, bulletproof I assumed. I could see a man who had definitely seen better days sitting down on a bench in handcuffs. He must have felt me looking at him because he turned his head and looked right at me. I had thought his tattered clothes were bad enough, but they were nothing compared to the damage someone had done to his face. He had two black-and-blue eyes and a split lip. I couldn't help but wonder what the other guy looked like.

I opened the door and made my way into the lobby. The man on the bench kept looking at me. When I made it to where he was sitting, I stopped and bent down to talk to him. "Are you okay? You don't look so well." Being up that close to him I could smell the scent of body odor and liquor. It was so strong I would have thought it was coming from my own body.

"What the fuck is it to you?" he replied in an extremely slurred voice. It never pays to be the good guy. I stood back up and made my way over to the front desk.

I could tell by the voice of the police officer behind the front desk, which was behind more bulletproof glass, that he was the same one that had answered the phone when I had called earlier.

"Hello, my name is Magen. I called earlier about Cindy Edwards. She's my cousin and I really need to speak to her."

I did my best to look shy and innocent. I had planned to get my flirt on, but this man was older than dirt. The creases on his face were so deep they made it look like it was cracked. The little bit of hair he had left on his head was as white as the driven snow.

"Let me give her a call and see if she has time to see you."

Strangely, I hadn't even given it a second thought that she might be too busy to see me. How busy can one be running an evidence room? Occasionally someone might come looking for evidence for a case they are working on. You find the evidence bag or box and have them sign the sign-out sheet. How tough can that be?

I am guessing the old police officer was also hard of hearing. He was speaking so loudly into the phone I could hear everything he was saying from across the room.

"Hello, Cindy… I'm doing great and you… I am happy to hear that… Hey look, I have your cousin Magen up here at the front desk… Magen… She said she is your cousin… Dirty blonde hair, about five feet five inches, about one hundred forty pounds… M-A-G-E-N." This wasn't sounding good. Though I had to admit he was spot on with my description and the spelling of my name.

He finally ended the call and walked back to the front desk where I was waiting ever so patiently.

"She said she will be right up."

Let's be honest here. She had absolutely no idea who I was. She was only coming to see who it was that was waiting for her. I was fairly sure we had only seen each other in person two or three times in our lifetimes. If I had to pick her out of a line-up after all these years, chances are I wouldn't be able to.

I considered going to sit down on one of the benches, but the drunk, beaten-up man was still sitting there in handcuffs, so I just leaned against the wall and waited for Cindy to appear. About five minutes later the side door opened and a heavyset woman walked into the lobby. She looked at me and then she looked all around the lobby. She had no idea who I was. After seeing no other women in the lobby, she approached me. "Hi, I'm Cindy. Are you the one that was asking to speak to me?" We would've both failed the line-up test.

"You don't remember me?" I asked in a tone I meant to sound semi-insulted. She looked me over from head to toe. I could tell she was trying to place me, but it wasn't happening.

"I was told you're my cousin Magen, but I don't have a cousin named Magen. Who are you exactly?"

By now the old police officer behind the front desk and the drunk man were both listening in on our conversation.

"Of course, you have a cousin named Magen. We haven't seen each other in some time. You always had the toughest time spelling my name. You insisted it was spelled M-E-G-A-N, but my mother always liked to do things differently than everybody else."

With that, I could see a light come on in her eyes. She looked me up and down again looking for confirmation that I was who she thought I was. Then a smile came over her face.

"I remember you! Of course, I remember my own cousin. My God, how long has it been?"

I had a feeling she was going to ask me that. I tried to remember the last time we had played together as kids. It had to have been at least twenty years ago. Where did those twenty years go?

"I think it was at my mother's second wedding. Remember we snuck a glass of punch and then acted like idiots all over the dance floor?" She busted out laughing. It was a great memory we shared.

"Now that was a good wedding." The wedding had been a good one, but the marriage was another failed attempt at a semi-normal family life thanks to my mother. "So, what brings you by today? Do you need help with something? I know it wasn't just to say hello after all these years."

A hunky police officer came out into the lobby and helped the drunk man stand up before walking him to the side door. The drunk man looked back and blew me a kiss. Luckily, he was so drunk his aim was way off and it landed on the old police officer's cheek. "Is there somewhere quieter we can go? I need to ask you a favor."

CHAPTER 15

Have you ever heard the saying 'Some things are better left unknown'? I always found that to be ignorant. Why would you not want to know everything you possibly could? Granted not everything you learned was going to be good. You had to take the good with the bad. Take it all in stride if you will. For someone with a curious mind like mine, I wanted to know everything there was to know about everything. Big or small. Good or bad. Lay it on me.

I followed Cindy through the side door and down a long hallway. When we reached the end of the hallway, we walked down two flights of stairs. Cindy's evidence room was on the basement floor. There were a lot fewer lights down in the basement and the air quality left something to be desired. There was even a scent of mildew floating in the dense air. I wouldn't last a single day working in that basement.

When we made it to Cindy's room, she unlocked the door, and I followed her into her office. I was relieved when she locked the door behind us. I didn't want any other police officers to hear our conversation. She sat down on the chair behind her desk, and I sat on one of the chairs facing her. "So, what kind of favor do you need, Magen?" I wanted to be as honest with her as I could be without making myself sound like a crazy lady.

"I'm not even sure if you can help me, but you are the only person I know who works for the police department. I don't want to bother you with all the details, so I'll just tell you the important parts. If you can help me, that would be great, but if you can't, I will understand."

I was stalling and she could tell. I was trying to figure out if I was overreacting. I had no proof whatsoever that Trent had anything to do with his wife's death.

"Why don't you start at the beginning and let me be the judge of what is important and what isn't important?"

There was absolutely no way I was going to tell her the whole story. I was not about to tell my cousin (second removed or not) that I had sex with a man before I even knew his name. Never mind a married man. I skipped the part about how we met and picked up on the day we went to the coffee shop.

"I met this guy Trent one day while I was out for a run. We got to talking and ended up going to a coffee shop about halfway between his house and mine. We talked for a while. The conversation was light and easy. We had a lot of things in common. I found myself attracted to him and I think he was attracted to me too. When we left the coffee shop, he kissed me on the cheek."

I needed to make sure I worded the next part exactly right or she was going to think I was a stalker.

"During our conversation, I had told him where I lived. Probably not a very good idea considering I didn't know him from Jack. Anyway, when I asked him where he lived, he was very vague with his answer. I found that to be odd as I had just told him where I lived. After he kissed me on the cheek, he turned and started riding his bike in the opposite direction of where I lived. I had nowhere else to be, so I started following him."

I could see by the look on her face she was already thinking I was a desperate crazy stalker. It was too late to turn back now.

"He rode his bike down a few blocks before turning onto a side street. I crossed the side street and hid behind a car so I could see where he was going without him seeing me." As I was saying this aloud, I realized that I really did sound like a desperate crazy stalker. Who in their right mind follows someone home just because they wouldn't tell you where they lived?

"When he made it to his house, the front door was open. There was a woman standing there waiting for him. I heard her say something that sounded like 'Where have you been? I have been calling you on your cell phone.' It was obvious she was upset with him. I assumed it was his mother considering she looked much older than him, and he had just kissed me on my cheek."

The look on her face changed to a look of concern. "Where are you going with this?" she asked me.

"The next time I saw Trent was two or three days later. He was standing near the waterfall on the running path I run on just watching the water splash off the rocks. When I approached him, I could tell he had been crying. I asked him what was wrong, and he told me he had found his wife dead, she had committed suicide."

Now her look turned more to one of puzzlement. "Before you say anything else, let me ask you a question." I couldn't figure out what she wanted to ask me. Then she asked me the question I was hoping to avoid.

"Did you have sex with this Trent guy?" I so wanted to deny it but isn't it against the law to lie to a police officer, or is that only during an official interview? In a much lower voice, I answered her question.

"Yes, I had sex with him, but I didn't know he was married. He never even hinted that he was married. I have regretted it ever since." I wasn't sure she was believing me. Was I even believing myself?

"So, the first time he mentioned the word 'wife', was when he told you he had found his wife dead?" I was starting to feel like I was in an official police interview. Was she not believing what I was telling her? Why would I admit to having sex with a married man I hardly knew if I didn't feel like I had to?

"Yes, that was the first time he mentioned the word 'wife' to me." I had given up trying to read her face. It seemed to be changing almost constantly.

"So, what is the favor you want to ask me?" With this new tone in her voice, I definitely started second-guessing if this had been a good idea. If my own distant relative wasn't believing my story, what would any other police officers think?

"There are some things he has told me since his wife died that I am finding hard to believe. I am starting to question everything he has told me. One of those things is if his wife really committed suicide."

I could tell I had piqued her curiosity with my last sentence. What police officer wouldn't be curious about a possible murder?

"Wait, wait, wait. Are you saying you think this Trent guy that you had sex with, might have killed his own wife two or three days after he kissed you on the cheek?" I couldn't tell whether she was trying to connect the dots that I had purposely left out or not. I was sure her next question was going to be asking me when I had sex with him. Luckily, she was too focused on the word 'murder'.

"How did he say she committed suicide?" I felt a bit of relief. It sounded like she was starting to believe me.

"He said she overdosed on her sleeping pills because she had found out about us having sex. I don't believe that's the truth. How would she have found out that we had sex unless he told her? Why would he tell her?" It was like I could see into her mind. All the wheels were turning like a hamster running on his wheel. She had a curious mind just like me.

"Have you seen him again since the day he told you about his wife committing suicide?" I took a deep breath and tried to relax. I wanted her to think I was calm, cool, and collected, not a paranoid lunatic.

"Yes, I saw him a few days ago at the waterfall again. I think he had been waiting there for me to show up. I asked him how he was doing. He told me 'Some days are better than others.' Then he told me he missed me and asked me out to dinner."

She now had the look of either shock or disgust plastered all over her face.

"Did I hear you right? A little over a week after this Trent guy's wife died, he told you he missed you and asked you out to dinner?"

It felt good to be talking to someone about this instead of keeping it all inside. It also felt good to know that I was justified in believing things with Trent weren't adding up.

"You heard me right. That's why I'm here now. The favor I wanted to ask you, is if you can look into the death of his wife. Is there any way to prove if it was or wasn't a suicide?"

I could tell she was thinking the same way I was. She was fully invested. Then she let the air out of my sails.

"Unfortunately, I am only in charge of the evidence room now. I don't investigate deaths anymore." I slumped back in my chair feeling defeated. "There is a detective that I worked with for over ten years that I trust completely. I could call in a favor of my own and ask him to look into this for you." I was trying to avoid getting any other police officers involved. If it turned out that it was a suicide and Trent wasn't involved at all I would feel like a fool.

"Would you be able to keep my name out of it? I wouldn't want it getting back to Trent that I had got the police involved."

What would Trent do if he did find out that I was talking to the police and asking them to investigate his wife's death? That was something I didn't want to think about.

"I will do my best," she said. With that, we both stood up and she walked me to the door of the evidence room.

"I will be in touch as soon as I have any information."

I thanked her and left the evidence room. I climbed back up the two flights of stairs to the main lobby. I was happy I didn't run into the drunk man again. I left the police station and walked over to my car. Just as I was about to pull out of the parking lot, I saw a car that looked familiar pull in. I hadn't been paying close enough attention to see who the driver was. As I waited for the driver to park and get out of the car, I remembered where I had seen the car before. It was parked in the driveway at Trent's house the day I followed him home.

CHAPTER 16

I sat there with my car halfway in and halfway out of the parking lot at the police station contemplating what I should do, until a police car pulled up right behind me blowing its horn for me to exit onto the street. A part of me wanted to pull right back in so I could see for myself who got out of the car. Just because it was the same make, model, and color as the car that was parked at Trent's house, didn't mean it was his car. There could be hundreds of them in the area.

I eventually talked myself out of going back to the police station because if it was Trent in that car, how would I explain being at the police station in the first place? I didn't want him to have the slightest idea I was looking into his wife's death. Besides, there was a part of me that wanted his wife's death to be a suicide. I was just having a tough time believing it after all the lies he had told me. Unless of course, I was wrong about everything, and he hadn't lied to me at all.

When I got back home there was a bouquet of flowers leaning against my front door. I couldn't remember the last time anyone had bought me flowers. I couldn't help but smile when I picked them up. They were beautiful and smelled like heaven. When I got into the house, I dug around in my kitchen cabinets for the only vase I owned. I filled it halfway with fresh water and plopped the flowers in it. I did my best to make them look nicely arranged. Then I took the little card out of the envelope that was sticking up in the center of them.

When I read what was handwritten on the card, I felt a cold chill run down my back. *'I miss seeing you every day. I hope you are not avoiding me. I will see you soon. Trent.'* I couldn't help but wonder if it was a coincidence that Trent had stopped by my house while I was at the police station. Never mind if it was him in that car that was pulling in just as I was leaving. For someone who doesn't believe in coincidences, they sure were piling up lately.

The more I thought about it the more I started freaking myself out. Had Trent been watching me? Had he followed me to the police station? I quickly walked over to my front door and made sure it was locked. Then I went around and locked every window in the house and the back door. I might've been overreacting, but I wasn't taking any chances. If I was right about Trent being involved in his wife's death, I didn't want to be his next target.

I reread what Trent had written on the card a few times. 'I will see you soon.' Was it meant to be a threat, or was I letting my imagination get the best of me? I tore the card into tiny pieces and flushed it down the toilet. I thought about throwing the flowers in the trash can, but I couldn't get myself to do it. They would be dead in a few days anyway.

Within minutes I was starting to feel like a caged bird. I didn't even want to risk looking out a window, never mind leaving my house. This wasn't sitting well with me. I had always been a free spirit. I didn't like feeling trapped inside my own house. Then it dawned on me that I hadn't gone for my run yet. Was I really going to let the possibility that I might bump into Trent stop me from doing what I enjoy doing the most? I had absolutely no proof whatsoever that Trent was involved in his wife's death. I did have a feeling that he was involved, but that was just a feeling.

I willed myself to put my running clothes and sneakers on. I put my earbuds in and searched for just the right song to listen to. With the words 'The winner takes it all' blasting in my ears, I headed out the door. If it was Trent at the police station earlier, maybe he was still there. What would be the chances of running into him at the waterfall? I had never gone running at that time of day before. It wasn't like he would just hang out at the waterfall for hours every day just in case I happened to go for a run. If he wanted to see me bad enough, he would just show up at my house like he had earlier.

There was a nice breeze blowing that was stopping me from sweating. It felt great to be out running instead of being trapped in the house. I got up to my full speed in no time at all. Surprisingly, there was no one else in sight. I felt my stomach tighten just a bit as the mist from the waterfall started hitting my face. I started slowing my pace as the waterfall came into sight. By the time I was about to take the last bend before the waterfall, I was almost slowed down to walking.

I hesitated for a moment before finishing the last of the bend. I couldn't believe my eyes. Trent was sitting on my bench. He turned around to look at me as I got closer to him. He said something but my earbuds were still in my ears. I sat down on the opposite side of the bench and took my earbuds out.

Then he repeated what he had said. "I told you I would see you soon. I hope you liked the flowers."

CHAPTER 17

Sometimes in life, we crave the attention of others. It often doesn't even matter if it is positive or negative attention. I once dated a guy who needed every bit of my attention every waking minute. If he noticed my attention was on anybody else except him, he would do whatever it took to get my attention back on him. It didn't matter whether we were with a group of friends or out and about. Let me give you an example.

One time we were hosting a New Year's Eve party at our house. We had moved in together after dating for a little over two years. Anyway, we had about ten friends over, most of whom were his friends. At one point during the party, I was in the kitchen talking to one of my friends, while he was in the living room talking to two of his friends. Sounds normal right? Not to him. He rudely called out my name across the rooms. I looked over at him and he gave me a displeased look. I knew what it meant, but instead of rushing over to him, I stayed where I was and continued my conversation with my friend. That wasn't working for him. He started making rude comments aloud. 'Did you hear me calling you?' 'Why are you ignoring me?' He was acting like a child. Everyone at the party was just looking at him. I was extremely embarrassed by his behavior. When I didn't respond to his comments, he went and locked himself in the bedroom. All our guests just looked at me. They had all come to accept this as his normal behavior. One by one they started leaving before the ball had even dropped. It wasn't until the last guest had left that he came back out of the bedroom. Every time he acted this way, I would ask him why he did it. His answer was always the same: 'Negative attention is better than no attention.'

As I sat there on my bench looking over at Trent, I felt like I was back in that apartment again. He wanted/needed my attention so badly that he was just hanging out at the waterfall waiting for me to show up. I was going to ask him how long he had been waiting there, but I was certain he would lie to me once again. Why had he set his sights on me? I was sure he had affairs with many other women although he had told me I was his first.

I hadn't answered his question, so he tried again.

"You did get my flowers, didn't you?"

I considered lying, but I wouldn't have been surprised if he had been watching me bring them into the house.

"Yes, they are lovely. Thank you." By the look on his face, he seemed pleased with himself. I couldn't stop seeing the car that I believed was his, pulling into the police station parking lot. What had he been doing there right when I was leaving? I wanted so badly to ask him about it, but I decided against it. If it wasn't his car, I would be letting him know I was at the police station for no reason at all.

"So, when are you going to let me take you to dinner?" he asked, in a noticeably confident voice. He was making it clear that he wasn't going to take no for an answer. I started feeling trapped. I was finding it hard to catch my breath. I was cursing the day I met him.

"I told you last time to let me know where and when. I haven't heard from you since. The ball is in your court."

I stood up and put my earbuds back in my ears. As I tried to make my way around him, he grabbed onto my arm and stopped me. I turned to face him. He must've seen the anger on my face because he loosened his grip on my arm immediately. With my free arm, I took an earbud out of my ear.

"What do you think you're doing? Let go of my arm before I scream."

He seemed shocked that I would've said such a thing to him. He let out a little sarcastic chuckle.

"I was just trying to get your attention before you ran off. There's no reason for you to want to scream."

Have you ever had someone talk down to you like you were beneath them? That is exactly how he sounded.

"Why did you want my attention?" Once again it came back to him wanting my attention.

"You told me to let you know where and when. That is what I was trying to do before you could take off on me again."

The absolute last thing I wanted to do was to go to dinner with Trent, but sometimes you have to do things you really don't want to do. That is especially true when it will enable you to get something out of it as well. "I am free tomorrow night at six. You decide where we are going. You don't mind driving, do you?" If I was going to have to sit across from him while trying to enjoy myself, I was at least going to see his car up close.

"I don't mind driving at all. This way I will be able to surprise you with where we are going." He flashed me a smile, so I forced myself to do the same.

"Sounds like a plan. I need to finish my run before I lose more daylight. See you tomorrow."

With that, I put my earbud back in and got the hell away from him. He was giving me the creeps. He was a mistake I knew I was going to deeply regret making.

CHAPTER 18

When I got home from my run, I took two long hot showers. After I had dried off from the first shower I still felt dirty just from being near Trent, so I jumped right back in the shower and scrubbed every inch of my body all over again. Fortunately, I don't know for sure, but I am guessing that is how women feel right after being raped.

I walked into the kitchen to grab a bottled water from the fridge. I somehow managed to forget about the bouquet of flowers Trent had left for me until I saw the vase on the counter. A bunch of questions were dancing around in my head begging for answers.

The first question was the most important one. The one I needed to know the answer to as soon as humanly possible. Was Trent involved in his wife's death, or was it a suicide? Fingers crossed I would hear back from Cindy sooner rather than later. If she was unable to get her friend on the squad to investigate Trent's wife's death, I would be stuck at a dead end.

Another of the questions was a newer one that had just joined the rest of them as I stood there looking at the vase full of beautiful flowers. Had Trent been watching my house? As I mentioned earlier, I don't believe in coincidences. With that in mind, was it an actual coincidence that Trent had stopped by to bring me flowers while I was at the police station asking questions about his wife's death? What were the chances of that just happening all by itself?

This brings me to another question that had been nagging at me. What had Trent been doing at the police station in the first place? Never mind how he managed to get there just as I was leaving. Of all days and times, he pulled in just as I was pulling out. How was that even possible unless he had been following me? I needed to find out one way or another if it was in fact Trent's car.

These were some of the other random questions that were stressing me out. What was it that Trent wanted from me? I had absolutely no idea how much money he had, but after seeing the house he now owned, he was definitely a rich man. He was also a very handsome and fit man. I had seen how many of the women had checked him out the day we sat at the window in the coffee shop. How many of them had he slept with before he met me? How many of them had he slept with since he met me? Why had he waited for me at the waterfall? Did he think this dinner was going to get him invited back into my bed?

I almost forgot the other biggie. Why was he nowhere on the internet? For a man his age, he should at least be on Instagram or Twitter. It made no sense at all that he would be nowhere. I was missing something, but I had no idea what it was. Maybe I just wasn't savvy enough to find him. Almost anyone could make themselves disappear if they really wanted to. You just had to know what you were doing to be successful. Was that what I was dealing with? Had Trent made himself disappear earlier in his life? Wiping out every trace of himself possible.

I was driving myself crazy trying to come up with answers to my questions that fit and made sense. Of course, the easiest answers were that Trent had done nothing wrong at all. That he had nothing to do with his wife's death. That he hadn't been following me or watching my house. That it wasn't his car at the police station. That he hadn't slept with any of the women from the coffee shop. That I was his first affair. That he just wanted to take me out to a nice dinner because he was lonely since his wife committed suicide. That he just needed someone to talk to that would actually listen to him. Sadly, we all know that the easiest answers are typically not the correct answers.

I had just finished my bottled water when my phone rang. I wasn't going to answer it because my head was still spinning from overthinking everything to death, but on the last ring, before the answering machine would've clicked on, I answered it.

"Hey Magen, it's Cindy. I was wondering if I could stop by your place on my way home. I have some information I think you might want to hear."

I paced every room in my house while waiting for Cindy to show up. I had pretty much begged her to tell me what she had found out over the phone, but she flat-out refused. She didn't feel comfortable talking to me about it over the phone. Of course, my curious mind was running at full speed. I couldn't slow it down even if I tried, so I just let it run. I hadn't really been expecting to hear back from Cindy so quickly, but I would be lying if I said I wasn't happy she called before I went to dinner with Trent instead of after.

Twenty minutes later there was a knock on my door. I ran to the door and opened it. Cindy was standing there with an older man dressed in a police officer's uniform. I assumed this was her friend that she had told me about. I let them into the house and closed the door behind them. The three of us sat around the kitchen table. I offered them drinks, but they declined the offer. I couldn't wait another minute.

"So, what did you find out?" I asked them both. Then I realized I hadn't even introduced myself to the older police officer. Cindy must've been thinking the same thing because she beat me to it.

"Magen, this is Officer Mack Andrews. Mack, this is my cousin Magen."

We nodded our heads and shook hands.

Now that the pleasantries were over, I waited on bated breath for one of them to answer my question. Cindy started the conversation.

"As you can tell, I talked to Mack about your concerns regarding the death of Trent's wife. He wanted to discuss it directly with you in person." I really didn't want to be telling the whole story again, but it seemed I didn't have a choice.

Before I could even say one word Cindy chimed in again.

"Please tell me those flowers aren't from Trent."

I didn't even say a word; I just nodded my head. Cindy got up from her chair and walked over to the vase of flowers. I knew what she was doing.

"I ripped the card up in tiny pieces and flushed it down the toilet." She looked over at me and I could tell she wasn't happy with what I had done.

"I didn't want it in my house. I almost threw out the flowers too, but I couldn't get myself to do it.

Then it was Mack's turn. "Do you happen to remember what it said on the card by chance?"

Did I ever? It was etched in my brain. 'I miss seeing you every day. I hope you are not avoiding me. I will see you soon. Trent.' When I finished telling them what had been written on the card, they both just looked at me.

Cindy again, "What did you think when you read the card?" I thought about lying at first. I didn't want them to think I was some kind of wuss, but in the end, I told them the truth.

"I thought it sounded like a threat." They nodded their heads at the same time in agreement.

They still hadn't told me what they had found out, but there was something else I needed to know while they were here. "When I was leaving the police station after talking to you, I could swear I saw Trent's car pulling into the police station parking lot. Do either of you know if it really was him?"

They both looked at me like deer in the headlights. They had no idea what I was talking about. "I could be wrong. It could've been someone else in the same kind of car, painted the same color." Their interest was so piqued I could smell it radiating off them.

Mack took out his notebook and opened it to an empty page.

"Can you tell me about what time you left the police station, and any details you might have about the car you believed to be Trent's?"

It was nice having people, never mind police officers, believing what I was telling them. While I told Mack everything I knew, he wrote it all down in his notebook.

"When I get into work tomorrow morning, I will check the security cameras and try to find the car, and hopefully the driver of the car."

I was feeling a little better, but I still had no idea what they wanted to tell me. I took my time repeating everything I had already told Cindy in her evidence room. Mack took notes the entire time. Occasionally, he would ask me to stop talking so he could catch up in his notebook. I was happy he was taking me seriously. When I finally finished my story Mack put his pen and notebook back in his pocket.

"As you know I can't talk to you about an ongoing investigation. I could lose my job if I did. Considering you are related to Cindy, I will tell you this, the investigation into Trent's wife's death is by no means an open-and-shut case. We are not totally convinced it was a suicide." That was all he said before they both got up and headed for the door. As they were leaving Mack turned around and said, "I will be in touch with you shortly. Do not repeat a word of what I just told you to anyone."

CHAPTER 19

Are you one of those people who always has to be right about everything, even if you are wrong? The kind of person who always has to get the last word in no matter what? If something happens, do you embellish the details when you tell someone about it to make it sound better or worse than it actually was? Can you accept negative criticism without your ego causing you to lash out?

After hearing what Mack said about Trent's wife's death not being an open-and-shut case, and that the police weren't totally convinced it was a suicide, I realized that sometimes being wrong about something is better than being right. I thought I would've felt vindicated, but instead, I felt even more concerned about going to dinner with Trent. Mack hadn't come out and said that they were looking at Trent as a suspect, but who else could there be with a motive to kill his wife?

I had one of the worst night's sleep that night that I had ever had. My mind was all over the place. It was moving on to a new thought before I had even finished the prior thought. After I finally fell asleep, I woke up in the middle of the night from what must have been one hell of a dream. When I opened my eyes, I was sitting straight up in my bed. I tried to remember what the dream had been about, but it was completely gone from my memory.

I skipped my morning run again that morning. Just the thought of possibly running into Trent at the waterfall, and then sitting across from him later the same day for dinner, was too much for me to handle. I wasn't okay with skipping my run, but hopefully, I would have all the answers to my questions soon. Then I could start putting this whole mess behind me. I was trying to be optimistic, but I was feeling pessimistic.

I did my best to stay busy. I didn't want to be thinking about Trent possibly killing his wife and then sending me flowers and asking me out to dinner less than two weeks later. Even if he had nothing to do with his wife's death, he shouldn't be sending flowers to another woman and taking her out to dinner so soon. It was wrong and creepy.

As the time grew closer to when Trent would be picking me up, I jumped in the shower. I was starting to second, or maybe even third-guess my decision of saying yes to Trent's invite. I would need at least one or two drinks just to be able to relax enough to eat. If I ended up drinking too much, I might let something slip about the police investigation. For me, it was always an exceptionally fine line between sober, tipsy, and drunk.

After I dried off, I stood in front of my closet trying to decide what I should wear to have dinner with a possible wife killer. What in the world was I doing? I was smarter than this. My only reason for saying yes to dinner was so I could see Trent's car. I could've just driven by his house to see his car, but what if he had seen me? What would have been my excuse for being in his neighborhood? Of course, if I had thought it through more, I would have realized that just seeing Trent's car wouldn't prove it was his car in the police station parking lot that day.

When I heard a car pull into my driveway, I slipped my heels on and headed for the door. I was sure Trent would come knocking on the door and I didn't want him in my house for even a second. As I was locking the door behind me, I realized that I hadn't told Cindy and Mack that I was going to dinner with Trent. How that had slipped my mind was a mystery to me. I was literally putting my life in the hands of a possible killer, and nobody knew about it. I thought of going back inside and leaving a note, but before I had a chance, Trent was out of his car and holding the passenger's door open for me.

As I got closer to the car, I could tell it was indeed the car that I had seen in Trent's driveway the day I had followed him home. Which meant it was indeed the car or a similar car to the one that had pulled into the police station parking lot just as I was leaving. While I was getting into the car, I thought of something I had not thought of before. If I had seen Trent pulling into the parking lot that day, what were the chances he had seen me pulling out of the parking lot?

CHAPTER 20

Trent had tried to make small talk with me during the entire drive to the restaurant. I think I heard about ten percent of what he was saying. I was too busy thinking about how many different ways he could kill me and dispose of my body without anyone ever suspecting a thing. I must've checked my seat belt at least five times. I had heard too many stories of people crashing their cars while the passenger didn't have their seat belt on, and the passenger went through the windshield. Some of them were accidents and some of them were on purpose.

When we arrived at the restaurant, I had to admit I was a bit surprised. Trent had brought me to the finest, most expensive steak house in the area. I had contemplated going by myself a few times, but after seeing their menu online I had talked myself out of it every time. Their prices were absolutely ridiculous. Trent got out of the car first then walked around and opened my door for me.

Once inside the restaurant the maître d' greeted Trent by his last name. How often do you have to eat at a restaurant before the maître d' knows you by your name? The restaurant was reservation-only and typically had a waiting list of over a week. Turned out Trent even had a usual table. The table was off in a corner all by itself, very private. All the outside walls were made of glass from top to bottom. Our corner table had the best view in the restaurant. I couldn't help but wonder if this was where he took all the women he had cheated on his wife with.

Trent ordered one of the most expensive bottles of wine on the drink menu. It cost more than most people's car payments. I made sure to drink my one glass nice and slow. We both ordered the special of the night, an eight-ounce filet with a baked potato and asparagus. I won't even tell you what that cost Trent. You wouldn't believe me if I did. I ordered my filet medium-well, while Trent ordered his rare. When he cut into his filet so much blood came out of it, I almost got sick. Though I would never pay that much for a meal, I do have to say, it was delicious.

By the time we finished eating, I had just finished my glass of wine. Trent, on the other hand, had drunk the rest of the bottle. Now we may both die in a car accident. Perhaps I should have driven. I offered to drive us back to my place, but Trent insisted on driving. Was he planning a murder/suicide? I hate to admit it, but Trent's driving after drinking three-quarters of a bottle of wine was better than mine when I was sober. It hadn't affected him at all. What did that say about his drinking habits?

I had been trying to get a read on Trent's intentions, but I was coming up blank. Our conversations in the car and at dinner were minimal at best. I had no idea what he wanted from me. If he thought he was coming into my house with me and possibly having sex, he was dead wrong. That would never happen again. I kept trying to bring up his wife and her death, but he kept changing the subject. There were so many things I wanted to know, but it was obvious I was wasting my time.

When we were only a couple of blocks away from my house, Trent pulled into an empty parking lot. My heart instantly started pounding like a drum. Is this where my life would end? There were two big, rusted dumpsters in one of the corners. Was one of them going to be my resting place until someone found my body, or what was left of it? Trent parked the car and killed the engine. My hand was on the seat belt release button in a second.

"I couldn't help but notice you keep asking a lot of questions about my dead wife. It is almost like you are obsessed with her. Why don't you go ahead and ask me anything you want to know, so we never have to talk about her again?" That is not where I was expecting this to go. What did he mean when he said I keep asking a lot of questions about his dead wife? Was he talking about tonight, or was he talking about with the police?

My palms had started to sweat. Was it really that important to know the answers to my questions? Was it important enough to put my life in danger? I looked over at Trent, he looked completely calm and composed. I couldn't see any sign that he was angry with me. Although a huge part of me thought it was a bad idea to ask him anything I wanted to, I couldn't stop myself.

"I am not obsessed with her. I had no idea you were even married until your wife was dead shortly after we slept together. Surely you can understand why I am curious about her and her death. I keep wondering if she had found out about us seeing each other and if it led to her committing suicide."

Surely you know some of that is complete BS, but I needed him to think I believed him about the whole suicide thing. It wasn't like he was going to confess to me that he had killed her.

What he said next threw me for a loop. To say I wasn't expecting it was a huge understatement.

"My wife did know about us, but not because I told her. She knew because she saw you hiding behind a car the day you followed me home from the coffee shop." My heart dropped. I had no idea she had seen me. Trent had never mentioned anything about it to me before. Why had he kept it a secret? What if it really was suicide? A suicide that was brought on by me following Trent home.

I suddenly had no more questions I wanted answered.

"Can you take me home now? I am not feeling so well." I didn't know how I was feeling exactly, but I knew I wanted to be home alone and close to a toilet. Another thing I knew for sure, was that I needed Mack to tell me Trent's wife had definitely been murdered. I know wishing someone had been murdered sounded awful, but there were too many ramifications for me if it had been a suicide.

Trent started the car and drove the two blocks to my house. I undid my seat belt and opened the car door. I thanked him for the dinner and got out of the car. When I opened my front door Trent was still sitting in my driveway watching me. I felt chills run up and down my back as I closed the door behind me and locked it.

CHAPTER 21

How do you deal with guilt? Do you let it fester and take over your life? Do you ignore it? Sweep it under the carpet as if it were another worthless feeling? I am by no means a saint, my mother would attest to that, but I do try my best to live a quiet easy-going lifestyle. I avoid confrontation as if it were the plague. I don't smoke, don't do drugs, and only rarely do I ever drink anything alcoholic. I deal with guilt like I do every other feeling, avoid, avoid, avoid.

When I woke up the next morning I felt like shit. I could swear I saw every hour pass by during my broken sleep. I kept hearing Trent's words on repeat, 'My wife did know about us, but not because I told her. She knew because she saw you hiding behind a car the day you followed me home from the coffee shop.' At the same time, I was trying to replay my actions the day I had followed him home from the coffee shop.

I could see it all clearly in my mind up to the part when I hid behind the parked car across the street from their house. I had been so focused on watching Trent's every move that I hadn't looked at the house until I knew for sure that it was the house he was heading to. How long had his wife, the wife I didn't even know existed, been standing in the doorway looking outside, looking at me? Had she spotted me before she even spotted Trent?

If what Trent said was true about his wife seeing me outside their house, and if that had led to her committing suicide, how would I ever be able to deal with that? There was only one answer. I got dressed, hopped in my car, and headed to the police station. I needed to talk to Mack, or Cindy, or Mack and Cindy. For all I knew, Trent could've been lying to me like he had plenty of times before.

When I made it to the police station I walked right up to the front desk. The same old police officer was behind the bulletproof glass. He walked over to me and asked, "Aren't you Cindy's cousin?" Either he had a great memory, or I had memorable looks. I tried my best shot at humor.

"Guilty as charged."

It worked; he let out a loud laugh drawing the attention of the other police officers close by. When he stopped laughing, he said "If you're here to see Cindy again, I am afraid you're out of luck. Today is her day off."

I guess I should've called first before heading over. I had one more chance, Mack. The old police officer must've wondered what I was doing just standing there looking at him not saying a word. Could he hear my brain working overtime? It wasn't until I went to ask if Mack was there, that I realized I had no idea what his last name was. I knew he had mentioned it once the first time we met, but for the life of me, I couldn't remember what it was.

I didn't want to sound unprofessional, but what other choice did I have?

"I was wondering if Officer Mack is here today?" Hopefully, there wasn't an actual Officer Mack working there. Now it was the old police officer's turn to let his brain work overtime. I could almost hear him working his way through the alphabet, listing off all the last names of the police officers that worked in the station. Luckily, he came up blank with the last name Mack.

"Do you mean Officer Andrews, Mack Andrews?" As soon as I heard him pronouncing the A in Andrews, I remembered it. Isn't that always that way?

"Yes, that's the one I'm looking for."

He picked up the phone receiver and pushed a few buttons. After what sounded like three rings, he said, "There is someone here to see you at the front desk." He hung up the receiver, looked up at me, and said, "He will be with you in a few minutes. Why don't you have a seat?"

I thanked him and then made my way over to one of the chairs in the hallway. I was relieved to see the drunk homeless man wasn't there to keep me company again.

While I waited for Mack, I ran through all the questions I had for him in my mind. They were starting to add up too quickly for my liking. The answers were what I needed. After about ten minutes the side door opened, and Mack walked out into the lobby. He spotted me right away and waved me over. I followed him through the side door, down the hall, and into what looked like an interview room. As he closed the door behind us, he said "It's better if we talk in here, more privacy." Did that mean he had things to tell me? Things he didn't want any of his fellow police officers to hear.

Once we were both settled into the uncomfortable chairs on opposite sides of the cold grey metal table, Mack said "You didn't waste any time getting here." I looked at him with my confused face, which is sometimes mixed up with my everyday face. I had no idea what he meant by what he said.

"I left you a message not even fifteen minutes ago asking you to stop by the station when you had time. Isn't that why you're here?" What is it they say about great minds?

"I must've already been on my way here before you called. I wanted to check in and see if you had any updates for me." I really didn't want to tell Mack about the day I had followed Trent home, unless I absolutely had to.

Just another crazy female stalker, but this one got caught by the wife. What would he think of me then?

"That's why I wanted you to stop by. I have a couple of updates that you may or may not want to hear." That wasn't sounding good.

"Should I be concerned?" I asked him. Willing him to say it was nothing to worry about.

"You can judge for yourself. The first thing I wanted to let you know is that we did confirm the car you saw pulling into the parking lot just as you were leaving last time, was indeed Trent's car."

I had to let that float there in the space between us for a minute while I figured out if that was bad or good. "Do you know why he came to the station?" What was Trent up to? Had he followed me to the police station or was it the biggest coincidence in the history of coincidences?

"That was the second thing I wanted to tell you. I spoke to the officer in charge of his wife's case. He is the one Trent saw that day. He had come in to ask for an update on the case." I looked at him with skeptical eyes.

"Why would he come here asking for an update on the case when as far as he knows the case is closed and listed as a suicide?"

Mack looked at me with one eyebrow raised and said, "That was my exact question."

It didn't make sense. If the police officer in charge of your wife's case tells you the case is closed and listed as a suicide, why in the world would you come asking for an update?

"Is there anything else you can tell me about how his wife died? I know there were a lot of pills in her system, and she died in their bed where Trent found her. Is there any way of proving one way or the other, if she took the pills willingly, or under duress?" Now instead of having one eyebrow lifted, they were both scrunched up as if to say, 'What the hell are you talking about?' I didn't like that look. What did he know that I didn't know?

"Where did you hear that from? She did have sleeping pills in her system, but she wasn't found in her bed. She was found at the bottom of their staircase." It felt like all the air had been sucked out of me after being sucker punched in the stomach.

"That's what Trent told me had happened. He said he came home and found her dead in their bed. An empty bottle of sleeping pills on the nightstand near the bed."

Why had Trent lied to me about how his wife had died? Dying in your bed is vastly different from dying after falling down a flight of stairs.

"Do you know if she was already dead before she fell down the stairs?" There was no way Mack should have been telling me the things he was. He could certainly get in a load of trouble if the higher-ups ever found out. They wouldn't be hearing about it from me.

"That's why the case isn't officially closed yet. We are still waiting for some more lab results to come back. They should be able to tell us what happened first, the fall down the stairs, or her death. If she was already dead before the fall, then there is no way it could've been a suicide. She couldn't have walked to the staircase if she was already dead. Unless of course, she had help getting there."

I found myself at a crossroads with no idea which way to go. Should I or shouldn't I tell Mack about my dinner with Trent, and more importantly, about what he had told me after that dinner? On one hand, Mack was risking a lot even talking to me about the case, but on the other hand, did I really want to insert myself into their investigation by admitting I had followed Trent home from the coffee shop? You know what they say about people that insert themselves into police investigations. Hello, target on my back.

I know it was probably the wrong decision, but I decided to not tell Mack anything about my dinner with Trent, or about what Trent had told me. I didn't see how it could help the investigation. I thanked him for seeing me and telling me about what he'd found out. He promised he would let me know when they got the rest of the lab results back and then he walked me out the door.

CHAPTER 22

What in the world had I got myself involved in? Reason number twenty-seven for why you should never bring someone home with you that you don't know: you might find yourself involved in a murder/suicide. I really needed to start paying attention to all the red flags everyone is talking about these days.

The question that kept me up that night was why Trent had told me he had found his dead wife in their bed when she had actually been found dead at the bottom of their staircase. If she had taken enough sleeping pills to end her own life, did it really matter where he had found her? Was he so used to lying that he couldn't help himself? I wasn't able to make it make sense no matter which way I turned it. It was like trying to fit a square peg into a round hole.

Even though I barely slept, I made myself go for my morning run. I wasn't going to let the fear of running into Trent mess up my daily routine anymore. The meteorologist had said there were rain showers headed our way. Hopefully, they would hold off until I made it back home. It felt good to be outside running again. I hate when I miss even one day. I hadn't seen one single person on the bike path, which was the norm for that time of the morning. I did, however, just miss running into a pile of dog shit someone had nicely left dead center of the path by less than an inch.

I was trying as hard as I could to focus on my breathing, but the thought of bumping into Trent at the waterfall kept forcing itself into my consciousness. I didn't know who I was more upset with, myself for letting Trent affect me the way he was, or Trent for getting me involved in whatever it was he was involved in. It is true what they say, every action has a reaction. Some are good and some are not so good.

As I got closer to the waterfall, I started to feel my stomach turning like a washing machine that is set on delicate. What would I do if Trent was there waiting for me? I should've thought about that before I left the house. Being unprepared is never good for anyone, no matter what the circumstance.

Right before the last bend before the waterfall, I turned around and started heading back home. It wasn't like I was running a shorter distance; I just hadn't stopped to rest. It was a great plan. I got my run in. I went the same distance. I burned some extra calories by keeping my heart rate up thanks to not resting. Sweat was dripping off me at an alarming rate and I smelled wretched. It was exhilarating.

I hadn't stopped running for even a second until I made it all the way back to where I had started. My eyes were burning from the sweat that had dripped into them. There were a few cars coming down my street. I waited for them to pass before crossing the street. I really wasn't paying attention to anything that was going on around me other than the passing cars. Once the last car drove past me, I crossed the street and headed for my house.

"I hope you don't mind me stopping by unannounced like this. You seemed a bit freaked out when I dropped you off last night. I just wanted to make sure you're okay."

You have got to be kidding me! I had switched up my run to avoid possibly running into Trent at the waterfall, only to run into him at my own front door. My head was spinning. I needed to sit down, but there was no way I was letting Trent into my house.

There were so many questions I wanted to ask him. The first one on the list, 'Why did you lie to me about finding your dead wife in your bed, when you actually found her at the foot of the staircase?' The problem with asking a loaded question like that one was how would I explain knowing the truth without letting on that I had been asking questions about him and his wife's death. He would know I had spoken to the police. I couldn't let that happen. At least not yet.

He had an innocent concerned look on his face. That might have worked on me a few weeks earlier before I started putting the pieces of who he really is together. Then the tiny light in my head switched on and started shining very brightly. I needed to get rid of Trent as quickly as I could no matter what it took. I had something much more important to do than stand there making small talk with a man I wished I had never laid eyes on.

We were now standing about two feet away from each other. Close enough for him to be smelling the wretched scent coming from every pore of my body. I overly exaggerated my tiredness and heavy breathing hoping he would get the hint.

"I am fine. You just caught me off guard last night. I had no idea you knew I had followed you home that day from the coffee shop, never mind that your wife knew." If he didn't believe the truth, there was nothing I could do about it.

His eyes looked glazed over as if he was trying to figure out if I was bullshitting him or being honest. For someone like him, telling the truth was a rarity.

"Thanks for checking up on me. I appreciate it. I really need to go take a shower in case you haven't got a whiff of my new perfume yet." He let out a little chuckle, which for some reason, made me want to punch him as hard as I could.

"I'm glad it's you that smells like that and not me. You could make dogs cry right about now. Go take your shower. Hopefully, we can get together again soon."

I watched as he walked away from me. If I wasn't feeling as nasty as I was, I would've probably followed him again. Where was his car or his bike? There was no way he would've walked all the way from his house to my house when he had a car that once belonged to his dead wife sitting in his driveway. Had he been at the waterfall after all? Was his bike chained to the same lamp post? Had he heard me running and then stop and turn around? I couldn't get inside my house fast enough.

CHAPTER 23

I was angry with myself for not realizing days ago that the answers I needed were very possibly just a phone call away. Instead of being nervous and on edge, I could be putting this whole mess behind me and getting on with my life. No more anxiety and stress messing with my sleep or disrupting my well-being. Isn't that what we all long for?

I peeked out my window to make sure Trent hadn't come back. For some reason, I was feeling overly paranoid. I was more certain than ever that he had been watching my every move from somewhere just out of eyesight. Satisfied that Trent had left, I picked up my phone and called the police department. I needed to talk to Mack again.

Twenty minutes later there was a knock at my door. When I opened the door, I was surprised to see Mack standing there in regular clothes. I had never seen him out of his uniform before.

"I can't stay long. I have a blind date tonight."

Have you ever been on a blind date before? If so, how did it turn out? Was it a love connection or a complete disaster?

"Who is the lucky lady?" I asked.

With a confused look on his face Mack replied, "If I knew who she was, it wouldn't be a blind date." He did have a point there. I nodded in agreement feeling a bit stupid.

"Sorry for calling you again so soon and asking you to come over on your date night. I promise this won't take long."

We made our way over to the dining room and sat down at the table.

"You said you had something important to ask me. What's it about?" I opened my laptop and turned it so we could both see the screen. Some things are easier to explain and understand when you can see them with your own two eyes.

I could tell by the way Mack's eyes were scanning the website I had opened on Google that he wasn't following what I was showing him.

"I meant to mention this to you before, but it somehow slipped my mind." He gave me a confused nod.

"What is it I am looking at here?" he asked.

Use your words, Magen, use your words.

This was no time to worry about embarrassing myself. It was time to get the answers I needed.

"I tried doing some research of my own about Trent, his wife, and her death. The page you are looking at now is what I was able to find out about Trent." Mack slid his chair closer to mine so he could get a better look at the webpage.

"I don't want to sound like an idiot, but what am I missing?" Okay, maybe the visual wasn't as helpful as I thought it would be.

"You aren't missing anything, that's the point. I tried every website I could find trying to get any information at all about Trent. Every website had the same result as the one you are looking at now, nothing. There is not one single thing online about a Trent Harper living in Massachusetts. How is that even possible? It's like he never existed at all."

I had no idea if what I was telling Mack was news to him, or if the police had already known about Trent's nonexistence online. If they had already known, why hadn't Mack told me about it?

The new look on Mack's face told me everything I wanted to know. The police had done little to no investigating into Trent. That confused me a bit. Wasn't it normal police procedure to investigate relatives when a family member dies or is possibly murdered? Even though I already knew the answer, I asked the question anyway. "Did you already know about this?"

Instead of answering me, Mack took his phone out of his pocket and angrily manhandled it. He walked out of the dining room and into the living room. I couldn't make out anything he was saying, but I could certainly tell his tone wasn't that of a happy man. I suddenly felt sorry for whoever was on the receiving side of his phone call.

After hanging up Mack walked back into the dining room. The reddish hue of his face was slowly turning pink.

"To answer your question, I didn't know about that. Because his wife's death had been ruled a suicide, and because we are extremely understaffed, Trent was never investigated. If the lab results we're still waiting for told us his wife was dead before falling down the staircase, then we would have started digging into his past." I couldn't tell if he was believing what he was telling me, but it sounded to me like he was making excuses for a sloppy investigation.

"We're going to start digging into this Trent Harper immediately. I will be in touch with you as soon as we have something. In the meantime, don't go near him. Don't even leave your house if you don't absolutely have to." Then he let out a low chuckle before saying, "I never was a fan of blind dates." I followed behind him as he headed for the door. As he was walking out the door, he said, "Lock your doors. Call me anytime if you think of something else."

I watched as he made his way back to his unmarked car. Then I shut the door, locked the lock, double-checked that I had locked the lock, then prayed Mack and his team would be able to find the answers I wasn't able to find.

Part Two

The Men

Zach

CHAPTER 1

What kind of household did you grow up in? Were you raised by your mother and your father, or were you raised by a single parent?

Was it a loving household? Were you shown love, kindness, and compassion? Were you taught the importance of caring and nurturing?

Was it a loveless household? Were you surrounded by arguing, swearing, and fighting? Were you shown hate, meanness, and cruelty?

I don't believe any of us are born good or bad. I don't believe there is an evil gene that can be passed down to us by our parents. I do, however, believe that we become good or bad in adulthood based on our life experiences as children. As children, we are very susceptible to good and bad behavior. The way our parents treat us, each other, and others often becomes what we believe is the correct way, the only way, to treat the people in our lives. A perfect example of this is prejudices. We are not born hating people of different races, people with different sexual orientations, or people who are different in any way from how we perceive ourselves. We learn prejudices throughout our childhood that stay with us throughout our adulthood.

If you were raised in a household with parents that were loving, kind, and compassionate then the odds are that as an adult you would be loving, kind, and compassionate. On the other hand, if you were raised in a household with parents that were always arguing, swearing, and fighting then the odds are that as an adult you would always be arguing, swearing, and fighting.

I was raised by my mother and father in a very dysfunctional household. It was an extremely toxic environment for anyone to live in. From as young as I can remember, there was always lots of screaming and fighting going on. The fighting would sometimes include hitting, slapping, punching, and pulling hair. Every swear word I know as an adult; I had learned by the age of ten.

My mother was always home with me while my father went to work. I often wondered why my parents ever got married in the first place. As far as I could tell, they had nothing in common. I tried to not pick sides between my mother and father, but the older I got, the harder that became. When I was younger, I would always run and hide whenever things started getting heated, which was pretty much every night. It was worse on the nights my father would drink.

When I got older, I started realizing that all the screaming and fighting was being caused by my father. That was when I finally picked a side to be on: my mother's. Night after night, I would sit there and listen to my father calling my mother the worst things imaginable. His voice would get louder and nastier with every new comment. My mother never dared to say anything back to him. She would just sit there and take it. Some nights he would close in on her until she was cowered in a corner just waiting for him to strike her. Those were the nights when I would do my best to work my way between them in hopes of calming the situation down.

Sometimes I yelled at my father to leave my mother alone. Sometimes I would break down in tears. I learned quickly that neither yelling nor crying had any effect on my father at all. His main goal in life was to break my mother completely. They hadn't slept in the same bed since before I was born. Our couch became my mother's bed. I spent more nights sleeping on that couch with my mother than I did in my own bed.

It wasn't bad all the time. Every minute my father was out of the house, my mother was able to be herself. She was funny, affectionate, caring, and very loving. I was the only good thing in her life, as she told me more times than I could've ever counted. She loved taking my picture, reading to me, and playing games with me, but mostly, she loved just holding me tightly against her chest. I never had to wonder if she loved me, I just knew she did.

CHAPTER 2

By the time I started high school, I was bigger and taller than my father was. He had started drinking more, which meant his tirades were louder and getting more violent. I hated leaving my mother alone with him, but I needed to start living my own life. I was given a ten p.m. curfew, which was strongly enforced. If I was even one minute late, I was grounded for a week.

Things got more complicated when I met my first serious girlfriend, Robin. We had become pretty much inseparable within the first month of dating. My mom loved her from the very first time they met. I put off introducing her to my father for as long as I could. I had no idea how he would act around her. Would he act like a normal father should while she was there with me, or would he act like the miserable, mean drunk he was and embarrass me?

Robin and I had been dating for almost six months before the inevitable happened. We were sitting at the dining room table helping my mother make a jigsaw puzzle when my father came home earlier than expected. It was clear to see he already had a few drinks in him. It was almost as clear as the way my mother's body tensed up the second he walked through the door. It wasn't until that second, that I wished I had told Robin about my father's drunken ways. His speech was so slurred we could hardly make out what he was saying.

The three of us just sat there frozen, afraid to say a word or move a muscle. Robin looked over at me while I looked down at the table, too embarrassed to meet her eyes. My mother, being the woman that she was, got up and tried to defuse what we all knew was going to happen next. My father, being the man that he was, pushed my mother so hard that she fell to the floor. Robin was out of her chair and rushing over to my mother before I had even had a chance to push my chair out from under the table. While Robin was comforting my mother and helping her sit back down in her chair, my father walked over to the table and threw all the puzzle pieces onto the floor. Robin and I stayed there with my mother that night until my father passed out.

Over the next few months, I did my best to only have Robin over when I was positive my father wouldn't be home. It didn't always work out that way. Although none of the encounters with my father were pleasant, none of them were as horrific as the first one. My father never even bothered to acknowledge Robin's presence, even when she was brave enough to acknowledge his. I promised myself so many times that I would never be anything like my father.

During my senior year of high school, I got a job at the car wash not too far from our house. It didn't pay much, but the hours weren't bad, and it got me out of the house. I had also become obsessed with working out. I know it wasn't the best goal to have, but my dream job was to work in a gym in some capacity. I started working out early in the morning five days a week. Then one of the worst days of my life happened. The day that changed my life forever.

I was always the first one up in the morning. Sometimes my mother would wake up when she heard me up and about, but she would go right back to sleep. When I woke up that morning, my mother was already up. She had been trying to be extra quiet so she wouldn't wake anyone else up. I was extremely confused when I saw her, and she was already dressed. My mother had spent more time in her housecoat than she had in street clothes.

When I walked into the kitchen to make my protein shake to take with me to the gym, my mother didn't even look at me. When I said good morning to her, she said good morning back to me in a voice that was so low I could barely hear her. Something was definitely going on with her. She had never been cold like that to me before. I asked her what was wrong, but all she did was shake her head, which definitely wasn't the truth. When I was done making my protein shake, I grabbed a bottled water from the fridge and said goodbye to my mother. The way she said, 'Goodbye, Zach' sounded so final, it sent shivers down my spine.

I walked out of the kitchen and headed for the door. That was when I saw it. My mother's packed suitcase was sitting right by the front door. I just stood there staring at it, lost for words. Where was she going that she needed a suitcase? I walked back into the kitchen. Again, my mother didn't even look at me. She knew I had seen her suitcase. Wasn't she going to tell me why it was packed and sitting by the front door?

I walked over to where she was and stood right on the side of her. She still wouldn't look at me.

Then I asked her, "Where are you going? Why is your suitcase at the front door?"

When I look back on it now, I see things much differently than I did then. On that day, when I heard my mother tell me she was leaving and not coming back, all I could think about was, after all the times I had stood up to my father in my mother's defense, all the times my father had hit me instead of my mother, all the days and nights I had devoted to my mother instead of living a normal childhood, she was leaving without me. She was leaving me behind with my father. How could she do that to the only good thing in her life?

These days, instead of thinking about what my mother's leaving would have meant for me, I think about my mother finally being brave enough to leave the hell my father had trapped her in for so many years. I was old enough on that day to take care of myself. I should've been proud of my mother. I should've called a taxi for her and carried her suitcase for her out to the taxi when it showed up. I should've been a better son, a better man. She deserved that from me.

Instead, I argued with her. I kept asking her, 'How can you do this to me?' I acted selfishly and immaturely. I could tell by the look on her face that the decision hadn't been an easy one for her to make. She was trying to hold back tears, but they started flowing out of her eyes like a dam had just let go. I tried begging and pleading with her to take me with her. I was acting as if I was still a ten-year-old boy.

I had raised my voice so much that I woke my father up. That was when things took a turn for the worse. Our washer and dryer were in the basement. My mother always hated the basement. It was dark and dungy and was known to house mice and spiders. She had done all the laundry the night before. Most of it was probably packed in her suitcase. When my father came into the kitchen, he instantly started screaming.

"What is going on in here? Do you know how early it is?"

My mother didn't say a thing. She just started backing away from my father. I could see the fear in her eyes. The second he noticed the suitcase near the front door she was going to get it. He would never allow my mother to leave him. That was when I did the thing I would regret for the rest of my life.

"She's leaving us," I said. I can still hear myself saying it to this day.

"Is that a fact?" my father screamed, as he moved closer and closer to my mother. What had I done?

The closer my father moved to my mother, the more she backed away from him. Her eyes were filled with fear; his eyes were filled with anger. My mother always made sure to close the basement door after coming up with the laundry, but for some reason, she had forgotten to close it the night before. Most likely, she had been too preoccupied with planning her escape.

I have watched what happened next play out in my mind at least a thousand times. My father closing in on my mother. My mother walking backward away from him. Me screaming out, 'Mom Stop!' right before she fell backward down the basement stairs.

CHAPTER 3

My father and I had just stood right where we were for what felt like hours. I kept waiting and hoping to hear my mother call out for me or to come walking up the stairs. My father was just standing there staring at the basement door. I can't remember seeing him blink. I think he went into a state of shock. It was me who finally got up the nerve to walk over to the basement door. I had to force my eyes to look down the flight of stairs. I let out a sound I had never made before when I saw the blood pooling around my mother's head. Her neck was twisted at an angle that could only mean one thing: my mother was dead.

I heard my father ask, "Is she dead?"

I couldn't get myself to respond. I wasn't ready to admit that the answer was yes. I backed away from the basement stairs and closed the basement door. I couldn't bear to see my mother that way for one second longer. The guilt took over my body instantly. What had I done? Why had I argued with my mother for finally being brave? Why had I raised my voice so loud that it woke my father up? Why had I told him she was leaving us? Why hadn't I stepped between them as I had so many times before? My mother was dead, and it was my fault.

In the next hour, my father and I came up with a plan. The first thing we did was unpack my mother's suitcase. We put everything she had packed back where it usually was and then put her suitcase back in the closet. Then we came up with the story we were going to tell the police and anyone else that asked. At first, my father wanted to just leave my mother down in the basement and not tell anyone. I couldn't let that happen to my mother. She deserved better than to rot away in the basement she hated. It took me mentioning the life insurance policy he had taken out on my mother for my father to agree about calling the police.

Once we had everything the way we wanted it to be when the police showed up, we walked out the front door leaving my mother dead at the bottom of the basement stairs. We needed to be away from the house long enough to give ourselves alibis. I changed that day, and I have never been able to go back to the way I was before.

The story my father and I had come up with started with me leaving for the gym before anyone else was up, which was what normally happened. When I got home from the gym, I would notice my parents' bedroom door being closed. My father would say that my mother hadn't been feeling well so he left her sleeping in the bed instead of on the couch. Then my father and I would leave for work at the same time.

I would be the first one to come back home like every other day. I would notice the bedroom door was still closed. I would open the bedroom door out of concern for my mother. I would notice the bedroom was empty and the bed wasn't made. I would frantically start searching the house and eventually find my mother at the bottom of the basement stairs. I would then make two phone calls. One to 911 and then one to my father at work telling him he needed to come home right away.

We both stuck to the plan. Neither of us had realized that by saying the basement door was closed when I had come home from work would be an error. If someone was going to commit suicide by throwing themselves down the basement stairs, they weren't going to close the basement door first. We needed to avoid suggesting suicide to the police and push for it to be an accident. An accident really didn't make sense with the door being closed either, but it wasn't like we could suddenly change our stories and say the basement door had been opened.

Luckily, the police officers that came by that day weren't the brightest. When the younger of the two police officers said the word accident, my father and I clung to it as if our lives depended on it. Watching them remove my mother from the house in a body bag was too much for me to take. I started crying so hard they wanted to take me to the hospital. They thought I was having a nervous breakdown. The amount of guilt I was feeling, first for being responsible for my mother's death, and then for lying to the cops about how she had died, was crushing me. I couldn't even look in the mirror for months. I didn't want to see the man who would be looking back at me.

CHAPTER 4

After the police officers left, I headed over to Robin's house. Although the story I had told her wasn't true, the tears that came along with it were real tears. Not only had I lied to the police officers about how my loving mother had died, but now I was lying to the girl I intended on marrying. That was when I realized that adding in the part about the basement door being closed was a mistake. Robin knew my mother. She knew my mother would never have closed the basement door behind her. I could see the doubt in Robin's eyes. The doubt that never faded.

As time went on, I tried my best to block out the events of that day. My mother's death was declared an accidental death. My father's and my secret was safe, at least for the time being. Robin and I got married. I had wished more than anything that my mother could have been there to celebrate it with us. My father had somehow found a replacement for my mother. A woman named Bonnie was now the new victim of his angry tirades.

Occasionally, Robin would mention her doubts about my mother's death. I refused to talk about it with her. I knew she never once suspected I was in some way responsible for what happened, but I was certain she thought my father was. Anyone who had ever seen the way my father treated my mother would've thought my father was responsible for what happened that day. I had hoped that one day Robin would let it go and just accept it was an accidental death like the police officers had, but unfortunately, that day never came.

Then one day while I was at work, I got a call from Bonnie. It was the first time she had ever called me. Her tone was profoundly serious as she told me my father had been rushed to the hospital. I shouldn't admit this to you, but a part of me hoped he would never come out of the hospital unless he was in his own body bag. Over the years my father had used the guilt I felt over my mother's death to get me to do things I didn't want to do.

'I would hate for people to find out what really happened that day', he would say. I can't remember a day when I didn't hate my own father.

I called Robin to tell her about my father being in the hospital. She didn't answer so I left her a voicemail. The tears I cried that day were forced tears. Maybe I should have set my life goal to becoming an actor. By the time Robin arrived at the hospital, Bonnie was in the room with my father and the doctor. I kept up the charade of being the concerned son while we waited for an update on my father's condition. When Bonnie came back into the waiting room, she let us know that my father had suffered a mini-stroke. He was going to be fine. Just my luck.

For one reason or another, the thought that my father could have died provoked Bonnie into asking my father questions about my mother and her death. He, like me, refused to talk about it. This led Bonnie, just like Robin, to be more curious about it, thus continuing to ask more questions. The difference was that my father had no patience whatsoever for people who didn't listen to him when he told them to stop doing something.

One day, rather unexpectedly, Robin asked me what my father's favorite food was. I was really confused. I knew she hadn't liked my father since the first day she met him. The next night my father and Bonnie were eating lasagna with us at our house. I couldn't wait for them to leave. I had nothing against Bonnie except that she was living with my father. Who knew that an innocent dinner for four, would lead to two of them disappearing?

My father had been taking a bunch of medications that his doctor had prescribed for him after his mini-stroke. Every one of them had a warning label on them stating, 'Do not mix with alcohol.' My father, being the alcoholic that he was, couldn't help but drink two glasses of wine with his lasagna. We all knew it was a bad idea, but telling my father he couldn't do something he wanted to do was never a good idea. I wasn't overly surprised when he called me saying he wasn't feeling well. He had made an appointment with his doctor and needed a ride.

I didn't know it at the time, but Robin and Bonnie had had a meeting of the minds in our kitchen while they were doing the dishes after our dinner together. The main topic of discussion was, of course, my mother and her death. While I was at the hospital with my father for his check-up, Robin drove over to my father's house and continued her secret conversation with Bonnie. My father and I would've been none the wiser if Robin hadn't put her perfume on. Bonnie didn't wear perfume.

When my father got home from the hospital, he smelled Robin's perfume as soon as he walked through the door. My father confronted Bonnie about Robin's mystery visit. She kept lying saying Robin hadn't been there. She tried making excuses for the scent of Robin's perfume, saying it was a new air freshener she had bought. When my father asked her to show him the air freshener, she then said it was a candle she had been burning. They went back and forth until my father had had enough of her lies.

That was when he started pushing and shoving her around the house. She didn't start telling him the truth until after the first punch to her face landed. Little by little she filled him in on everything that had been said during both of their conversations. At that point, he knew for sure that

Robin suspected it wasn't an accidental death, and that she thought he had pushed my mother down the basement stairs. Then Bonnie made the biggest mistake of her life. Instead of at least pretending to not agree with Robin's suspicions, she asked my father straight out if Robin was right.

The next time I talked to my father he told me what had happened. I couldn't believe what I was hearing. He told me that they had argued and fought. He told me about Bonnie lying to him about Robin's visit. He told me everything Bonnie had told him about Robin's suspicions. Then he told me about pushing Bonnie down the basement stairs. The same basement stairs my mother had fallen down. Then he told me about the hole he had dug in the basement floor, and how he had buried Bonnie's body. He knew the police wouldn't have believed two women had fallen down the same basement stairs and died. Bonnie had no close relatives or friends that would come looking for her. I wanted to scream at him at the top of my lungs. I wanted to push *him* down the damn basement stairs. What was he thinking?

CHAPTER 5

I had no idea what to tell Robin about Bonnie. I didn't want her to know that I knew about her visit to my father's house, or that I knew about the two conversations she had had with Bonnie regarding my mother. Part of me was angry with her. Why did she think it was her business what had happened that day? It wasn't *her* mother who had died. Also, why had she been involving Bonnie in it? I had told her several times that whatever had happened between my parents was none of her business. Why wasn't that good enough for her? Why had she insisted on sticking her nose where it didn't belong?

I knew I had to mention something about Bonnie to Robin as soon as possible. If I waited too long and then she found out that Bonnie wasn't living with my father anymore, it would make her even more suspicious. When I told Robin the story about how my mother had died, I messed up saying the basement door had been closed. When I told her about Bonnie not living with my father anymore, I messed up by using the word 'gone'. Bonnie being gone didn't sit well with Robin. One little word was all it took for the second disappearance to happen.

Robin just couldn't let it go. No matter how hard I had tried to convince her that *gone* meant my father had thrown Bonnie out of his house, she kept asking about her. On the same Friday night that Robin had surprised me by cooking steaks on the grill and buying movie tickets for our first Friday night date in months, my father called to tell me he had seen Robin in Stop & Shop. He told me that she had brought up Bonnie's name. He was convinced that she had gone shopping at the same time as him so she could purposely provoke him into saying something about Bonnie. I tried telling him he was crazy, but he wouldn't listen to me.

It seemed like everything around me was spiraling out of control. The last thing my father had said to me before hanging up, 'She has to go', made me feel like we were on a collision course with no way of stopping it. I knew my father was right. Too much was at stake now. Robin had already been suspicious about my mother's death. Now she was also suspicious and asking questions about Bonnie being gone. There was no way she was going to stop until she had answers. Answers that would put me and my father behind bars for the rest of our lives.

Although neither of us had actually pushed my mother down the basement stairs, we had both lied to the police with our made-up stories of that day's events, waited hours to call 911 to give ourselves alibis, and unpacked my mother's things to hide the fact that she had been intending to leave us. Once you add to that what my father had done to Bonnie, and my failure to report him to the police for doing it, we would be in serious trouble if Robin ever found out the truth. We couldn't let that happen.

I had been a bit surprised when Robin hadn't argued with me about taking my father along with us on our hiking trip. When we picked my father up that morning, I had been expecting to see at least the slightest sign of remorse for what he had done to Bonnie, but there wasn't any. You would never have guessed that he had buried a woman in his basement less than two days earlier. Our original plan was for my father to bring the sleeping pills he had just picked up from the Stop & Shop pharmacy the day Robin had bumped into him, with him. I had put the backpack with the bottled waters in the back seat figuring that was where my father would be sitting. I would distract Robin while he added the sleeping pills he had crushed up to the bottle I would hand her. We had to adjust the plan when Robin moved into the back seat so my father could sit in the front seat.

Once we made it to the hiking trails my father slipped the little baggie with the crushed-up sleeping pills to me. While my father and Robin applied the bug spray and sunscreen, I poured the crushed-up sleeping pills into one of the bottles and set it aside. To be completely honest with you, the thought of playing Russian roulette with the bottle was an option that had been bouncing around in my head since my father and I had made the original plan. Which one of us deserved that bottle more than the others? It certainly wasn't Robin.

I was worried at first that Robin would notice the little white pieces floating in her bottled water, but the label was hiding most of them. My father had already assured me that they had no taste. We just needed her to drink enough of the water for them to take effect. We walked slower than we needed to so Robin would have more time to drink the water. When I made it to the bench at the lake, I looked back and noticed she was swaying a little bit as she walked. Extreme guilt flowed through my body. How was I allowing this to happen to the woman I loved? I wanted nothing more than to take the rest of her water and force my father to drink it. I felt like I was choking on guilt, and it was all his fault. I hated him more in that moment than I had ever thought possible.

When I saw Robin sitting on the water's edge just innocently watching the fish swimming around in circles, I could taste vomit working its way up my throat. I wanted to rush over to her and tell her what we had done to her. I wanted to rush her to the hospital and get her stomach pumped. I wanted to drink the rest of her water and die right there by her side. I wanted to do so many things, but instead, I just went and sat next to her. I was just about to tell her that I loved her when she fell over onto her side. My father came over and helped her sit back up. Then we did the unimaginable. We both stood up and took one of her hands into ours. We helped her stand up. She was very unsteady on her feet. After glancing around to make sure nobody else was close by, we walked with her slowly into the lake. She was so out of it by then, I don't think she even realized she was waist-deep in water. Then one by one we let her hands slip out of ours. She instantly fell face-first under the water. In our original plan, we had thought she would struggle to get out of the lake. One of us was going to have to hold her head under the water. She didn't struggle at all. Either she didn't have the strength to struggle, or she had just accepted her fate for what it was.

My father and I walked out of the lake and watched as the last of her air bubbles made it to the surface of the lake. It took every ounce of my being to not crawl up into a ball on the ground and cry my eyes out. The two women that I loved the most in the world were now dead, and the man I hated the most was standing on the side of me. How had I allowed this to happen? Once we were certain she was dead, we walked back into the lake, pulled her back up onto her feet, and walked her back to the bench. My father sat down on the bench, and then I sat Robin's dead body right on the side of him. While they sat there like two people resting during their hike, I ran all the way back down the trail. I wanted to make sure there was no one else around that could see what we were about to do.

After not seeing anybody, I ran back up the trail. My father quickly turned his head when he heard me coming up the trail. He relaxed when he saw it was just me. The trail wasn't wide enough for the three of us to go down side by side, so instead, I grabbed Robin's arms, and my father grabbed her legs, then we slowly made our way back down the trail. When we made it down to the opening, we stood Robin back up and walked with her between us over to the car. We laid her down in the back seat and got out of there as fast as we could without looking like we were up to no good. I drove us back to my father's house. We left Robin in the back seat while we went into the house. We dug a second hole in my father's basement floor while we waited for it to get dark outside. Once the sun had set, we carried Robin into my father's house and then we buried her right next to Bonnie.

It wasn't until I was back home sitting at the dining room table that the reality of what we had just done hit me. I ran as fast as I could to the bathroom and threw up everything that was inside of me. Robin wasn't like Bonnie. She had parents who loved her, parents who would want, or rather, demand answers, as to where their daughter was. Hopefully, my acting skills would be good enough to convince them that she had packed her stuff while I was at work and left me without saying a word to anyone.

The next six to nine months were extremely stressful. Robin's disappearance became the biggest story in New England. Her face was in all the newspapers and local news reports every day. There were flyers in every possible store window. We did searches and held candlelight vigils. We let purple (her favorite color was purple) balloons go. The police were at my house more times than I could count. Everyone always assumes the husband did it, which in this case, was true.

By the time the one-year anniversary of Robin's disappearance came around, most people had moved on. She had become second-hand news. Just another missing woman out there somewhere. My life was starting to get back to normal, though I did still get weird looks from the people who believed I was responsible for whatever had happened to Robin. Like Robin, my face and name had been all over the news. When it seemed like the worst of it was over, I dropped my first name and started going by my middle name, Cole.

Cole

CHAPTER 1

Over the next few months, I managed to get certified to be a personal trainer at the gym I had been working out in all these years. Most of the stigma that had been following me around eventually dissipated. I was in my mid-twenties and single. I had more clients, mostly female, than any of the other trainers that had been there a lot longer. Things were finally starting to look up.

I had been trying my hardest to distance myself from my father. If I could've had it my way, I would never have seen him again after the vigil we attended on the one-year anniversary of Robin's disappearance. He had been living alone, so to speak, and he didn't like it. He had nobody to take care of him or do everything around the house for him. He had gotten even worse once he was semi-forced out of his job and put on disability. Most days he just sat around the house all day by himself. He would call me at least once a week to go visit him. More times than not I ignored his calls and voicemails.

I decided to stop by his house after work one day after almost a month of not hearing from him. When I walked into his house, I couldn't believe my eyes. The place was a complete pigsty. Every dish and glass he owned was dirty in the sink and all along the kitchen counter. There were disgusting smells coming from the rotting food he had left on the plates. I was quite sure he hadn't showered in weeks. He looked like shit warmed over.

Although I hated the man, he was still my father. I couldn't leave him living like that. I tried to get him to move in with me, but he refused to leave his house due to what was buried in his basement. So instead, I sold the house Robin and I had lived in and moved back into the house I was raised in. The house my mother had died in, the house with two dead bodies buried in its basement. It took us almost a month to clean up the mess he made of the house.

Living under my father's roof again was constantly stressing me out. I started drinking his alcohol instead of pouring it down the drain to prevent him from drinking it. After one too many DUIs, I lost my driver's license.

My only means of transportation was a ten-speed bike. My life was once again going to shit. A few months later, two major events happened in my life, one good and one bad. Depending on how you look at it, it might have been two good things.

I will start with the one that could be good or bad. One day when I came home from work the house was eerily quiet. Normally I would hear the television at a relatively loud volume. My father had started losing his hearing though he refused to admit it. On this day, the television was off and there wasn't even one dirty dish or coffee cup in the sink waiting for me to wash. I started calling out for him but got no reply. I found him dead in his bed. He had never even gotten out of bed. His skin was cold and clammy to the touch. I wish I could tell you that I cried that day, but I am being as honest as I possibly can with you. I was free of him at last, or was I?

I found myself in a sticky situation. My father was dead in his bed and there were two more dead bodies buried in his basement floor. I knew I should've called 911 and let them deal with my father's body, but I was too nervous to let them in the house. In the end, I did the only thing I could think of. I dug a third hole in the basement floor right next to Bonnie.

I continued living in that house in hopes of preventing anyone from noticing the lack of activity. Every month when my father's disability check came in, I deposited it into his checking account. Then I used it to pay all the bills that came in. No one suspected a thing as far as I knew. I was getting better at making plans when people died.

CHAPTER 2

The good thing that happened was that I met a woman. She had come into the gym with whom I later learned was her sister. She was at least twenty years older than me, out of shape, insecure, reserved, and rich. This may freak you out a bit, but the thing that attracted me to her the most was that she reminded me of my mother. She was living the life my mother could have been living if she had married the right man.

I didn't want to come on too strong and scare her away. I somehow managed to get her to sign up for some training sessions with me. She was so nervous just being around me at first. It was very flattering. Don't get me wrong, I didn't find myself sexually attracted to her, but there is more to a relationship than just sex. By our third session, we were talking about all kinds of things. I was learning more and more about her every session. When she told me about the way her ex-husband had treated her, it made me feel like I was listening to my own mother telling her story. She liked to talk, and I liked to listen. I genuinely enjoyed our talks. They reminded me of when my mother used to tell me stories when I was younger.

I could tell she was starting to fall for me. One of my other clients was this large-breasted blonde chick that I had banged a few times. Anytime Kari, the new woman in my life, saw the blonde trying to flirt with me, her jealousy showed through her unattainable façade. It was cute to watch. Before I knew it, I started having feelings for her too. It was like I was having a second chance at being a good son.

It felt weird when I asked her out on a date. I wanted to spend more time with her without having all the curious eyes following us around at the gym. I knew she would say yes, which she did, but for vastly different reasons. With all the insecurities she was dealing with, I was sure it would take a while before she was ready to take things to the next step. She was happy. I was happy. What could go wrong?

Occasionally Kari would ask me about my family, but I always managed to evade answering her. What was I supposed to tell her, that my mother accidentally fell down our basement stairs and died, and that my father was buried in the same basement? I had put off being intimate with Kari for as long as I could. If I stalled any longer, she would've known something was askew. When the time came, I tried to block out the images of my mother's face that kept trying to present themselves and replaced them with images of the blonde from the gym. It worked well enough to get the job done.

I always made sure to treat her the way my father should have treated my mother all those years. I know this all sounds messed up to you, but I think I was trying to atone for everything that my father and I had done to my mother. A short while later, two more major life events happened almost simultaneously. Again, one was good, and one was bad.

Whenever someone tells me they have good and bad news, I always opt for the bad news first in hopes that the good news will outweigh the bad in the end. In case you are like me, I will start with the bad again.

A new threat to my family secrets presented itself in the form of Kari's sister, Heather. I had never even noticed Heather until the day she brought Kari into the gym with her. She was just another face in the crowd. Then one day after Kari and I had started dating, they came in together again. Heather put on quite a little show when she came over to formally introduce herself to me. She made a couple of inappropriate comments that made Kari uncomfortable. I was relieved when she walked away from us and headed to the treadmills.

After our awkward encounter at the gym that day, Kari insisted on inviting Heather out with us on some of our dates. She was feeling guilty that she had found a man to spend time with, while Heather was home alone all the time living like a spinster. It had become obvious rather quickly that Heather was suspicious of my intentions toward Kari. At first, I had thought it was just sisterly jealousy, but there was more to it than that. She wasn't as blind to all the red flags as Kari was. Trouble was brewing and it wasn't smelling good.

CHAPTER 3

Then one day it happened. I was sitting at home after work waiting for Kari to pick me up when the doorbell rang. I thought it was odd because Kari never rang the doorbell. She had always just tooted her horn a couple of times. When I opened the door Heather was standing there. What the hell was she playing at?

I hurried her inside the house before anyone had a chance to see her standing at my door. Did she know I was waiting for Kari to show up? Is that what this was all about? When I asked her what she wanted, her response wasn't what I had expected. She told me she had been stopping by my house when she knew I was at work so she could meet my father. She didn't like that I hadn't introduced Kari to my father. She knew I was hiding something, and she wanted to know what it was. I didn't have time for her and her suspicious mind.

I tried to remain as calm and collected as I could. After all, there was nothing to see here. I didn't know whether it was my imagination or not, but for the first time since I had moved back into my father's house, I thought I was catching a whiff of decay coming up from the basement. I had to get her out of the house immediately.

I told her, "Not that it's any of your business, but my father is on vacation in Florida. Now if you don't mind, Kari will be here any minute." What would happen if Kari showed up and saw Heather's car sitting outside my house? It was then that the new plan started coming together.

Less than five minutes after Heather pulled out of my driveway, Kari pulled in. I couldn't help but wonder if they had passed each other on the street. I had been a bit unnerved by Heather's visit and Kari noticed it during dinner. That was the first night she had taken me to what became my favorite restaurant. It was a very fancy, awfully expensive steak house. Never before had a steak tasted as good as it did that night. Kari even had a favorite table, which had been her and her ex-husband's favorite table. It would become our favorite table, at least for the time being.

This is the part of the story that I was referring to earlier, the bad life event. When I got home from our delicious steak dinner, my new plan was the first thing I thought of. I didn't want to do it. I had tried so hard to not be like my father, but unfortunately, it wasn't turning out that way. I found the bottle of my father's sleeping pills when I was going through his things shortly after he died. I took half of what was left in the bottle and crushed them up. If there was any other way, it failed to present itself to me.

With crushed-up sleeping pills in one hand, and a screwdriver in the other, I headed out the door. I knew where Heather lived thanks to the couple of times we had picked her up when she had decided to grace us with her presence on our dates. It was an easy twenty-minute bike ride from my front door to hers. When I made it to her house, I checked to make sure none of her neighbors had any lights on. When I was satisfied the coast was clear, I walked my bike to the side of her house out of sight of anyone who might drive by.

I checked under the bigger stones and the flowerpots near her front door hoping to find a spare key. Finding nothing, I was glad I had brought the screwdriver with me. I was just about to stick the screwdriver into the lock on the front door when I saw a light come on in her neighbor's house. I dropped to the ground and didn't move an inch until five minutes after the light had gone back off. Back at the front door, I worked the screwdriver into the lock. It wasn't as easy as I had thought it would be. The damage to the lock was very noticeable, even in the dark of night.

The sound of the lock popping sounded so loud in the stillness of the night. I wouldn't have been surprised if it had awakened her. I opened the door as quickly and quietly as possible. I was in her house within seconds. I closed the door behind me and then just stood there for a couple of minutes. Not hearing anything, I made my way to the kitchen. The layout of her house was remarkably similar to Kari's house.

My original plan included me filling a glass with tap water. After careful consideration, I decided I didn't want to risk how loud the faucet might be if I turned it on. Instead, I opened the refrigerator and grabbed an open bottle of vodka. I was silently thanking myself for putting gloves on before I left my house. I emptied the crushed-up sleeping pills into a glass and then filled it with vodka.

I was as quiet as a mouse as I made my way over to the staircase. I paused at the bottom of the staircase listening for any movements coming from the second floor. Hearing nothing but my own heartbeat pounding in my ears, and the clicking of the second hand on the grandfather clock, I started climbing the stairs one at a time. I was cursing my father under my breath for turning me into the man I had become as I climbed the stairs. If my mother could see me now, would she even recognize me as her son, the best thing in her life?

Once I made it to the top of the stairs I paused again. One can never be too careful when planning the perfect murder. After waiting two minutes I crept down the hall to the master bedroom. The door was wide open. I could see Heather fast asleep in her bed. The sound of quiet little snores making its way across the room. I couldn't believe what I was about to do. Another innocent woman was about to pay the price for my and my father's sins. There is no truer statement than, 'Life just isn't fair.'

When my eyes had fully adjusted to the darkness of Heather's bedroom, I realized she was wearing a sleeping mask. Not a part of the original plan, but a welcomed edit. I basically slid my way over to her bed. I didn't want to risk waking her up by taking actual steps. Once I made it to the side of the bed, I put the glass of vodka on the nightstand. I was going to need two free hands for the next part. Thanks to all my time in the gym I was very agile and flexible.

In one quick movement, I went from standing on the side of the bed to being on top of Heather on the bed. I had one knee on each of her arms and my hands over her mouth. She hadn't even had a chance to scream. I had planned to tell her that she should have minded her own business and that she didn't have to worry about Kari, I would take care of her, but considering she couldn't even see who I was with her mask on, I decided to stay silent. Would she know her life was about to end? Would she know it was me that was taking her life from her?

I quickly leaned over and grabbed the glass from the nightstand. I stuck two fingers between her lips and then between her teeth, just enough to be able to start pouring the vodka into her mouth. She gagged a little and tried biting my fingers. Little by little, I managed to pour the whole glass of vodka laced with sleeping pills down her throat. With the glass empty, I just sat there with my knees on her arms and my hands over her mouth waiting for nature to run its course.

It only took about fifteen minutes before I felt her whole body just relax. I knew at that point it was only a matter of minutes before she would be dead. I climbed off her and wiped the vodka that had dripped down the side of her face. I then turned her head to the side so she would be in a more believable sleeping position. I adjusted her sheets so whoever it was that found her, wouldn't be able to tell that someone else had been on the bed with her. It wasn't until I checked the surface of the nightstand to make sure the glass hadn't left a water ring that I noticed she had the same exact bottle of sleeping pills as my father sitting right there the whole time.

With my gloved hand, I picked up her bottle of sleeping pills and poured half of them into one of my pants pockets before placing the bottle back in the same exact place it had been. If the police officers investigated her death and looked into the last time she had refilled her pills, they would think she had overdosed on the ones that were now in my pants pocket. Before leaving her bedroom, I bent down and checked her pulse. She didn't have one.

I couldn't wait to get out of that house. I had just taken the innocent life of Kari's sister, the only living relative that she had ever told me about. The sister she loved more than she loved herself. That was when the plan for the good life event started forming. Before I can get to that… I made my way back down the stairs, washed the glass in the kitchen sink, and put it back where I got it from. Then I headed out the front door. I made sure the door with the messed-up lock was locked before getting on my bike and heading back home. The screwdriver in my back pocket jabbed me a few times while I rode my bike. Instead of feeling pain, I felt alive. What did that say about me?

CHAPTER 4

I wasn't surprised by how little sleep I got after my late-night activity. I kept replaying everything I had done over and over in my head. Had I left something behind that could point to me? Was she really dead, or had she just been unconscious? Had one of her nosy neighbors seen me leaving on my bike?

For the time being, I had to stop thinking about all the mistakes I might've made. It was time to focus on my future. I knew I couldn't just leave things up to chance anymore. I needed to act, and I needed to act right away. Things between me and Kari were about to turn upside down. I needed to do whatever I could before she found out about Heather. If not, I was going to lose her forever just like my real mother.

I took a shower, got dressed, and with my little surprise in my pocket, I headed off to work. It was going to be Kari's last session with me. I made sure to block out all my appointments after hers. I had no idea what her reaction was going to be, but I wanted to be ready for all possibilities. It took me a bit to put a name to the feeling I was experiencing when she walked into the gym. It had been some time since I had felt nervous. I hadn't even felt nervous when I was inside Heather's house. Yet, there I was watching Kari walk across the gym, and my nerves were jumping. Was I afraid of rejection?

Considering it was Kari's last session with me, I didn't hold back on her. We worked every muscle group in her body. By the time we finished, I was surprised she was able to move. It was almost *go* time. I patted my hand against my pocket to make sure I hadn't lost my surprise. I had Kari lie down on the stretching mat. I grabbed onto her feet and told her I wanted her to pull herself up from the mat and touch her toes. She thought I was crazy. There was no way she could possibly do that without moving her feet. I could see her focusing as I counted down from ten. When I hit five, I took my surprise out of my pocket and held it between my fingers.

At the same exact time as I said zero, Kari started pushing herself up. She was incredibly determined to at least make it to a sitting position. I checked to make sure the overhead light was shining directly down on my hands, leaving nothing to chance. Kari had the biggest smile on her face as she sat up. She had done it; she was sitting straight up. When she looked over at me, I looked down at my hands. I couldn't see if her eyes had followed mine but when I heard her gasp, I knew they had. I teased her with the surprise a little bit to get her to finish the stretch and touch her toes. I didn't even bother waiting for her response to the four magic words. I took her reaction as a yes. Then I gently slid Robin's engagement ring onto Kari's finger. It was a perfect fit.

I know that might have sounded morbid, but I looked at it as a way to remember Robin, to honor her short life. When Kari left the gym, I hoped she would've asked me to go with her, but she didn't. I had a strong feeling I knew why. I found out a few hours later that I was correct. She had gone over to Heather's house to show her the ring I had given her. She knew Heather was dead, most likely due to an overdose. Everything was about to change once again.

Everything I thought would happen when Kari found out about Heather happened, and then some. She tried her hardest to get the police to do a formal investigation into Heather's death. She kept using the messed-up lock as evidence that it hadn't been a suicide even after the medical examiner concluded it was a suicide. I was thanking God for incompetent, lazy police officers, while she was cursing them. She was spending more and more time locked away in her house, only allowing me limited visitations.

Then one night I brought up our wedding. I wasn't even sure if she still wanted to get married. At first, I thought she was making excuses to call it off, but once I sold her on the idea of quietly eloping, she got on board. Two weeks later we stood before the justice of the peace with two total strangers as our witnesses and became man and wife, or son and mother depending on how you looked at it.

I moved the little belongings I had from my father's house into Kari's house. When I left with the last of my belongings, I made sure all the windows were locked and the blinds were all closed. I didn't want any neighbors trying to peek into the house. Then I locked the front door and the storm door. I knew the mailman would be dropping the mail through the mail slot on the storm door. With the storm door locked, I would be the only one that could access the mail. Another well-thought-out plan put into action. All that was left was for me to stop by every so often to collect the mail, deposit my father's disability check, and continue paying the bills.

Although we were living together, Kari was still keeping me at arm's length. She was busy working her way through the tremendous grief she felt after Heather's death. I was fine with the way things were between us. I didn't need us to be sexual together; I was getting that from the blonde again. Trust me, she was more than I could handle. She loved the idea of having sex with a married man.

Eventually, Kari started acting more like her old self. She still had her dark days, but she had started going out of the house again. I even convinced her to start going back to the gym. She really wasn't ready to be around people yet, but she went anyway. I think she was just trying to make me happy. I hated seeing her sad and depressed all the time. I knew I would never be able to take Heather's place in her life, but I wanted to try, nonetheless. After all, I was the one that had taken Heather from her life. In my defense, I did it so Kari and I could have a future together. Was that really such a dreadful thing?

CHAPTER 5

Why do all the good things in life always have to come to an end? I was being the best husband/son I could be to Kari. I was always there for her when she wanted to talk or needed a shoulder to cry on. I was always trying to boost her self-esteem by giving her compliments, even if they weren't deserved. I wanted her to feel beautiful and desirable. Isn't that what every woman wants? I ran errands for her and kept the house tidy. I gave her amazing foot massages, even when her feet were dirty and stank. I made sure to keep her satisfied sexually whenever she wanted me to.

Things started heating up again with me and the blonde. I keep referring to her as the blonde because I can't even remember her name. That's how much she meant to me. She kept pushing me to spend more time with her. The only way I could do that was to lie to Kari about where I had been if she asked. I didn't like lying to Kari, but I did. The only reason I lied to her, is because the blonde said she would tell Kari about us screwing if I didn't do what she asked me to. What else was I supposed to do? I made my beds, I had to lie in them.

I'm not sure how much of this part is true, but I will tell you about it anyway. One day Kari wanted to surprise me for lunch. She knew I always went to the Subway closest to the gym. She drove to the Subway and waited in the parking lot for me to show up on my bike. She wanted to surprise me. Turns out, she was the one that was in for a surprise when I showed up in the blonde's car, instead of on my bike. Kari sat in her car watching us through the window. When I pushed the blonde up against her car and kissed her, Kari was two cars behind us. She had seen everything up close and personal. I only know about this because Kari had the nerve to confront me about it. I tried lying my way out of it, but she wasn't having it. In the end, I confessed my sin and promised to end things with the blonde, which I did like a good husband.

After a couple of months of good behavior, I honestly thought our marriage was solid until Kari's motherly instinct kicked in. After Heather had died, Kari was left with no family. She was an adult orphan. The more she thought about that, the more she pushed for me to spend time with my father. She couldn't understand why I was being so nonchalant about being distant from my father. She wanted to fix it for me, just like every mother would want to.

I didn't know it, but Kari had been driving by my father's house just like Heather had, trying to meet him without me knowing about it. Yes, I will admit her intentions were good, but the outcome of her efforts was anything but good. She had been so nosy; she even noticed the mail between the doors before I had a chance to collect it. Timing is so important in the larger scheme of things.

Speaking of timing, the day after I stopped by my father's house to sort through his mail, Kari had gone back once again. From what she told me later that day when she noticed the mail was gone, she decided to hang around with the hopes of talking to one of my father's neighbors. It was Doris from the house after my father's house that she met up with and questioned. That conversation was the beginning of the end for everything in my life pertaining to Kari.

When I got home from work that day, I found one of the envelopes from my father's house sitting on the table. At first, I thought maybe I had brought it home with me and Kari had found it. That thought didn't last long. I had always made sure to never bring one of the envelopes into our house. I knew if Kari had seen one, there would be a million questions for me to answer. That could only mean one thing, I needed a new plan.

I picked up the envelope and walked into the living room where Kari was waiting for me. I didn't waste any time with small talk. I knew what had to happen that night. I couldn't allow myself to deviate from the plan. I could see on Kari's face that she was upset with me, maybe even more upset than I was with her. I showed her the envelope and asked her where she had gotten it from. That was when she told me the story I mentioned earlier, about the conversation she had with Doris after seeing my father's mail was gone. The questions, suspicions, and accusations flew out of her mouth one after another, after another.

I tried my best to hide the anger that was building up inside of me. It might have been my best acting ever. I got up and headed to the kitchen. I told Kari I was getting a beer and asked if she wanted a glass of her favorite wine. I knew she would never say no to a glass of her favorite wine, not even if she was on her deathbed.

I had hidden the sleeping pills I took from Heather's bedroom in the cabinet in the downstairs bathroom. I made my way quickly to the bathroom to get the sleeping pills. I crushed up the pills, grabbed a beer and the bottle of wine from the fridge, poured the wine into one of the dark-tinted wine glasses, then added the sleeping pills. I watched as the crushed-up pieces fell to the bottom of the wine glass before returning to the living room. I could tell Kari was confused by the sudden change in my mood, which had allowed her to let her guard down just enough for her to start drinking the wine without giving it a second thought.

I turned the television on to keep Kari distracted enough that she wouldn't realize the effect the sleeping pills were having on her. She finished her glass of wine before I had finished my beer. It wasn't long before I noticed her body starting to sway. She tried saying something but all she could manage was jumbled-up noises. It was time for the finale of the plan.

I walked over to where she was sitting and picked her up in my arms. She had a smile on her face as I carried her over to the staircase like Prince Charming sweeping her off her feet. She was too heavy to carry up the stairs, so I put her down and helped her climb the stairs one foot at a time. When we made it to the top of the stairs, I knew she was expecting me to pick her up in my arms again and carry her over to the bed, but instead, I left her standing right at the edge of the top step and backed away from her.

I stood there watching as her body started swaying again. She was trying to tell me something, but I couldn't make out what it was she was saying. As she fell over backward down the stairs, I found myself thinking how ironic it was that Heather's sleeping pills would be found in Kari's body if they did an autopsy on her. Life is funny that way sometimes. When I heard her head smash onto one of the stairs, I couldn't help but walk over to where she had fallen from. The sound her head made when it smashed the second time almost made me throw up. I was certain her skull had cracked.

As I stood there at the top of the staircase looking down at Kari's lifeless body, instead of seeing her, I was seeing my mother's lifeless body at the bottom of our basement stairs. I sat down on the top step completely overcome by all the loss I had experienced in my life. So much loss just to keep a secret safe. Had it been worth it in the long run? Who could honestly say if it was or wasn't?

I dialed 911 and told them I had just got home and found my wife dead at the bottom of the stairs. As I waited for the police to show up, I washed the wine glass Kari had drunk from making sure there was no trace of the crushed-up sleeping pills. If I had any luck, the police officers would be just as clueless and lazy as they had been before.

There was only one part of the plan left. I needed a new name. I knew from what had happened when Robin disappeared that me and Kari's names would be all over the news for a while even if they considered her death an accident. Kari was a very wealthy woman, especially after collecting everything she did from when Heather died. I never cared about her money like everyone else thought I did. I just wanted a second chance to be the son my mother deserved.

Trent

CHAPTER 1

In the week leading up to Kari's death, I met Magen. Let me back up a little bit. During Kari's grieving time, when she wanted to be left alone most of the time, I found myself with a lot of free time on my hands. If I wasn't meeting up with the blonde from the gym, I was out riding my bike. There was a bike path about seven blocks from Kari's house. In the middle of the bike path, there was a waterfall with a few benches in front of it that people could sit down on and watch the waterfall. I found the sound of the waterfall to be very relaxing.

On nice days I would ride my bike from Kari's house to the beginning of the path. Then I would chain my bike to one of the lamp poles and walk to the waterfall. On one such day, while I was sitting on one of the benches watching the waterfall, I was surprised to see a beautiful woman approaching the benches with sweat dripping off her and music blasting from her earbuds. Within minutes, I found myself in Magen's bed having sex with her.

The next day I purposely made it to the waterfall at the same time as the day before. I had hoped Magen had a set time she ran every morning. At almost the same minute as the morning before she came running around the bend. I smiled at her, but to my surprise, she just kept running right past me. I knew we hadn't exchanged names and phone numbers the morning before, but was that reason enough to completely ignore me?

I waited at the waterfall for about fifteen minutes expecting Magen to pass me on her way back home, but she never did. I knew there was only one other way to get back to her house, the long way. Instead of wasting more time waiting for something that wasn't going to happen, I headed in the direction she had come from. I got to her house before she did. When she saw me waiting there for her, I couldn't tell if she looked happy, surprised, or pissed off.

She was a little reluctant at first to talk to me, but she quickly caved and invited me into her house. I sat at her kitchen table while she took a shower. I had contemplated joining her in the shower, but I didn't want to push my luck. I should've been more prepared for the conversation I knew was coming as soon as she finished in the shower. One of her first questions was the one I was waiting for, the one I should've put more thought into. She asked me what my name was.

I thought of saying it was Cole but quickly decided against it. Then I thought of saying it was Zach, but again I decided against it. I was angry at myself for not thinking about this earlier and having a name on the tip of my tongue. Then I thought about a conversation I had had with Kari. We had talked about the possibility of having a baby before she was too old to do so. She had told me if she ever had a son, his name would be Trent.

Although Magen had not told me what her name was, I answered her question. "My name is Trent, and yours?"

We talked for a little bit longer. She kept trying to get me to tell her things about myself, but I wasn't ready to share anything real with her that soon. When I got up to leave, I told her I would see her the next day. I left before she had a chance to turn me down.

CHAPTER 2

I was running a little late the next morning. I had also forgotten that I had a training session scheduled at the gym that I couldn't get out of. It was with the blonde that I thought I had seen the last of. When I made it to the waterfall, Magen was just about to give up on me showing up at all. She seemed a bit off as we sat down on the bench. I couldn't tell whether it was because I was late showing up, or that something else was bothering her.

When I asked her if something was wrong, she seemed to hesitate before answering. It was like when you want to say something, but you lose your nerve, so you say something else instead. When she asked me why I wear jeans to go running, though she had never seen me running, I knew it wasn't what was really bothering her. It seemed I wasn't the only one hiding something. Was her secret as bad as mine?

Before I had a chance to tell her that I had to head to work, I heard an alarm go off on her phone. She seemed surprised when she heard it as if it wasn't coming from her phone. I couldn't help but wonder if the player was being played. We both agreed that we would meet up again later in the afternoon, then we went our separate ways.

When we met up for the second time that day, I brought Magen to my favorite coffee shop. That was when she found out I rode a bike instead of driving a car. She didn't seem to mind at all. We sat at the same table in the front window that I always sat at. I loved the attention I got from almost every woman, and some of the men, as they walked by. I never batted for the other team, but attention is attention.

Magen was once again trying to get me to tell her personal things about myself, which I wasn't comfortable doing. Why are all women so bloody nosy? When she caught onto the fact that I wasn't going to spill my guts to her, she became a bit distant and chilly. We hung out at the coffee shop making small talk that neither of us really cared about. When I noticed the time, I realized I needed to get home or there would be hell to pay. How was I going to explain why I was getting home from work so late without Kari getting suspicious?

When we left the coffee shop, I kissed Magen on the cheek, hopped on my bike, and headed home to Kari. I hadn't even made it one block when my phone started ringing. I stopped riding to see who was calling me, it was

Kari. She wanted to know where I was and when I would be home. After we hung up, I noticed I had missed calls from her that came in while I was with Magen in the coffee shop. During the rest of my ride home, I couldn't shake the feeling that someone was following me. I had a bad feeling about the night ahead of me. When you play with fire, someone is going to get burned.

The next time I saw Magen was two days later. I had made it to the waterfall before her. I made sure I was standing in front of the waterfall when I heard her coming around the bend. By then, I had mastered the skill of crying on demand. It was time to put my acting abilities to work again. This time, I was once again playing the grieving widower. When Magen noticed I was crying she asked me what was wrong. In my best shaky voice, I told her my wife had committed suicide the same night we had gone to the coffee shop.

Magen wasn't a good actress. She sucked at hiding her feelings. Her facial expression told me more than her words did. She may have told me in words how sorry she was to hear that my wife had committed suicide, but her facial expression told me she was infuriated that I had a wife in the first place. I needed to calm her down. I needed to play on her sympathy or lack thereof. I could feel the forced tears dripping down my face as I told her about being the one to find my wife dead. No one wants to be the one to find their spouse dead.

That was when I messed up. I was so focused on not using the word 'wife' again, that when I was telling Magen about finding Kari dead, I mistakenly told her that I found Kari dead in her bed, instead of at the bottom of the staircase. It was Heather that was found dead in her bed. I was so busy trying to sell the lie, that I hadn't even realized what I had said until later. By then, it was too late to correct myself. It wasn't like I could have a do-over.

Her facial expression never changed. I wasn't even sure she had heard anything I had told her, except the word 'wife'. I tried to smooth things over by telling her that she was the only woman I had cheated on my wife with. It was another lie of course, and it was obvious she wasn't buying it. I could tell she was going to need some time and space away from me and I was okay with that. I did have a funeral to plan after all.

CHAPTER 3

It was strange enough going to Heather's funeral knowing how she had really died; it was even worse going to Kari's funeral. There were so few people there that it was impossible to hide in the crowd. I swear I could feel everyone's eyes burning holes through my back. After the priest said some prayers and gave a little speech he asked if I had anything I wanted to say, I didn't.

What was I going to do, stand there spewing a bunch of lies at a funeral? It just didn't feel right. So instead, I walked up to Kari's coffin, placed a single rose on it, and then walked away. I could hear the disgust coming from everyone else there including the priest. That was when I saw her. Magen was there at my wife's funeral. Just her head sticking out from behind a tree. As quickly as I spotted her, I bowed my head to look at the ground and continued walking back to the limo. I didn't want her to know I had seen her, just like she didn't want me to know she was there. I had even changed my name in the death notice just in case she looked for it, which it seems she had. I definitely wasn't the only one keeping secrets.

I waited a few days before heading back to the waterfall. I wanted to see Magen again, but I didn't want her to think I was heartless. I had no idea how long a husband grieves for his wife when she dies. I was sure it was more than a few days, but there was something about Magen that kept me wanting more. She was the first woman in my life who had a backbone. She had no problem standing up for herself. I found that incredibly attractive. She was constantly keeping me on my toes. Perhaps I had finally met my match.

When Magen showed up at the waterfall, I was so excited to see her that my tears on demand failed me. I did my best to look upset without tears when she asked me how I was doing. If I had to guess, she was seeing right through my widower façade. I may have gone too far when I told her that I missed her. Instead of stopping there, I went on to ask her out to dinner. Talk about forcing doubt down her throat.

The next day I stopped by Magen's house and left flowers at her door. I didn't bother knocking because I noticed her car wasn't in the driveway. I just wanted her to know I was thinking about her. After that, I headed to the police station in Kari's car. I still didn't have a license, so driving to the police station wasn't one of my brighter ideas. When I was pulling into the parking lot of the police station, I could have sworn I saw Magen's car pulling out. I knew I had to be wrong, she had no reason to be at the police station.

Even though they had declared Kari's murder as an accidental death, I thought if I showed some fake interest in the case, it would make me look good to the police, and to Magen. I spoke to the incompetent police officer that was in charge of the case and asked him if there were any updates I should know about. He politely told me he had nothing new to tell me. I wasn't surprised or shocked at all. The only thing the police cared about was clearing up cases and moving on to the next one. I was perfectly fine with that.

I know this is going to sound a bit obsessive, but the next day I visited the waterfall at least once an hour hoping to run into Magen. I was quite sure she only went running in the morning, but she wasn't there at her usual time, and I had the day off from the gym, so I just kept going back. It finally paid off. She was definitely surprised to see me there waiting for her. I asked her about the flowers, and she said they were lovely. That brought a smile to my face.

I again asked her about taking her to dinner, but her answer was vague. Then things got a bit weird. She had put her earbuds back in her ears and started running away from me. I grabbed onto her arm to stop her. I wanted a definite answer about dinner so I could make a reservation for us. The steak house was now reservation-only. She didn't appreciate me grabbing onto her arm. She told me to let go of her or she was going to scream. What the hell was going on with her? Why was she suddenly acting like she was afraid of me?

Before running away from me, she finally committed to dinner the next night at six. The weird thing about it was that she was very insistent that I be the one to drive us to the restaurant. She knew I didn't have a driver's license. She was up to something, but I had absolutely no idea what it was.

CHAPTER 4

The next day dragged by like molasses. I couldn't wait to bring Magen to the steak house. I wanted to impress her as much as I could. She had definitely been focusing on all the negative things about me. It was time to change that. I needed to get back into her good graces.

I showed up at her house at exactly six p.m. I had left my house a bit too early in case there was traffic. I parked a block away from her house and waited there instead of showing up early and making her feel like she was being rushed. When I saw Magen opening her front door, I got out of the car, walked over to the passenger's door, and held it open for her. I think women still like chivalry. I tried making conversation with her several times during the drive to the restaurant, but she seemed to be somewhere else entirely.

I thought I saw a little sparkle in her eyes when I pulled into the parking lot for the steak house. I was hoping for a smile, but we weren't quite there yet. I made sure to open the car door for her again and held it until she was standing right next to me before closing it. When we walked into the restaurant the maître d' greeted me by my last name, which definitely seemed to impress Magen. She didn't need to know that when I called to make the reservation, I said there would be an extra-large tip if the maître d' called me by my last name. Leave nothing to chance.

When Kari died, everything she had was left to me. I didn't really want all her money, but now that I had it, I might as well spend it. I ordered a bottle of the most expensive wine they had. I ended up drinking most of the wine while we ate our dinners. Things got a bit awkward when Magen kept trying to get me to talk about Kari and how she died. I couldn't understand why she was doing that during our first official date. Was I reading her all wrong? Were we even on a date?

When we were getting close to her house, I pulled into an empty parking lot. I didn't want our date to end on a bad note. As I put the car in park, she instantly grabbed the release button for the seat belt. I think she thought I was looking for a little car action, but that was the furthest thing on my mind. I turned to look at her and told her she could ask me anything she wanted to. Chances were, I would probably end up lying to her, but how would she know the difference?

She only ended up asking me one question that night. She wanted to know if Kari had known about us being together. She couldn't stop wondering if that was the reason behind Kari's suicide. It was a loaded question for sure. I did an imaginary flip of a coin in my head. Heads, I would tell her the truth. Tails, I would tell her another lie.

Before the coin had a chance to land, I had decided I would mix the truth in with a lie. I told her that Kari did know about us seeing each other because she had seen Magen hiding behind a car when she had followed me home from the coffee shop that day. I told you I thought someone was following me, and I was right.

Just so you know, the truth part of what I told Magen was that Kari did see her hiding behind a car. The lie part was that Kari thought she was just a woman bending down to tie her shoe. When I looked out the window and saw it was Magen she was talking about, I told her I couldn't see anyone. It did make me smile knowing Magen had followed me home. A bit stalkerish, but still flattering.

After hearing me tell her that Kari knew about us, Magen's face looked like it was turning green. I was certain she was going to throw up in the car. Instead, she asked me to take her home because she wasn't feeling good. That I knew wasn't a lie. For once her face matched her words. I did feel a little guilty for making her feel somewhat guilty for Kari's death, but she would get over it, just like I did.

CHAPTER 5

I knew something was really bothering Magen. I assumed it was based on the guilt she was dealing with over Kari's death. She hadn't seemed the type that would let guilt eat her alive, but did I really know her at all?

I had a feeling she was avoiding me. That feeling became a reality when I was waiting for her at the waterfall the next day. Instead of coming around the bend like she always did, I heard her turn around and start running back the way she had come. I snuck a peek around the bend just to make sure it was, in fact, her, and there she was running and bouncing to the music blasting in her ears.

Although I felt a little disappointed in her, I didn't let it deter me. I ran as fast as I could (which isn't half as fast as Magen can) back to my bike and rode it over to her house. I didn't think I would make it there before she did, but miracles do happen. I hid my bike on the side of her neighbor's house so she would be surprised when she saw me standing there waiting for her.

The look of shock on her face, when she saw me, wasn't what I wanted to see, but it was what I had expected to see. I told her I was sorry for showing up unannounced. I just wanted to make sure she was okay after the bombshell I had dropped on her the night before. She assured me she was fine. I wasn't getting the feeling that she was feeling guilty as much as she was feeling anger toward me for not telling her that Kari had seen her hiding behind the car.

If she had any idea how many other things I hadn't told her, she wouldn't be talking to me at all. She used the excuse of needing to take a shower to get me to leave her alone. Considering the stink that was coming from her was making my eyes water, it wasn't like I could argue with her. I told her I hoped to see her soon. Then I watched her as she walked through her front door.

The next time I saw Magen was when she was on the witness stand during my trial testifying against me. I had a feeling early on that she would be the one to put an end to my reign of terror. She wasn't like the other women I had been involved with. My innocent boyish charms didn't work on her as they had on Robin and Kari. To be completely honest, I feel a sense of relief that for the first time in my adult life, I can stop the charade of trying to live a normal life. I can finally stop compiling lies on top of lies, and just let the truth come out. It is time to pay the piper. The player had definitely been played.

Epilogue

Mack

If it hadn't been for Magen, our police force would still have egg on its face. The word 'incompetent' is not strong enough. I would like to say that I was not the lead detective on any of the cases involved, but I still feel extremely embarrassed by how many mistakes were made by my fellow police officers. How they had failed to make so many obvious connections between the cases is mind-blowing to me.

When I met with Magen at her house and she showed me all the websites she had used to try to find any information at all about Trent Harper, none of which had produced any results, I knew something was amiss. I headed back to the station, and with help from Cindy (the only other police officer I trusted), we turned Trent Harper's life upside down and inside out.

I am an honorable man. I always give credit where credit is due. Having said that, it was Cindy who made the first connection we so desperately needed. We didn't have any better luck than Magen did finding anything online about Trent Harper. That was when Cindy pulled the file for the case of his dead wife. The case that Magen had originally come to us about.

There wasn't anything useful in the file due to the lack of an investigation into his wife's death, but it did get Cindy thinking. What did we actually know about his dead wife? There was nothing about her on social media as Magen had told us, but when Cindy ran her name through our database, she struck gold. There were several incident reports that involved Trent's dead wife Kari, and her ex-husband. Seems neither of her marriages had been happy.

We both kept digging into Kari's life. What we found was alarming. Since the time she met this 'Trent' guy, not only had she died from accidentally falling down her own staircase, but her sister, Heather, had died from an overdose in her own bed. After reading that, I pulled the file on Heather's death. There were three things that caught my eye. The first thing was that Kari was certain her sister would never have committed suicide. The second thing was that she had been certain it wasn't a suicide because of damage to the lock on the front door. I took a close look at the photo in the file of the messed-up lock. It was obvious to me that someone had jammed something into that lock. It was a forced entry. My embarrassment regarding my fellow police officers multiplied when I read in the report that they had told Kari they believed Heather had caused the damage to the lock herself. The third thing was that Kari had told the police officer that she had stopped by her sister's house to show her the engagement ring Cole had just given her. Who the hell was Cole?

We didn't stop there, we kept digging. We searched for any missing women in the area. If 'Trent' had killed these two women, chances are he had done it before. It took us about thirty minutes before we found the connection that would be putting 'Trent' away for the rest of his life.

I vaguely remembered a missing persons case from about five years back. The woman's name was Robin Harper. She was in her early twenties, married, and an editor for the local newspaper. One day she just disappeared into thin air never to be seen again. I remember her mother had kept calling the station asking if there was any new information. She refused to believe that her daughter would've just left without telling her where she was going. While I was reading what we had in our database about her case, Cindy grabbed the actual file we had on her missing person's case.

When I heard Cindy yell "Holy shit!" I knew we had him. Inside the file, there was a photo of Robin on her wedding day. Standing on the side of her was her husband, Zach AKA Trent. Hello nail, hello coffin. We kept on digging. The next connection came when we found the case involving Zach's mother's accidental tumble down their basement stairs. What are the chances that two women in one man's life would die by accidentally falling down a flight of stairs? Don't overthink it. The answer is, there are no chances at all. Unless your name is Michael Peterson.

While Cindy was looking at the case file for Zach's mother's death, I dug a little bit deeper into Zach Harper. I checked our database for his real name. I found that he had lost his license after getting several DUIs. I couldn't believe my eyes when I saw the picture of his driver's license. His middle name was right there in black and white: Cole. It was my turn to yell out "Holy shit!"

We now had connections between Zach, AKA Cole, AKA Trent, and three deaths, and one missing woman. Who knew how many others there were that we didn't know about yet? Cindy and I were beat. We had been at it for hours after already working our regular shift earlier in the day. We still had lots of unanswered questions. The one at the top of the list was what really happened to Robin. Our strategy for the next day was to take a trip out to Zach's father's house. How many of our questions would he be able to answer?

The next morning Cindy and I met at the police station, then I drove us over to the house Zach had grown up in. I couldn't help but wonder what those walls would say if they could talk. As we pulled into the driveway, we could tell right away that we were in for another interesting day. The grass looked like it hadn't been mowed in months. There were shingles from the roof all over the yard. All the shades were pulled down. It looked like the house had been abandoned quite some time ago.

Cindy and I got out of the cruiser and walked up to the front door. I tried to open the storm door so I could knock on the front door, but the storm door was locked. Who locks their storm door? I tried ringing the doorbell, but it went unanswered. Having no luck with the door, we split up. Cindy went one way around the perimeter of the house, and I went the other way. We tried every window to see if any of them were unlocked, but again no luck. The house was sealed up nice and tight.

When we came back around to the front of the house there was a little old lady standing at the edge of the driveway. Cindy and I walked over to her. We didn't want her getting any closer to the house in case it turned into a crime scene. After we all made quick introductions, Doris asked if we were there because of the woman who had been asking her questions a couple of weeks ago. When we asked her for a description of the woman, she described Kari almost perfectly.

With that added information, we now knew that Kari had visited Zach's father within days, if not on the day that she had died. Just another coincidence, I think not. Cindy then asked Doris when the last time was that she had seen her neighbor. With a suspicious look on her face, she told us that was what the other lady had asked her. Doris then added that she didn't believe the other woman was who she said she was. The other woman had told Doris that she was married to Henry's son Cole, but Henry's son's name wasn't Cole, it was Zach. Then she finally told us that she hadn't seen her neighbor in almost two years.

Cindy and I just looked at each other in complete bewilderment. I had arrived at the station about ten minutes earlier than Cindy that morning. While I waited for her, I looked into the ownership of Zach's father's house. I wanted to make sure he still owned it before we headed over. From what I could tell, the house was still in his name and all the utility bills were up to date. If he hadn't been seen in almost two years, who was paying all his utility bills? The more interesting question was *why* was someone paying all his utility bills?

I walked over to the trunk of the cruiser and grabbed the crowbar. Cindy followed me to the front door. Doris attempted to follow right behind Cindy, but we told her she needed to stay on the sidewalk. I used the crowbar to pry the lock on the storm door and then the lock on the front door. It was dark and musty in the house. It was obvious that no one had lived in the house for a while. We walked down the short hall into the kitchen. The next thing I heard was a shriek coming from behind me. A mouse had run across Cindy's foot. She doesn't much care for any kind of rodents.

While Cindy was pulling herself together, I walked over to the basement door. At first, I thought I was smelling the remains of something the mouse had found to eat, but once I opened the basement door, I realized I was smelling something much worse. Once you smell the remains of a body rotting, you never forget that scent. I closed the basement door and walked back out of the house with Cindy right behind me. There were calls that needed to be made.

Within the next twenty minutes, the crime scene unit had showed up, and went straight down to the basement. While they did their thing, Cindy and I searched the rest of the house. Although we found nothing of importance, the crime scene unit had much better results. All the house's secrets were buried in the basement. They dug up the remains of three bodies: two females and one male.

We later confirmed through dental records and DNA testing, the identity of two of the bodies. The male was identified as Zach's father, Henry. His cause of death was determined to be a heart attack. Why he had been buried in his own basement was another mystery we may never know the answer to.

One of the females was identified as Zach's first wife, Robin. Her cause of death was determined to be from drowning. At least now her parents would have the answers they had been waiting for all these years. The second woman's identity is still unknown. Her DNA wasn't in any databases, and we weren't able to match her dental records. We checked all the missing person reports, but we couldn't find one that matched our Jane Doe.

Zach was arrested and charged with twenty-eight different offenses ranging from murder to false identity. He pleaded not guilty. He has never admitted to doing anything wrong. For every question we asked him during our nine interviews, he pled the Fifth every time. I find solace in knowing that he will spend the rest of his life behind bars. He will never be able to hurt another woman again.

About the Author

Alan Sakell is the Author of
The Boy, Who Am I? |
The Jane Brooks Story, and
Last Breath.

He was born and raised in Fall River, MA. After living on and off in Miami, FL, and Medford, MA, he has since moved back to Fall River. He has been doing accounting for a non-profit organization based in Miami, FL, for the last eighteen years.

Printed in the USA
CPSIA information can be obtained
at www.ICGtesting.com
CBHW060020070524
8168CB00011B/533